BOYFRIEND GOALS

By
Riley Hart

Copyright © 2022 by Riley Hart
Print Edition

All rights reserved.

No part of this book may be used, reproduced, or transmitted in any form or by any means, electronic or mechanical, including photocopying, recording, or by any information storage and retrieval systems, without prior written permission of the author, except where permitted by law.

Published by:
Riley Hart

This book is a work of fiction. Names, characters, places, and incidents are products of the author's imagination or are used fictitiously. Any similarity to actual persons, living or dead, is coincidental and not intended by the author.

All products/brand names/trademarks mentioned are registered trademarks of their respective holders/companies.

Cover Design by Cate Ashwood
Cover Image by Wander Aguiar
Edited by Keren Reed Editing
Proofread by Judy's Proofreading, Karen Meeus, and Lyrical Lines Proofreading

Milo

Unusual. Quirky. Different. I've heard it all. I've accepted I'm not for everyone. Maybe not anyone.

When I find out I inherited a bookstore and apartment on a small East Coast island, I jump at the chance for a new life.

Turns out, I've also inherited a sexy, tattooed guy who not only rents the space next to my store for his tattoo parlor but my apartment too.

Did I mention he's really hot?

And surprisingly sweet?

Gideon

I wasn't looking for a roommate, but it's not like I can stay at Milo's place while he's banished to a hotel.

Our unlikely friendship is instant. According to Milo, we're bestie goals.

And if he doesn't wear pants at home, who am I to complain?

Milo's not like anyone I've ever known. I like laughing and flirting with him. He's adorably honest, eager, and sexier than he realizes.

Now I just have to figure out how to convince him that maybe it's time for an upgrade from bestie to boyfriend goals.

Dedication

To anyone who has ever felt like you don't fit in, this is for you.

Special Thanks

To my sensitivity readers: Sam, Abbie, and Davi. While everyone is different and there's no one way to tell anyone's story, it was important to me to share Milo's journey as authentically as possible. Thank you for reading, providing feedback, and your willingness to answer questions. Your help was invaluable.

CHAPTER ONE

Milo

*P*ORN IS CONFUSING.

I liked it well enough. The whole point was to get you off, and most of the time when I tried, I succeeded even if it took a while. I just didn't understand all the grunting and loud noises. All the exaggerated sounds and pleas of *fuck me*. I mean, why did he have to beg the other guy to do what he was already doing? Why did he continue to ask for what he already had? From the look of pleasure on the top's face, I didn't think he would be stopping anytime soon, so why didn't the bottom just shut up and enjoy the ride?

I stroked my hand up and down my shaft before glancing at the clock on the nightstand. I kept it there despite my phone sitting beside it because…well, just because. I didn't need a reason.

I only had five more minutes. If I didn't come before

that, I'd have to stop because it would be time to start getting ready for work. Nighttime jack-off sessions were easier to squeeze in, but I had a million things on my plate today, and I'd already decided I needed to go to bed early.

My gaze traveled back to the TV. "*Yes, fuck. Oh my God. Right there.*"

"Shut up! You're annoying," I told the man on the screen. My dick was going soft. I hated when I pulled myself out of it like this. Why did sex require so much talking? Begging? Screaming? It was just awkward and got into my head. Or maybe that was just how it was in porn and not in real life, but if I'd be expected to do all that, I wasn't sure I'd ever be getting off with anyone other than myself.

I would *never* be able to *say* those things—and I might never trust someone enough to have sex with them at all, but I chose not to concentrate on that at the moment.

I used my free hand to hit Mute on the remote. Sometimes I could finish with the annoying dirty pleas, other times I couldn't. Apparently today was going to fall into the latter category.

The blissful silence helped some. I paid attention to the cock pounding in and out of the bottom and…oh, there we go, my dick was hardening again. My balls were full, my cock throbbing, and I really wondered what that would feel like—to be inside someone or to have them inside me…maybe. I hadn't decided if I'd ever be able to bottom. Whomever I slept with had to be okay with that. And he had to be nice…and hot…maybe a little bigger than me, but not one of those meathead guys because…just no. Someone who was interesting. I really wanted to have sex with someone interesting. *And* who didn't annoy me, but that was really hard not to do. Most people frustrated me sometimes, but he wouldn't…oh… I squeezed tighter, stroked faster, before playing with my nuts, which was one of my favorite things.

A really hot guy who wasn't irritating and didn't make strange sex noises and didn't want me to ask him to do what he was already doing.

Heat shot up my spine. My balls drew up, my vision blurry as I shot my load all over my chest.

I fell back into my pillows, breathed a couple of deep breaths because that had felt *so* good. Only now the sticky release on my skin pulled all my attention. I didn't typically like strange fluids touching me—or anything, really. Ketchup was the worst. Who could eat that stuff? I got it on my hand once as a kid. I swear I nearly died.

But cum…I kind of liked that. I'd never eaten it or anything because I'd only been around my own—and that was definitely *not* something I ever planned to do—but I was curious about it. I liked the feel of it on my skin because it represented pleasure, something I was more interested in than I could explain.

Pleasure was basically the best thing ever, next to not wearing pants.

I looked over just as my five minutes were up. Perfect timing.

I made my way into the en suite. I wiped my release away before turning on the shower to just the right temperature. I went back into my bedroom for my underwear, work shirt, and tie. I laid them on the bed, took my shower, brushed my teeth, then pulled on the clothes I'd laid out.

It was Monday, which meant two scrambled eggs, toast, and oatmeal. I didn't do coffee, something my mom didn't understand. I was pretty sure it pumped through her veins.

I didn't always eat the same foods for every meal, but I tried to for breakfast, especially Mondays. I liked to start my days a certain way, and the beginning of my workweek never wavered. It was the most important meal of the day after all. Over the years, I'd learned to be more flexible with lunch and dinner.

I cooked and ate my food, along with my cup of orange juice.

Once I had everything together and couldn't put it off any longer, I pulled on my pants, which rested over a rack by the front door, then put on my dress shoes. I made sure to lock up on the way out.

There was a car waiting for me in front of my San Diego apartment building. "Hello, Bradley," I said to the driver after I climbed into the back seat. "Good morning, Mom." She was seated beside me. She had an apartment in the same building, and we worked together too. She was slightly overprotective, only without the slightly part.

"Good morning, Mr. Copeland," Bradley replied. "Milo," he amended, likely seeing the scowl on my face. I didn't like to be called Mr. Copeland, though people had been saying it all my life.

"He's just being professional, Milo," Mom said.

"Yes, but I don't like it. Isn't it also professional to call people what they want to be called?"

She sighed. I made her do that a lot. "How was your morning?"

"Noisy," I replied, thinking about all the *fuck mes* I'd heard before hitting Mute.

Mom frowned but didn't ask. She'd learned there were times she shouldn't ask me what I meant because I had a habit of always being honest.

It took forty-five minutes to get to Mom's financial firm, where I worked as an accountant. She'd built her business from the ground up with her own sweat and hard work. As overbearing as she could sometimes be, there was no one in the world I respected more than my mom.

She didn't need anyone.

She didn't let anyone take advantage of her.

When Dad left me, she stayed.

We talked work the whole way; that was what we almost always discussed on our journey to the office. Neither of us had much of a social life—Mom because she often scared people and didn't much like them, me because I didn't always know how to relate to them and they didn't know how to accept me.

We took the elevator up. I was comfortable with the one in this building because I knew it was checked regularly. "You should come over for dinner tonight," Mom said. She didn't ask, but it wasn't as if I had anything to do anyway.

"I can do that."

Once we exited, we went our separate ways, each to our own office.

The morning was spent going about the same routine as I'd had since I started working there. I didn't love numbers, but I was good at them, and I didn't really know what I loved. Maybe there was nothing. Most of the time I was okay with that, but others it upset me in ways I couldn't really put my finger on. Maybe sort of like wanting to have sex but being picky who I had it with and how we did it. Sometimes I was my own worst enemy.

It was noon, thirty minutes before my lunch hour, when my assistant called from the front. "Milo, you have a call from a lawyer in Portland on line one."

I frowned, wondering who it could be. "Can you put them through?"

"Of course."

A few seconds later, a man's voice was on the line. "Hello, is this Milo Copeland?"

"Yes, may I ask what this is in regard to?"

"My name is Chester Harrington. I'm based in Portland, Maine. Your grandmother hired me to represent her estate."

My stomach twisted, but then my brain kicked in and took control. This had to be wrong. "This must be a mistake. My grandparents are both dead. They passed in a car accident before I was born."

"Your mother is Beverly Copeland from Little Beach Island in—"

"Maine," I finished for him, trying to mentally sort through what was going on.

"Wilma Allen was Beverly's biological mother. From what I understand, they didn't have a relationship."

I opened my mouth, but nothing would come out. My thoughts were spinning, my chest too tight. "I don't…I don't understand," I finally managed to say. Mom was adopted, and she'd never told me?

"I don't know the whys behind their relationship, or lack thereof. And I'm sorry. I hate to be the one to tell you that your biological grandmother passed. It's not much, but she left her bookstore to you—that and the apartment upstairs, the whole building, actually—but she rents the store next door to a gentleman, Gideon Barlow. He runs a tattoo parlor out of the space and—"

"I own a tattoo parlor?" I didn't even have tattoos. Why would someone choose to permanently carve something into their skin?

He chuckled. "Well, no. You own the building, and the space is rented to Mr. Barlow. She asked in her will that you continue to allow him the space. And there's the issue of the apartment to figure out, but it would be easier if we could do this in person. I'm not sure what you want to do with the properties, if you'll want to keep them or—"

"I want them," I blurted out, surprising myself. What I was going to do with a bookstore, an apartment, and...Gideon Barlow, I didn't know, but I had a grandma and she'd wanted me to have them.

A grandma Mom never told me about.

A grandma who was dead.

"Okay, I can send the documents over, if you'd like. You can sign that way, or we can meet up if you're planning on coming out right away."

His words were muffled after that, Chester Harrington telling me things I was sure I needed to know but couldn't sort through at the moment. The pressure in my chest grew. This was...different and out of control. Those things always overwhelmed me.

"Milo? Are you there?" he asked. Clearly, he'd spoken, and I hadn't replied.

I counted down from three, and strangely, wondered about Gideon Barlow and why my grandma wanted to make sure he kept the shop but wanted the building to go to me, and...what an odd name Gideon Barlow was. This tattoo guy was already strange to me, and I hadn't even met him yet.

"I'll, um...be there. I'm coming. There. To Portland." I'd never been to Portland in my life. Maybe I should say no. I couldn't do this. Why would I want to do this? It was so out of my routine. I didn't do impulsive. It made everything too overwhelming, but…I had a grandma…and she'd given me a bookstore, and that intrigued me. "Can you give me a week or so to get my affairs in order?"

See. I could do this. I needed to do this. I *wanted* to do it, which was what made me push forward, toward more independence, which I craved.

"Yes, of course. Let me give you my number." My hand shook as I took it down and ended the call. I gathered my things, stomach tense, but I forced myself to hold my head high when I walked out of the office.

MOM HADN'T TOLD me… Why hadn't she told me?

"Marybeth, I have some personal family business to attend to. I'm taking the rest of the day off. Can you cancel my schedule?"

Her mouth dropped open, probably because I'd never taken time off. I was killing this independence thing already. "Yes, of course. Do you need me to call you a car?"

"No, thank you." I went straight down the hallway toward Mom's office.

"Hi, Mr. Copeland. How are you?" one of our newer advisers asked.

"Terrible. My mother is a liar." I *hated* lies. I didn't understand why anyone told them. How hard was it to just tell the truth?

"Oh... I..."

I didn't hear their response as I pushed open the door to Mom's office. "Milo...what are you doing?"

"I have a grandma...well, had. And she lived on the same island her whole life, which means you knew about her. She died, and she left me her bookstore and a tattoo parlor and Tattoo Guy."

"Who is Tattoo Guy?" Mom asked. I studied her face, looking for sadness, because it hit me then that I was talking about her mom.

"My tattoo guy," I said, which made no sense. I didn't like tattoos, or want tattoos, and he wasn't mine. But I couldn't sort through my thoughts enough to figure out what to call him.

She sighed. "Come in and close the door so the whole office doesn't hear us." She'd always cared what other people thought. I knew it bothered her that people thought I was odd, though in this case, it wasn't so much about appearances but rather love. As angry as she made me, I knew there was nothing she wouldn't do for me, no battle she wouldn't fight, even though I didn't want anyone fighting on my behalf. If need be, I would do it myself.

"Why didn't you tell me? About Wilma Allen?"

She flinched, either at my question or the name, before steeling her face again. "Because she wasn't my mother. My parents died in a car accident. She might have given birth to me, but that's where our relationship ended."

I looked down, a little sad and a lot confused. "You still could have told me."

"You're right," Mom admitted. "And I apologize for not doing so."

"What happened? With Wilma Allen? Why did she give you up for adoption?"

"I don't know. I don't care. I don't want to talk about it. We can talk to someone about putting the building up for sale. We'll compensate employees and this tattoo man and—"

"No," I cut her off. Her assumption about what I wanted to do and the way she automatically took over told me I was making the right decision. I didn't want to sell. I didn't know what I would do with it, but I was pretty sure I wanted to try and figure it out on my own.

"You're not going to Little Beach," Mom said.

"I'm twenty-four years old. I'll do what I want." Wow. I was pretty sure I sounded more like a teenager right then than I ever had.

"You have a job here and—"

"I quit." This wasn't what I wanted anyway. I just did it because I didn't have anything else to do, because I was good at it and it was what Mom did.

"You've never lived more than two floors away from me. Even when you went to Franklin University, you stayed home with me. I know you're capable of taking care of yourself, Milo, but—"

"No," I cut her off. "You don't." I'd always known it but had never said it out loud. She knew I was smart, but she didn't think I could take care of myself. Mom expected everyone else to know she didn't need anyone, that she was strong and independent, but she had never seen it in me.

"Little Beach has nothing to offer you, Milo. It's small and small-minded. I was never happy there, even when my parents were alive. I never felt like I fit. I don't want that for you."

I don't fit here either. I might never fit anywhere.

Almost every decision in my life had been made for me by my mom—going to Franklin U because it was close and she knew the dean. My career. My apartment. She was a good mom. When my dad said there was something wrong with me, when he was hateful about it, she chose me. But she'd never let me have my own wings either. And as much as I loved her, I knew I would never have them while we were close. And maybe it took inheriting a building to realize how much I wanted that. "I have to go. To see what it's like. You left, didn't you? To figure out who you are?"

Because in San Diego, I was just Beverly Copeland's weird son, the one everyone tolerated because my mom mattered and she lined their wallets.

"And you think you'll find yourself there? You don't know anything about it. It's a small island where everyone is expected to be just like everyone else."

And I wasn't. We both knew that. But I didn't really care. I still wanted to try something of my own. "Maybe things have changed. It's been a long time. I'm going to go. And I'm sorry about your mom."

"She wasn't my mom."

While her distance bothered other people, it didn't bother me. I understood it in my own way, so I just said, "I'll let you know how it goes."

It was there, in her eyes—Mom wanted to ask me to stay. She wanted to demand it. But she wouldn't. That wasn't how she was built.

Mom nodded, and I walked out.

CHAPTER TWO

Gideon

"WHAT'S UP, BUTTFACE?" my brother, Orlando, said as he walked through the door of my tattoo parlor, Conflicting Ink. We were complete opposites, he and I. He was blond, I had dark hair. His skin was untouched, mine was tattooed across my chest, arms, and stomach. I had my right daith pierced, as well as my nipples, left eyebrow, and a labret beneath my lower lip; Orlando had none.

He'd played sports in high school and dated cheerleaders. I'd been in the closet and then secretly hooking up with my bi best friend who I'd been in love with. Orlando had married the girl he'd been dating since he was sixteen, only left home to go play college baseball and get his degree, then go to law school, while I'd run away from here with my tail between my legs after telling Kris how I felt at our high school graduation party, only to find out it was all just a little fun for him. He'd thought I felt the same—bros secretly getting each other off. It had killed him to hurt me. The guy couldn't help it if he hadn't loved me, but it had been enough to get me off Little Beach Island for what I'd thought was for good.

I was out as fuck now, even though I was one of the only out queer men on Little Beach. I was still best friends with Kris and still the odd one in my family. Dad and Orlando were spitting images of each other. Mom was closer to them than to me, and I was just…Gideon—the only one who hadn't gone to college and who liked to put holes in his body and ink in his skin.

Still, we were all close, even if I never felt like I totally fit with them.

But Orlando was also the kind of guy who called me buttface while looking all prim and proper in his suit. "Has anyone ever told you you're ridiculous?" I asked, finally responding.

"Nearly every day, brother. I can always call you *Snacks* if you'd prefer."

I rolled my eyes while I continued to clean up the supplies from the ink I'd finished not long before he'd come in. "Don't call me Snacks."

"It's so cute, though! It reminds me of when we were kids, when you used to waddle around with some kind of candy or cookies or chips in your hands."

I'd had a thing for treats when I was younger—still did in some ways. Sweet or salty, both did it for me. I'd always get caught sneaking an extra snack, hence the name. "Don't you have the world to save? A case to win, a little old lady to get out of a tree or something?"

The lawyer and the tattoo artist. Again with the opposites.

Orlando laughed and crossed his arms. "I think you mean a cat."

"This is Little Beach, so you never know. I wouldn't be surprised if we had little old ladies getting stuck in trees, and if we did, you'd be the one to rescue them."

He also had a habit of being in the right place at the right time, once witnessing a car accident and getting the driver out. Another time he'd done the Heimlich on someone choking at a restaurant. He was not only Mom and Dad's golden boy, but the island's too. How the fuck did you compete with that? Not that I wanted to, but it had made me feel less than when I was a kid. I didn't want to make it sound like there was animosity between us, because there wasn't. My parents loved and supported me just as much as Orlando. Everyone just knew he was a little more perfect than the rest of the world—or at least in Maine.

"I guess I should be on the lookout for old women stuck in trees, then."

"Yeah, you should." I placed the tattoo machine in the cabinet and washed my hands again. "To what do I owe this visit from the perfect one?"

"Ha-ha," Orlando replied. "Heather is having dinner with friends tonight, so I thought I'd come over and see what my troublemaker brother had going on."

"Oh yeah, such a bad boy. Was it my tattoos that gave me away?" I teased.

"I think you're a wannabe bad boy. Like you want to project that image, but really, you're just a big pile of mush inside while sending off that don't-give-a-fuck, Mr. Brooding attitude. Do the guys dig that?"

"Clearly. Can't you tell by all the men I have lined up for a piece of me? They travel from all over the state for Gideon Barlow. Also, if you just came to bust my balls, you can see yourself out."

Orlando chuckled. "I didn't come for that. It's a perk. I just wanted to hang out with one of my favorite people. Do you have any other appointments coming in?"

"Nah. I was going to hang out and see if I got any walk-ins. Freddy's on his way. I can bail when he arrives, and if we stay close, he can hit me up if anyone comes in while he has appointments."

"Sounds good."

The tattoo business wasn't booming in Little Beach, but I did enough to get by. We weren't really one of those destination islands where tons of rich folks or family vacationers came to stay for the summer. Sure, we had some; we were on an island after all. People trickled in, and we had our own little tourist season, but there were a whole lot more places off the East Coast that people wanted to visit ahead of Little Beach, which was fine by me. The money would be nice, though.

Thinking about that made my thoughts head straight for Wilma. Christ, I missed her. It had nothing to do with the fact that she'd owned the building where I had my shop as well as the apartment upstairs where I lived. Real estate wasn't easy to come by in Little Beach, but I'd trade it all to get the crazy old woman back into my life. She'd been a hoot, one of the best people I knew, and now her big-city grandson would be coming in to…what? Take over? Sell the building? Start trying to gentrify Little Beach Island?

Who the fuck knew?

Hell, we hadn't even known she had a grandson before I found out he'd inherited the building. It was all the talk around Little Beach—about how a woman named Beverly had been her biological daughter, much to everyone's shock. I was too young to have known Beverly, but others did. It was maybe the first secret that had ever been kept in Little Beach.

Freddy arrived a couple of minutes later. He was in his fifties and had married a local. He hadn't gotten into tattooing until later in life, traveling to Boston to work. After we'd both moved back home and Wilma had rented this place to me, I offered him a chair here.

"I'm gonna grab a bite with Orlando," I told him. "If anyone comes in wanting some ink, text me."

"Will do," Freddy replied, tying his long hair back in a ponytail. He had a thick beard to match.

Orlando opened the door, and the two of us walked out. We didn't even discuss where we were going, both of us turning toward the Lighthouse, the local bar and grill that served some kick-ass food. It was built around a lighthouse replica—which wasn't functioning and wasn't even right on the water.

Townsfolk looked up when we entered, some saying hello, others offering a wave or a smile. The bar counter was to the far left, crescent-shaped to fit inside, and there were booths and tables on the right. In the back they had billiards tables, an old jukebox, and a stage for when locals came in to perform.

Orlando and I found an open booth and slipped inside just as Patsy, one of the waitresses, stepped up. "Well, if it isn't the Barlow boys, different as night and day."

I tried not to grimace. Sometimes I couldn't believe that was a thing people actually said to us. I mean, yeah, I highlighted our differences, but it was one thing when I was the one doing it, another when it felt like people were saying *it's Orlando and his sidekick*—one who just wasn't quite as good as he was.

"Good evening, Patsy," Orlando said.

"Ma'am," I added.

"What can I get you boys?" There were menus on the back of the table, in the clutches of a fake lobster, but neither of us needed them.

We both got beers, and Orlando, being a good New Englander, ordered seafood while I got a steak. I was a bit of a carnivore.

"You hear anything about the building?" Orlando asked when Patsy left.

"Not much. The lawyer said he reached out to the grandson and that he'd be here soon. And he told him Wilma requested that he continue to rent the space to me for at least a year. I understand why she wanted to keep it in her family, but it fucking sucks. She rented to me for cheap, and there's not a whole lot available if he's a dickhead." Which meant I might have to go back to the mainland and work in someone else's shop. If that was the case, I'd likely move. Maybe that was a good idea anyway. I'd licked my wounds long enough. I'd run from Little Beach, then run away from the city. Maybe it was time I made a plan and moved *toward* something instead of hightailing it away.

"Whatever happens, we'll figure it out," Orlando replied. It was such a typical Orlando answer. "There might be an apartment coming up for rent, I heard, over on Half Moon Bay Lane. If that doesn't happen, or while you're waiting, you can always stay with Mom and Dad or me and Heather."

Because that was every twenty-six-year-old's deepest desire. Move back home, and then in with your parents. I'd be getting laid even less since I wouldn't be able to hook up with the guys who occasionally came over from the mainland.

"No offense, but I'd rather die."

Orlando rolled his eyes. "You're so dramatic."

"*You're so dramatic,*" I mocked. My brother always seemed to bring out the inner twelve-year-old in me.

"Why so grumpy, Snacks?" He grinned, and I flipped him off.

"I hate you with every fiber of my being."

"I love you too, little bro."

I tried not to grin. He was so fucking annoying.

Patsy brought our beer, and we changed the subject, talking about work and life. He asked about Kris and his wife, Megan, as if they didn't see each other as much as Orlando and me.

I couldn't stop thinking about Wilma's grandson, though, the one who hadn't given enough shits about her to ever be in her life, but he sure was finding his way to Little Beach Island fast enough to claim his inheritance. I hated the fucker already.

CHAPTER THREE

Milo

CHESTER WAS ODD. I knew I shouldn't think things like that. People thought I was weird, and while I knew that, I didn't understand why they felt it, but Chester really was. He kept *looking* at me funny. And he had a strange mustache that he touched all the time. It curled up at the edges and like…why? What was the point in that? It reminded me of a cartoon character. But what really annoyed me was how he kept asking if I was sure I wanted Wilma Allen's building, if I thought I could handle it.

"Do you think I'm stupid?" I finally asked, sitting across from him in his office, which literally smelled like old socks and cheese.

His eyes widened as if he hadn't expected me to ask. People were like that; so many didn't say what they meant or what they were thinking—again, something I couldn't wrap my brain around—and every time I did, when I spoke whatever words flitted through my head, they looked at me like I was crazy, didn't expect it, and oftentimes ended up speechless.

There would be a whole lot less problems in the world if everyone just spoke the truth.

"What? No," Chester sputtered.

"You've asked me five times, in five different ways, if this is what I want. The first was within two and a half minutes of meeting me. Is it because you don't think I'm smart enough? I might not have ever owned a bookstore, or a tattoo parlor, though I guess I don't own that, just the building, so no, I've never owned a building where I ran a business and rented space for another or was a landlord, but I can do it. And if for some reason I decide I can't or I don't want to, I'll let you know. Okay, maybe not you because I'm honestly not sure I like you, but someone. I'll let someone know."

He stared at me, his mouth opening and closing like a dying fish. Wilma Allen chose this guy? If she were alive, I'd have had a word with her about her judgment—in the kindest way possible, of course.

"My apologies, Mr. Copeland."

"Milo," I replied.

Things went more smoothly after that. There was a

lot of talking, a lot of reading, because I didn't believe in signing papers I hadn't read, and then a lot of giving my signature as well. My phone kept ringing, Mom on the screen each time. I muted it. How did she expect me to concentrate with the incessant buzzing?

"Wilma Allen didn't have a house?" I asked when we finished. He hadn't mentioned one. There was the apartment above the store, but Tattoo Guy lived there. He and Wilma Allen must have been very close.

"She sold it years ago to buy the building. She lived in the apartment for a long time before she moved in with her gentleman friend."

"She had a lover?" Gentleman friend was a dumb thing to call someone.

Chester sputtered again. People were so odd about sex. On the one hand, lots of fluids were going back and forth, so if you thought about that part of it, I could see where the gross factor came in, but that wasn't the issue. It was something no one wanted to talk about; they were more comfortable discussing or witnessing violence than sex. I'd read a lot about it.

"I don't know the nature of their relationship," Chester replied.

"Oh, I'll ask him. Can you write down his name and address?" I'd stayed later than I'd planned, and I still needed to get out to Little Beach Island, which totally needed a new name. I'd also have to find a hotel to stay in, and I hated hotels.

"I'll give you his name and phone number," Chester replied.

"That will do."

I packed up all the papers he gave me in the bag I'd brought up with me. I now had the address for the building, leasing information for Tattoo Guy, and anything else I would need. He handed me keys next, each one labeled for what it went to. I didn't know if it was Chester or Wilma Allen who had done that, but I chose to believe it was Wilma Allen. Labels were *awesome*, and maybe it meant I had something in common with her.

"Thank you very much." I held out my hand for him, and we shook. Hopefully I'd never have to see him again, and if I did, I prayed he shaved the mustache before that happened.

Since elevators weren't my favorite thing, when the opportunity arose, I chose the stairs. I took those down and went to the parking spot where the car service I'd hired was waiting. My belongings were in the trunk, along with a couple of small bags in the back seat. I could have bought new things, but I liked my old stuff. There was often an adjustment period for me, and I'd already have to deal with that when it came to a bed. Once I was settled, I'd pay to have my old one shipped.

"Mr. Copeland," the driver said, opening the door.

"Milo," I replied. I was so over being called Mr. Copeland.

I climbed in, and he closed the door behind me. I should probably start using an app to find a ride, but would there even be many options on Little Beach Island? In San Diego I used Mom's driver, and the current one was a service I'd found for airport transportation. I wouldn't be using them consistently, and while I was good with money and had some saved, I didn't want to waste it. I also didn't want to accept any from my mom because I wanted to prove to her that I could handle this on my own.

I enjoyed the scenery as we drove. It wasn't what I was used to growing up in Southern California. There were tons of cliffs and rocky, rugged beaches with lighthouses in the distance; more greenery too.

We had to drive to the ferry, which he was riding with me because I had my things and needed to search for a room. We were almost to the boat when I glanced at the speedometer.

"You're going five miles over the speed limit," I told

the driver, whose hands tightened on the steering wheel.

"Sorry about that."

I thought about apologizing—I hated it when someone told me how to do something they couldn't do themselves—but speed limits were there for a reason. It wasn't as if I followed every rule there was, but driving stressed me out, hence why I didn't do it. Someone should have considered another career if they couldn't follow basic driving rules.

We finally got to the ferry. Little Beach was, luckily, only a thirty-minute ride from shore. Knots formed in my gut as we made our way over the ocean and closer to my new life...to a bookstore and Tattoo Guy and an apartment I probably couldn't live in, and I really hoped Tattoo Guy didn't suck. After Chester, I questioned Wilma Allen's choices in those she associated with.

As much as I wanted to just relax and take my pants off, I'd given the driver the address of my bookstore instead of the hotel first.

He pulled up in front of a white brick building with seafoam-green accents. There were two doors—one for the bookstore, the other for the tattoo parlor. I sat there for a moment, just looking out the window. The left side had a sign that said *Conflicting Ink*, and the right read *Little Beach Books*. It had a stack of books on each side of the name. Tattoo Guy had gone with a similar theme, though his sign featured the torture device he used to draw on people's skin.

And what was up with that name? *Conflicting Ink.*

Each store had a large front window, the bookstore's with a display behind it, even though it was clear the store was closed down.

There was a cobblestone area along the right side, which was basically the cutest thing ever. I wondered if Wilma Allen had put tables there at all. It would be a nice place for customers to sit outside and read or to chat with friends.

I had a feeling the driver was mad at me because he didn't say anything, just started to take my bags out of the trunk. It was so foreign to me sometimes—the things people got upset about. I hadn't meant to piss him off, but he was the one speeding, so why was it my fault?

Apparently we wouldn't be going to the hotel together. No matter, I'd figure it out. I didn't like or want to be around him either.

I got out of the car, pulled my remaining bags from the back seat, and he mumbled something I couldn't hear before getting in his car and driving away. I stood there on the sidewalk, people walking by, the smell of the ocean around me, and oh God, I really, really wanted to take my pants off.

But the town was cute. It reminded me of a postcard—the main street lined with beachy businesses, ice cream parlors, restaurants, and shops.

I tried to imagine Mom here, growing up in this place, and the image didn't fit right in my brain. She felt too California for this. I was sure she was blowing up my phone, but I still had it on *do not disturb*.

I started walking my bags to the door of the bookstore. I'd been given the number for a woman named Rachel. She had worked for Wilma Allen and would be willing to do so for me too. Little Beach Books hadn't been open since Wilma Allen's passing.

I had…a lot of bags, probably too many, but I chose to pretend that wasn't the case. Once I had them all around me, basically blocking me in, I fumbled for the keys, pulling them out of my pocket and reading each label until I found the one for the front door.

Everyone should label everything…even though I didn't. But I appreciated the effort when others did.

Just as I pushed the key into the lock, I heard, "Oh, hey. You must be Wilma's grandson."

I turned around to who I immediately assumed was Tattoo Guy. He clearly liked them even more than I liked labels, and he used them more too. From his wrists up were dragons and random designs and… Was that a top hat?

He wore shorts and flip-flops, which were probably one of the worst inventions ever. How could you walk around with something stuck between your toes? The torture devices were uncomfortable and ridiculous, but he did have nice feet. He scored points for that.

There were more tattoos on his calves and shins, but without bending down, I couldn't make out what they all were.

His shorts were nylon, like basketball shorts or something, but he didn't look like a basketball player. Did basketball players have a look? Maybe that was one of my judgy moments. I tried not to have them, I really did, but sometimes it was hard, which I definitely would be too—hard, I meant—if I didn't quit looking at Tattoo Guy.

Did that stop me? Nope. I couldn't make my eyes focus on anything but the piercings at first—lip, eyebrow, ear. I shivered because how could that not hurt? Did I mention he had great lips? Wow, did he have an awesome mouth. I'd never been into the whole bad-boy thing, but I had to admit, he was hot.

"Does someone else have a key?" I sputtered out, realizing I'd been staring for who knew how long.

"Huh? No. Just me and you that I know of."

"Because you said I must be her grandson, instead of just *hi, Wilma Allen's grandson*, since you don't know my name. That made me wonder if someone else had a key."

He stared at me, his dark brows pulled together like he wasn't sure what to say or think. I got that response a lot, but instead of asking a question or continuing to gawk at me like I'd sprouted another head, he just gave me a slow, lazy smile and said, "What's up, Wilma Allen's grandson? I'm Gideon Barlow. I rent the space from you next door and an apartment upstairs."

He held his hand out, bags between us, and wow, I couldn't believe he'd just gone with the flow like that. Even if others did, they still gave me a look that told me they thought something was wrong with me, but Tattoo Guy didn't.

My gaze shot down to his hand. It was nice, strong-looking, with lots of veins. Who knew veins were my thing? I certainly hadn't. It was weird that they were even a thing that could be hot.

Tattoo Guy dropped his arm. Shit. I'd waited too long. I hadn't reached for him, and now he'd think I was rude and, "You're very attractive." I smacked a hand over my mouth the second the words came out. Why in the hell had I told him that? Yes, I thought the truth was important and wanted more people to say how they felt, but I also didn't like fighting and really didn't want to get beaten up. I knew karate—Mom made me take lessons so I could defend myself—so I could probably incapacitate him before he could hurt me, but I didn't want to. I didn't like violence. "I would appreciate it if you didn't punch me. I should have figured out if you're homophobic before I complimented you, and why is that what they call it anyway? Shouldn't it be homojudgmental? Or I don't know, just an asshole?" Great. I was rambling.

Tattoo Guy gave me another slow, easy smile. He was very good at those. He must practice them a lot. "I can promise I won't punch you, and I'm definitely not homophobic—though I probably had a little bit of internalized homophobia when I was a kid. Also, thank you. You're very attractive too."

Wait. Did he just… Was he… "Internalized? That means you're…"

"I am." He crossed his arms. "*You're* not going to punch *me* now, right?"

"What? No!" I said before it hit me that he was joking. "I think we should really shake hands this time."

"I think we should too." For the second time, he held his hand out and again introduced himself. "I'm Gideon Barlow."

"Milo Copeland. Please don't ever call me Mr.

Copeland. I hate it. But I might call you Tattoo Guy sometimes. If you hate it, I'll try not to, but that's who you've been in my head, so it'll take me a while to get used to Gideon. Plus, you do have a lot of tattoos." He barked out a loud laugh. Sometimes when people did that, it felt like they were laughing *at* me, but it didn't with Tattoo Guy. Gideon. "Your name is kinda different."

"I've heard that before. Have I been in your head a lot?" The right side of his mouth kicked up.

I frowned. "Huh? No…*oh*." That sounded like the guys in porn when they were—"Was that flirting? Oh my God. I think it was, which is strange. I don't even know you, and well, I guess I told you I think you're attractive, but wow. I'm not sure I've ever been flirted with before. Or are you just being friendly?"

"Actually, I'm not sure," Tattoo Guy replied without hesitation. "Friendly and flirty? Flirt-ly? It just sort of happened."

The sea of bags separated us, and I suddenly got even hotter. Great, good-looking guys made the weather worse. This was going to be a problem for me…and I had so much to do. The last thing I should be worried about was attractive tattooed guys who lived in my apartment and had a shop next to mine. "We should probably talk at some point, but right now, I'd like to look at my bookstore. And according to Chester—whom I'm not sure you've met, but he's an odd guy—Wilma Allen maybe had a lover. I need to call him. Do you know anything about him?"

"Gene...he's a good man. He loved your grandma a lot." His gaze darted away. "I'm sorry for your loss. I should have said that earlier. She was a great woman. Treated me real good. We'd sit around and talk for hours sometimes. I gave Wilma her one and only tattoo."

My eyes bugged out. "Wilma Allen had a tattoo?"

"Yep. It was two pink tulips."

I opened my mouth, but nothing came out. I finally managed to whisper, "That's my mom's favorite flower."

"I'm sure she got them for the two of you, then."

Maybe she had. I hated that I would never know. I hated that I didn't know why she hadn't raised Mom or if they could have had a relationship. I felt...a little empty, hollowed out. Like there was a Wilma Allen-shaped hole inside me I hadn't known was there until just this moment.

"I also have to check into my hotel. And find a ride."

Unlike many others, Tattoo Guy didn't stumble to keep up with me and my random subject changes. He just gave me a simple nod. "I'll leave you to it, then. You know where to find me."

He watched me for a moment, then gave me another of his smiles and headed next door.

CHAPTER FOUR

Gideon

MILO DEFINITELY WASN'T a dick. I couldn't say what word I would use to describe him, but I'd been working on a tattoo for the past couple of hours since our chat, and I was still thinking about him. I was still smiling while doing it too. That had never happened to me before, but I had a feeling that Milo had that effect on a lot of people.

It took me another hour to finish up the ink—a skull with fire. We talked as I worked, but my thoughts were next door. I didn't know anything about Milo. Townsfolk knew his mom, of course. She'd left at eighteen when her parents had died and had never come back. Then Wilma had passed away, and it came out that she had a biological daughter—Milo's mom. Wilma hadn't talked about her to me or to anyone else that I'd heard.

Was Milo going to keep the store? With all those

bags, it looked like he planned to stay, but maybe it was only for a few months and he'd sell? Or maybe he'd want to put something else on this side of the building, and I'd lose my shop. I dreaded that possibility. But then…

"You're very attractive."

That definitely wasn't what I should be thinking about.

"What are you smiling at?" asked Mario, the guy I was inking.

"My handiwork," I replied, even though it had been the memory of Milo's confession. I sure as shit hadn't seen that coming, but was pleasantly surprised by it.

I was also wondering what he was doing and how he'd get a ride to the hotel with all those bags. And maybe I was a little intrigued by the guy, so kill me. There was something really fucking interesting about him. So when Mario was out, I told Freddy goodbye and headed next door. For all I knew, he wasn't even there anymore, but there was no way I couldn't try. He felt new in a way nothing around Little Beach ever did, or hell, maybe nothing in my life did at all. It was just my luck I'd get this experience from the guy who had the means to take my livelihood away from me.

Typical day in the life of Gideon Barlow.

I peeked through the glass, and I could see Milo there.

His bags were by the door, and he was pacing up and down the front aisle. His arms and hands were moving all around. He was on the phone, and…oh yeah, he definitely wasn't happy. It looked like whoever was on the other end of the line was getting an earful.

I wasn't sure if I should go in, but what if it was something I could help with?

I knocked lightly on the glass before opening the door just enough to stick my head in.

"I'm a twenty-four-year-old adult and—" Milo's gaze snapped toward me, locking on mine just as his foot caught on the edge of a rug, and he tripped, stumbling forward slightly. I tried to push the door out of the way to get in and catch him, but I was too far, and besides, he didn't need it. He righted himself, straightened his shirt as if it had been messy, and said, "Tattoo Guy is here. I have to go." I could hear the other person speaking when Milo ended the call.

"Moms, huh?" I asked, shoving my hands into my pockets, a nervous gesture, which was weird as fuck. What did I have to be nervous about?

"How did you know that's who I was talking to?"

"Because I have one myself. They're great. No one will love you more, but sometimes they can be…"

"A lot? Overbearing? Treat you like a child?"

I chuckled. "Yeah, I guess. All that."

"She makes me crazy! Sometimes I just want to…to… Well, I don't know what I want to do because I know it comes from the heart. They're stupid, I think."

Curious, I leaned against the wall, arms crossed, and asked, "What are?"

"Hearts. They're very complicated and make things a lot messier than they need to be. At least, that's what I've witnessed in other people."

There was an uncomfortable heaviness in my chest. I understood what he was saying. That muscle had caused a whole lot of difficulty in my life. "I agree."

"Why are you here?" he asked bluntly.

"Ouch."

Milo frowned. "I didn't mean… Was that rude? It was a legitimate question of why, not because I don't want you here. I'm not saying I do either because I don't even know you."

I smiled. Jesus, this guy. What was it about him? "No, it wasn't rude. I like that you say what you're thinking. I came over to see if there's anything I can help with. I'm not sure what your plans for the store are, but if you need a ride to your hotel or whatever, I can do that." Basically, I'd help him today or any other day was what I was trying to say, but suddenly I couldn't seem to speak coherently.

He cocked his head slightly. His auburn hair was short and styled neatly. He didn't run his hands through it like I did. Somehow, I knew that wasn't something Milo ever did when he was uncomfortable or unsure. Freckles danced across his nose and cheekbones. He had wide doe eyes, the color of the sky on a perfect spring day, and apparently the ability to inspire poetry-like thoughts because I sure as shit didn't usually think of things that way.

He bit into his bottom lip, not trying to be sexy even though it was. He was thinking, dissecting, trying to figure me out. I had a feeling that was how Milo looked at the whole world, trying to sort through it and put things into different boxes. I didn't mean in a judgmental way, just an organized one, so he knew where everything fit.

"I'm very hungry," he said, "and I've been told I go from hungry to hangry at the drop of a hat—strange saying, don't you think? I don't really get it. Do people drop hats often? Where did it come from? I'll look it up tonight and tell you next time I see you."

An unfamiliar flutter danced around in my gut, something that felt like…happiness? Enjoyment? I didn't know. Milo was just fun. "We can do it right now." I pulled out my phone, but he shook his head.

"We'll look it up at dinner because I'm tilting slightly more toward hangry. I guess I could walk, but I don't know where to go." A flare of what looked like panic flashed in his eyes, like maybe it just hit him he'd traveled to a town he didn't know and wasn't sure how to deal with that.

"I'm an expert on food. I can put a whole hell of a lot of it away."

"You have a great body, though. You don't look like you eat too much."

"This old thing?" I winked. "Glad you like it. I was blessed with a fast metabolism. Let's lock up and head out."

"Should I leave my bags here? Will we come back before you take me to my hotel?"

"We're walking to dinner. We'll come back for them." I appreciated that he was spending time with me, that he was willing to go have dinner and let me take him back to his room. It was maybe a silly thing to feel grateful over because technically it was me helping him, but I couldn't help wondering how typical this was for him. Or if, for whatever reason, Milo trusted me.

He nodded, shoved his phone into his pocket, and grabbed his keys. I went out first and waited for Milo to lock the bookstore.

He fell into step beside me, both of us quiet for a moment. There were people out and about, a few saying hi, others calling me by name, and all looking at Milo and wondering who he was...or wondering about his mom's history with Wilma Allen. How had she never told anyone Beverly was her daughter?

"People here stare a lot," he said, making me chuckle.

"It's because you're new. Small towns are like that. Where are you from?"

"San Diego. Why do you wear flip-flops?"

My head snapped toward him at the strange change of subject. "Um...I don't know. I don't always. Is something wrong with my feet?"

He shrugged. "No, I suppose as far as feet go, they're nice. I'm not really a foot person, but yours aren't glaringly bad or anything. It's not like I've never seen anyone wear flip-flops. I see it all the time, I just don't get it. It's bizarre...showing them in public. And the part between your toes, how is that not the most uncomfortable thing in the world?"

"Not glaringly bad? You're going to give me foot insecurity. I'll have you know I used to sleep with this guy who loved toes and thought I had particularly sexy ones."

"Oh my God! What did he do with them?" He looked at me wide-eyed, as if he didn't know what to think. There was interest there, and maybe a little disgust too.

"I'm sure you don't want to know." Shit. Why in the fuck had I mentioned it?

"I do," Milo replied. "If you want to tell me, that is, and I really hope you do because…I mean…*toes*."

Again, I found myself laughing. "First, don't knock other people's kinks. Second…Jesus." I ran a hand through my hair, suddenly embarrassed. He had the ability to make me feel that way when I typically didn't. I glanced his way. Milo was still walking but watching me expectantly, and damn, I didn't want to disappoint him.

"He liked to suck on them. What else would he do with them?"

"I don't know. You're attractive, but I definitely don't want to suck your toes. Do you like that? Is that what you want guys to do to you? Did you do the same to him? Isn't it gross?"

"Okay, we're getting off track here." I pointed toward the restaurant. "That's where we're going." Only Milo didn't move. He was rooted to the sidewalk, so I stopped too. His head angled down, and there was no doubt in my mind he was going through the topic of our conversation.

"Sorry," he said, "but they just don't do it for me, and

I don't think I can move until I know if they do it for you. Not because I'll judge you, but because, oh my God, I have to know. How can I not know?"

A woman and her daughter walked by with ice cream cones, looking at us like they weren't sure what to think. I honestly didn't either, but it was refreshing. I sighed.

When they were safely out of earshot, I said, "No, I don't expect that, and it doesn't particularly turn me on, but turning on my lover does, so it was hot for me because he liked and got off on it. No, I didn't return the favor, and also, I will never, ever wear flip-flops around you again. My toes feel like they should go into hiding." I curled them down.

For the first time, I heard Milo laugh. It was smooth and clear like his voice, this little burst of happiness that made me feel the same.

He started walking toward the restaurant, and I followed. "They're not terrible toes."

"I didn't use to think so."

"Did I really make you insecure, or are you joking?"

I nudged him with my arm. "I'm joking."

"I can't always tell."

"Eh, I can't either. People are hard to read sometimes. Nothing wrong with that."

Again, Milo openly stared at me. He didn't try to hide

it, or his look of concentration, the slight downward curl of his lips, which I could tell wasn't an unhappy frown, just a confused one, like maybe he was searching for some kind of answer.

"You're different," Milo said.

"I think the same thing about you."

"Yeah, but most people think that about me. Do they with you?"

The question made my thoughts stumble slightly. Milo made me think in ways I wasn't familiar with. "Yes and no. I stand out in my family. I'm not like them. Then being the only queer kid around growing up, that kind of thing. But I don't think that's what you mean."

"No." He shook his head. "It's not."

When he didn't add anything more, I wasn't sure what else to say, so I motioned toward the Lighthouse. "Are we going to go in so you don't get hangry?"

He startled. "Wow…I forgot to even get mad about being hungry. Why did you have to remind me?"

"Well, then hurry, let's go before it's too late." I put my hands on his shoulders and steered him toward the door.

Milo chuckled, opened it, and we went inside.

He took a couple of steps before stopping without notice, and I ran into him. "Shit. Sorry."

"It's a little loud in here."

It didn't feel that way to me, but I knew it would be later on. "Too loud? We can go somewhere else."

"No, it's fine. Maybe we'll just hurry?"

"Let's pick somewhere else." The last thing I wanted was to make him uncomfortable.

"It's okay. I know you're trying to be nice, but I said I'm fine. Believe me, I'll let you know if I'm not. I need you to trust me when I say something. I don't like it when people push or try too hard to fix things for me. If I can't handle something, I'll say so." I hadn't meant to do that, and I think he could read my discomfort on my face because he added, "I know you're trying to be helpful. It's just…important to me."

"Okay. Done."

The relief was clear on his face, making a strange feeling of pride settle inside me that I'd said the right thing. I often said the wrong thing, so it felt like I scored unexpected points in a challenge I didn't know I was participating in.

"You gonna take a seat or block the walkway?" a familiar, playful voice said from beside me, but Milo immediately tensed up.

"There's plenty of room. We're not blocking anything," he replied, back straight, arms crossed, and head held high. Milo's response hadn't been said in the same joking tone as Kris's.

Kris and Megan looked at him, then me. Fuck. It wasn't often I didn't want to see my best friend, but for some reason, tonight was one of those evenings.

"We didn't mean... He was joking," Meg said.

"Oh. Strange joke. It's not a very good one," Milo said, and I bit the inside of my cheek to keep from laughing.

"Milo, this is my best friend, Kris, who thinks he's funny but isn't. And this is his wife, Megan, who could do better, but I guess she feels bad for him."

"Ha-ha." Kris wrapped an arm around my shoulders and tried to playfully put me in a headlock.

I shoved him off. "Guys, this is Milo, the new owner of Little Beach Books." And my shop, but I wasn't going to say that.

Recognition sparked in their gazes, which then turned curious and leery because no one knew his plans for the building. We were protective of our space on the island. We didn't want to be one of those places that was all for show and more touristy than anything else.

"Nice to meet you," Megan said.

"We're going to eat," I replied.

"Want to sit together?" Kris asked.

"No," I rushed out and saw Milo relax, but the truth was, I hadn't done it for him. I wanted to spend more time getting to know him. "We're going to be quick. Then I need to get Milo to his hotel."

Kris's brows pulled together, but they said goodbye. We sat on opposite sides of the restaurant. The second we were in our booth, Milo said, "Your friend is weird."

"That he is, but he's a good guy." I grabbed the menus from the lobster's grasp and handed one to Milo.

"Is now a good time to mention I'm a vegetarian?"

"Hey, Gideon, who's your friend?" Daria asked. She and I went to high school together, and now she waitressed here part-time.

"We're not friends," Milo answered, and Daria's eyes practically fell out of her head in confusion.

"There you go, hurtin' my feelings again," I teased.

"I didn't mean we won't be, but we just…we only met today. We don't know enough about each other yet." Milo looked at Daria. "Wilma Allen was my grandmother. She left me the building where he lives and works." He always called her that, I'd noticed, by her first and last name. Because they'd never met? To keep himself at an emotional distance?

"I'm sorry about your loss."

"It's okay. I didn't know her. I wish I had. I'm going

to talk to her lover soon. I'm excited to learn more about her," Milo said honestly.

I grinned.

"Oh…um…wow. What can I get you guys to drink?"

"I'll just take water, and I'm getting really hungry, so can I order a salad? All veggies, please. No meat. Cheese is fine. And a side of…hmm…French fries. Or mozzarella sticks. Do you want to share those with me?" His gaze met mine.

"Sure." I turned to Daria. "I'll have the chicken club."

"Will do. I'll get that right out to you both," she replied and left.

"Does she not like Gene?" he asked.

"No, I think she's just not used to people calling him Wilma's lover."

He shrugged. "That's what he was, wasn't it? I can say boyfriend, but that sounds odd for them too. Anyway, it doesn't matter. We're going to chat tomorrow. Did I tell you?"

"Nope, you didn't."

"I'm also going to meet Rachel at the bookstore to make plans to reopen. I have so much to learn, though…"

"So you're planning to reopen? Stick around?" I held my breath even though he'd basically just said so.

"Of course. It was Wilma Allen's dream. Plus, I don't love being an accountant. I feel like I haven't found that special thing that's mine. You know, the one I want above all else. I guess I'm trying to find my place in the world."

"You and me both," I replied, but for whatever reason, I hadn't expected it from him. Milo just seemed to know who he was, to be that person, and nothing else mattered.

"Really?" he asked.

"Yep. I mean, I know I love tattooing. That's what I want to do. And I love my shop, but outside of my career…" I shrugged. "Who the fuck knows?"

He smiled widely. "Maybe we'll figure it out together."

My pulse drummed against my skin. I wanted that. "Maybe we will, though you should probably figure out if you want to be friends with me first." I winked.

"I'm working on it. I'll let you know soon." A slow pink crawled up his cheeks.

Damned if I didn't need him to say yes.

CHAPTER FIVE

Milo

I HATED THIS hotel. Like, if I knew I wouldn't hurt anyone or go to jail, I would love to burn the whole thing down. I'd have to be super positive about avoiding incarceration because no way I could survive it. And also the keeping-people-safe part because the thought of hurting someone made me want to vomit. But the point was, this was *the worst* hotel there ever was.

That was all I could think about as I waited for Gideon to pick me up and take me to the bookstore.

My face burned hot, the heat traveling down to my stomach at the thought of him. Gideon was nice. We'd talked all through dinner the night before, and just like he'd promised, we'd made it quick so we could leave when the Lighthouse still wasn't too busy. He didn't complain when I told him I wanted to go and didn't question it when I asked for two bills—because we weren't on a date and we were still figuring out if we were friends, so I didn't want him to pay for me like he'd asked.

The conversation had continued to flow as we'd walked back to the bookstore and piled my things in his truck. When he'd dropped me off, he offered to pick me up this morning, and oh, that was another problem with this hotel. It was too far from the store. I could get a car service, but I was worried about how reliable they'd be and how many options there were on a small island like Little Beach.

My phone buzzed, and I knew without looking that it was Mom. My hunch was quickly proven correct.

Are you still ignoring me?

I rolled my eyes. **I wasn't ignoring you. I told you I would talk to you later. I'm waiting for Tattoo Guy to pick me up. Oh! And Wilma Allen had a lover! I'm talking with him today too! I'll call you tonight. Promise.**

I wasn't surprised when a reply came back almost instantly. **What is up with this tattoo guy? What's his real name?**

I sighed. **Gideon Barlow. I can take care of myself.**

And when his black truck pulled up in front of the Sleepy Island Lodge, I couldn't help smiling. I hiked my bag up onto my shoulder, walked over, and climbed in. "Their breakfast is terrible. Have you ever tried it? It's omelet day, and they ruined omelets. How do you even do that? I understand they're hard to get perfect, but these were rubbery. Eggs should never taste like rubber."

He chuckled, a rich laugh that was unexpectedly soothing. "Does that mean I'm in danger of hangry Milo?"

"Yes, also lack-of-sleep Milo. The bed squeaks, and the mattress is too firm. And it's very loud at night. People walk and laugh down the hall at all hours. I tried to sleep, and when I couldn't, I read for a while, then tried again. It didn't help. I need another hotel. I don't know if I can handle it. Actually, I just need to rent a house…or an apartment. I don't need a whole house just for me. Do you think there are many apartments available?"

Tattoo Guy had already pulled away from the curb and was driving. He frowned. "Honestly, apartments are hard to come by on the island, but technically, you already have one."

"You live in it, though."

"That doesn't mean it's not yours. It wouldn't be fair of me to sit comfortably in something you own while you suffer in a hotel where you can't sleep. Or for you to deal with the struggle of finding something else."

"It wouldn't be fair of me to take your home either.

You live there. That would feel gross." My gaze darted from his eyes downward and—"Oh my God! You're wearing shoes! Did you do that because of me?"

He cocked a dark brow before returning his attention to the road. "I was wearing shoes yesterday."

"I don't think you were. Those were toe-torturers. Don't your feet feel so much better safely tucked away in sneakers? Not that they were necessarily bad toes, but we went over this yesterday. Also, the drop of a hat originated in the nineteenth century when it was how they'd begin a fight. They'd drop a hat and then shoot."

"Yeah, that makes sense. I probably should have known that."

"I thought the same thing! I can't believe I didn't."

"Well, we know now." He reached down and scratched his thigh beneath the shorts he wore. His were looser than mine, baggy but not overly so. Like, I knew that when he stood, the band of his underwear likely peeked out the top, which would be super hot.

He waved his hand. "Hello? Earth to Milo."

I snapped my gaze away from his thigh that I now wanted to lick. Shit. I'd been staring…and hopefully not drooling. "Yes?"

"Did you need me to stop somewhere so you can get a better breakfast?"

I shook my head. "I can do it. I'd like to do some exploring of the places I can reach on foot. I have a lot to figure out, and I don't want to have to depend on you to help." My list was growing between bookstore stuff and Wilma Allen stuff and apartment stuff and transportation stuff, but if I were in San Diego, this was where Mom would try to take over even though I didn't need her to.

Tattoo Guy pulled in behind our building, where he'd been parked the night before too. "Okay. Well, I'll be around."

I couldn't help but grin. I liked that he was so easy to get along with. He just went with the flow, didn't question me, or try too hard to help like some people did. They assumed there was something wrong with me when there wasn't. Neurodivergence wasn't wrong…just different. But not once so far had he made me feel that way.

"Wow…something must be good?"

"Hmm?" I asked.

"Your smile is bigger than your face. I'm not sure I've ever seen that before."

"That's not possible."

"One would think that, but they aren't looking at you right now. It's cute as shit—and there it goes, getting even bigger. Damn, you can go on the road with this act."

"That was a terrible joke, and you're very strange." When his brows pulled toward his hairline, I asked, "What?" though I knew what he was saying: why was I the one calling him strange? But it didn't bother me at all. I knew how he meant it, and again, I knew I was unusual to a lot of people. Something about Tattoo Guy made me feel comfortable, though, because if someone else I'd known for less than twenty-four hours had done the same thing, I probably would've given them a piece of my mind.

"What, what?" he asked.

I shook my head and tried not to let my smile take over my face again. "I have to go."

"No one is stopping you."

He was right. No one but me. *I* was stopping me because he was fun. We hadn't even done anything, and I was having a good time. So I just said, "You're exactly right," and unclicked my seat belt and opened the door. "Thank you for the ride."

"You're welcome for the ride."

"Are you staying there all day?" I asked after climbing out.

"Stop being obsessed with me. First you won't get out of my truck, and now this."

My heart dropped somewhere near my sneaker-covered feet. Oh God. Did he think I was some obsessed stalker? I opened my mouth to plead my case just as the familiar curl of the right side of his mouth kicked up again. "I know that was sarcasm. Do you think you're very good at it? I'm not an expert, but you don't seem to be."

Gideon playfully clutched his chest like I'd just dropped my hat before mortally wounding him. "Ouch. I thought I was funny before I met you. You've done nothing but bust my balls."

"Yours are in your chest?" I asked as seriously as I could, but he just rolled his eyes.

"Not that I'm aware of, but I've heard my brain is in my dick before, so I guess you never know."

We shared a laugh before I grabbed my bag and forced myself to walk away.

It wasn't until I unlocked the door and was safely tucked away in the bookstore that I realized I'd thought of him as Gideon instead of Tattoo Guy.

ALL THE PASSWORDS and information I needed were in the paperwork Chester had given me, and the first thing I discovered was that Wilma Allen had badass bookkeeping skills. I was honestly impressed with that part of it, but what had me a little worried was the fact that she was making less and less money. As in, toward the end, she was in the red. Part of that was because she'd worked less herself and had hired more people to help. I'd be full-time, which would help, but I couldn't ignore the feeling of discomfort settling at the base of my spine.

Which made my brain start going too fast and too many thoughts sprint around the damn thing. She'd left me a business that could fail—logically, all businesses could, but this one had steadily declining profit for years. And according to my research, she was charging Gideon less than the going rate for rent on his space and the apartment upstairs.

She was lucky she owned the building outright. If she hadn't, I wasn't sure how she would have continued to make it work. And I so, so, so needed to do that…to make this work, not just for Wilma Allen, but for me. She had built this with her own hard work and then had entrusted it to me. I didn't want to let down this woman I didn't even know, and God, did I want to prove I could do it.

Yesterday I'd been too busy to really let myself take much in. The bookstore was definitely outdated. There weren't many reading spaces. I didn't really get why people liked to read in public, but I knew that was a thing. Or they came to bookstores to drink coffee and talk to their friends, and Little Beach Books wasn't set up for that. Were bookstores without coffee even a thing anymore? I figured they were, but probably not a very popular one.

Her book stock was good, though. It was your typical small store, with a little bit of every genre. It appeared she had a lot of the popular, newer titles—the ones that released before she passed away, at least.

I'd always been good with money and had some saved. My brain told me it was stupid to invest a lot of money into a business I wasn't sure would ever be profitable. It wasn't as if I'd wanted a bookstore all my life, but again, I was pretty sure I did now.

Mom would think it was a terrible idea. She would fill my head with all sorts of reasons why I should sell and come home, but...how would I know if I didn't try? When had anything in my life really been my choice? I wanted this to be.

So I sat down, pulled out my planner, and started with a list. Lists were *awesome*, just like labels on a key chain full of keys.

When I was done with that one, I made a second about the first, because really, you could never have too many.

I was just about to look at the time when there was a knock on the glass door. I glanced up to see a woman with braids in her dark hair, and she was smiling at me. I'd gotten so busy making plans, I forgot Rachel was coming.

I went over and unlocked the door. "Rachel?"

She gave me another kind smile. "That's me."

"I'm Milo Copeland. Please don't call me Mr. Copeland."

"Right? It makes me feel old when people do that…and…I don't know, it's too professional. I'm afraid of saying or doing something wrong."

I was pretty sure hearts shot out of my eyes. Not the romantic kind because while I could see that Rachel was beautiful, I was only attracted to men, but that one statement had been plucked right out of my head. "Exactly. I know it's a respect thing, but it's also respectful to call people what they'd like to be called."

"I agree. It's so funny you said that. Wilma was the same way."

A confused feeling washed over me, one that was both happy and sad, because while it was cool to hear we had something in common, it also hurt that we hadn't been able to discover that together. I wished I knew why she hadn't been in Mom's life. There had to have been a good reason.

But then I couldn't help wondering if it mattered that I called her Wilma Allen, which I did because…well, because that's who she was to me. I didn't *know* her, and calling her Wilma or Grandma felt too close, as if we'd had a relationship when we hadn't.

"Come in," I said belatedly.

She did, and I locked the door behind her. Rachel looked like she was about my age, with smooth skin that was a creamy, light brown like maybe one of her parents was Black, but the other wasn't. She wore a spaghetti-strap shirt and had a couple of tattoos on her arms, ear piercings, and a hoop in the left side of her nose.

"Did Gideon do your tattoos?" I asked, even though he likely hadn't. It wasn't as if he was the only tattoo artist in Maine.

"He did this one." She pointed to an *Alice in Wonderland* tattoo with Alice, the cat, and the man in a top hat. Around it was the quote about being mad and bonkers and how the best people were.

"You know, I've never actually read it…or seen the movies."

Rachel nudged me with her arm, as if we'd known each other for longer than five minutes. "Good thing you own a bookstore. You should read it, and then we'll watch the movie together. The Tim Burton one."

My pulse danced excitedly against my skin. "I'd like that…I think. If I don't like the book, I might not want to watch the movie."

She laughed. "You just let me know."

I nodded. "You helped W—" It felt peculiar to call her Wilma, but now I couldn't help but worry about calling her Wilma Allen. It made my head spin a bit, so I found a way to switch direction. "Here a lot?"

"I did. I love this place. I live with my parents, and I go to school online. I got pregnant at seventeen, and while I wouldn't take it back because Cammy is the best little girl in the world, it's made things difficult. This was my first job at sixteen, and Wilma had always been supportive. My parents too. They help while I'm working on getting my degree. I don't know what I'd do without them."

I was always interested in people's stories. It was crazy how diverse everyone's experiences could be. It was hard sometimes because I liked rules and structure, but humans weren't always like that, life wasn't always like that, and while it stressed me out, other times it fascinated me or made me like someone or respect them.

"She's seven," Rachel added.

"Is she loud? Sometimes I get annoyed with loud

kids."

Just as I wondered if I'd said the wrong thing, Rachel laughed. "I like you, Milo. And, not really. I mean, she's a kid, so sometimes she's a little wild, but she's mostly just really fucking cool."

"I hope I get to meet her," I said honestly.

"I hope you do too."

"I have ideas…about the bookstore…"

Her smile grew. "I can't wait to hear them."

CHAPTER SIX

Gideon

I WAS IN the back room, stocking supplies, when I heard the bell jingle, alerting me that the door was opening. Freddy had left to grab himself some dinner, so it could be him coming back.

I looked out toward the main part of the building to see the door was open just enough for a head to stick through, which it did, all neatly styled auburn hair as Milo peeked around, his body still outside. Did he not want to come in? That looked to be the case.

He was so damn adorable I couldn't help watching for a second while his gaze darted around, checking things out. He took a step in, paused. Then another, and pause. "Tattoo Guy?"

I set a small box down on the shelf before stepping into the doorway and leaning against the jamb. "Boo."

"Hoo?" he said as if it was a question, and I chuckled.

"Check you out. Making a joke so bad you cried."

"You're lucky I tried. I typically don't, though I make people laugh sometimes, but it's not on purpose and it's usually not a good feeling."

I crossed my arms. I didn't like the sound of that. I didn't want Milo to ever feel he was being laughed at. "Well, those people suck."

"I agree, though sometimes I don't think they mean it…or realize it. People are strange and confusing, even to themselves."

"You can say that again."

"Most of the time I don't like people." His brows pulled together, small thought wrinkles settling in on his forehead. "I like you, though. That's not normal for me—liking someone so quickly."

I grinned, my chest feeling uncharacteristically fluttery, like there was a butterfly race going on inside. I opened my mouth to say something about being special when he added, "And Rachel. I like her a lot."

Oh, well, scratch that whole me being exceptional; apparently, Rachel was unique too.

"That reminds me of why I came. We had the best day! I have so much to tell you. Can we have dinner together again before you take me to the hotel? I was so distracted I didn't have time to look for another place to stay… I'm going to be incredibly pissy tomorrow, by the way. I don't know if I'll be able to sleep. I need to find another hotel. Maybe I should skip dinner with you. Yes, I think that's what I'll do. I can give you my good news tomorrow or in the truck since you're driving me. Are you sure that's still okay? Why are you grinning at me like that? It's creepy."

"Creepy wasn't the vibe I was going for."

"Did I hurt your feelings?"

I shoved off the wall. "No." God, he was refreshing. I didn't know another word to use for him other than that. I never knew what to expect, and everything was so damn pure with him. I couldn't help wanting to spend more time with him, couldn't help wanting to be his friend, and really, I hadn't wanted much in a long time. "We can grab a quick dinner upstairs if you want. It's your apartment, really, and you haven't even seen it. You can tell me about your day, and we'll figure out the sleeping arrangement." As soon as I said it, I remembered he was a vegetarian. "Shit…hopefully we can piece together a full vegetarian meal. I don't grocery shop with that in mind."

"Yes, let's do that. I'm really good at figuring out ways to eat."

On cue, Freddy slipped inside, and Milo turned to him. Freddy was a big guy—six foot four, barrel-chested, and that long, thick beard of his. He had more tattoos than I did. They started at his fingers, crawled up his hands, arms, all the way to the top of his neck.

Milo said, "I think you should be Tattoo Guy from now on."

"Huh?" Freddy asked, looking from Milo to me, clearly confused.

"It's what I call Gideon. It was the name in my head for him before I met him. I haven't gotten it out yet, but I've called him Gideon twice now. I'm Milo Copeland, but please don't call me Mr. Copeland. Who are you?"

"Um…Freddy," he replied, his gaze darting back to me again.

"Freddy's the other artist working here." I went over to them, giving my attention to a very confused, bearded man. "Milo's Wilma's grandson."

"Oh shit. I'm so sorry for your loss."

"Thank you. I hope this isn't rude, but we're going upstairs now. I'm going to raid Tattoo—Gideon." His head whipped in my direction. "I can call you Tattoo Gideon!"

"Do you have to?"

"Of course not. I would never call you something you don't like. That reminds me—I have a question about Wilma Allen, but I'll ask when it's just us."

Freddy's scrunched-up face told me he wasn't sure what to think, and while I sometimes felt that way with Milo, I didn't like seeing it from Freddy. That affection I already felt for Milo wasn't there. But Milo was a grown-ass man who could take care of himself—and also, he was someone I hardly knew, I reminded myself. I had no reason to feel protective over him.

"You good here?" I asked Freddy.

"Confused but good."

"I have that effect on people," Milo said. "Let's go. I'm excited."

Curious electricity sparked inside me. I wanted to know what he had to say—and hoped it wasn't that he was going to sell or something crazy like that.

"I'll see you tomorrow, and if you get any walk-ins tonight, you can text me to see if I want to come down. I don't know what time Milo will be heading out."

"Will do," Freddy replied. "Nice to meet you, Milo."

"You too," Milo told him.

We headed for the door, then around the building to the stairs out back. I went up first, unlocked, and stepped aside, signaling for him to go in. Milo did.

"Oh, look. It's your toe-torturers." He pointed to my flip-flops by the door. "Do I need to take mine off?"

"Nah, it's fine, and you be nice. I happen to like

them."

"I just have concerns for your feet."

I watched as he went farther in, looking around as he did. It was a large apartment. The living room, dining room, and kitchen were open-concept. The kitchen was to the left, and a long breakfast bar separated it from the dining area to the right and the front room ahead, which ended at four picture windows along the far wall that looked out over the street below.

There was a short hallway on the left, with two small bedrooms and a bathroom. It was clear that whoever designed it had wanted more space in the main areas rather than where they slept.

"It's kind of perfect, isn't it?" Milo asked, his hand brushing the bar as he walked by, heading straight for the windows.

Guilt ravaged my insides. This was his. He should be living here, not me. "It is. Listen, I wanted to say—"

"Wait! I have good news I need to share first. And we have to cook. I might make myself at home in your kitchen. I hope you don't mind. I need to distract myself anyway."

I cocked my head, watching him as he made his way to the fridge, opening both it and the freezer. "Distract yourself from what?"

"I'd rather not say. It's not really appropriate." He didn't look my way, kept his eyes on what he was doing.

Was he talking about his attraction to me? Because I didn't think that was inappropriate. I thought it was hot. "Okay, well, obviously you don't have to, but you can tell me anything if you want."

"I know…which is weird. You have stuff for a salad…and…zucchini. Do you have marinara? There's mozzarella."

I had no idea where he was going with this, but I went to the cabinet and pulled out a jar.

"Perfect! We can slice these lengthwise, put some sauce and cheese on top and bake them like little cheese pizzas."

"That's not pizza."

"It's different pizza. Different can be good."

Still no eye contact. I couldn't help wondering if he was saying more than it sounded, if we were talking about more than simply his zucchini and marinara.

"You're right. I like unique. It makes things more fun." When he stared at me and grinned, I added, "Let's do this."

"If you have pizza crust, we can use that."

"I don't. Plus, I like to try new things."

Milo pulled the supplies from the fridge. I asked him

the temperature to preheat the oven, and he told me, and then we washed our hands and got to work, making zucchini pizza and salads. I wasn't going to lie. I was pretty sure I'd miss meat, but I figured I could eat some when he left…if he left.

"So…your exciting news?" I prompted, the two of us standing side by side and working together.

"I can't believe I almost forgot. I want to remodel the bookstore. I did some research into permits and what I'd need to do. The store is great, but not very up to date. I think I can do that while keeping the similar feel the people of Little Beach probably like, but the space could be worked so much better to have an area for comfy chairs to read. I thought about a kids' area, and I'm going back and forth because they're loud and sometimes too much for me. We really need a café. Nothing major, but coffee, pastries, and tables for people to meet up to chat or do work. I talked to Rachel, and she has some great ideas too. She's also not in a position where she has to get back to work because she lives with her parents. I think we can still make good use of the space with these changes and not affect Conflicting Ink. I would never do that."

He wouldn't, and somehow I already knew that about him. I'd been so worried about what would happen, and now Milo was here, and suddenly I was feeling guilty for that worry and for not thinking of his business. "I appreciate that, but you also have to consider what's best for you. My space is smaller than yours, but if you need to knock down the wall to expand, you should. I can find something else."

He stopped chopping and looked at me. "What? No. It would be weird without you there."

"It's only been a day."

"Yeah, but I have that idea in my head now. If I didn't like it, you'd be in trouble, but I do, and now I can't imagine it any other way. Even thinking about that stresses me out. I like things the way I like them, and I like my bookstore with Conflicting Ink next door, and wow…that was cool. I just automatically thought of it as *my* bookstore. Maybe this is me."

"I'm glad you like it, but you don't need a bookstore to tell you who you are, Milo. I might not have known you for long, but it's true."

"Yes and no…and it's not something I always have a choice in. Some people can hide things about themselves. I can't." He shifted. "Like it's totally inappropriate, but it's killing me not to take my pants off right now."

"Huh? Ouch! Shit!" A burning sensation shot through my finger with the slice of the knife.

"Oh my God. I'm so sorry. I made you cut yourself."

Milo grabbed my wrist and tugged me to the sink. He turned the faucet on, pulling my hand under the water. "Does it hurt bad?"

I watched him, fascinated by this man who was my new friend. "No. I didn't get it good. Just a little slice. Can we get back to the pants thing?"

Red climbed over his cheeks and freckles. "I'm not propositioning you for sex. I just hate pants—shorts too. I'm able to place the times I wear them into these boxes in my head. Like…I really don't want to walk around the grocery store without them, but when I'm at home, taking them off is always the first thing I do. Something's telling me I'm home, so I need to remove them, but it's strange because I'm not home. My boxes are getting messed up, and I don't like it."

He used his free hand to rub over his face, discomfort rolling off him. I hadn't seen this side of him before, not really. He took a step back and then another, and damned if I didn't want to fix those fucking boxes. I'd climb inside his brain if I could and sort them out just the way he liked them.

"What if you were?" I asked.

"Were what?"

I turned off the water. "Home. I mean, technically, your boxes aren't messed up. You own this building, so this apartment is yours. I've been thinking about it all day, and…I don't feel right, staying here while you're in a hotel or looking for a rental on an island that rarely has them crop up. Plus, you don't drive, so this would make it easy for you to get to work. You should live here, Milo. My parents are on Little Beach. I could always stay with them or my brother and his wife." The thought sat heavy in my chest, made my stomach tighten because I loved this apartment, but it was the right thing to do.

"Do you want to live with your parents or your brother and his wife? Do you want to move out?"

"I'm not sure that matters."

"It does to me. Wait." He turned and went for the hallway, didn't ask, just peeked in the bathroom, then opened the spare bedroom door, followed by mine. "I think I could do it. I think I could live here with you. I had to see the rooms first, and I've never had a roommate, so I'll probably be annoying, and *you'll* probably be annoying, but I'm willing to try."

"I…" Really fucking loved that idea, but he needed to be sure. "You could live with someone who's not a friend?"

"I can't tell if you're being sarcastic or not, but I think we are friends now. Which is odd. I said that earlier when I told you about Rachel, though, how I like you both and normally it takes me much longer. So, we're friends, if you want to be friends with me, that is."

I grinned. It was a stupid, wide grin that was much too happy for the situation. "I do want to be your friend."

"Do you want to try and be roommates?"

"As long as you promise that if you don't like it, you tell me. Or if there are things I do that bother you, you tell me that too." I wanted this to work out for him, for us. I didn't want Milo making a sacrifice for me that would leave him feeling uncomfortable or out of his element. I didn't want to be the reason any of his boxes were out of whack.

"Obviously. Why wouldn't I?"

I chuckled. "It's a deal, then." I held out my hand.

"I'm not shaking that. You were just bleeding."

"You grabbed my hand to wash it."

"Your wrist, but that was in the moment, and now the moment has passed and all I can think of is that I could have gotten your blood on me. No offense to you. I don't want anyone's blood on me."

God, he was really great. "Well, then we'll pretend we sealed the deal. Should we finish making dinner now?"

"Not you. You're done for the night. I…can't. Sorry. Do you have a Band-Aid? I know it's not bleeding anymore, but it'll stress me out."

"Okay, new plan. You make us food. I'll bandage this up."

"Second deal." He nodded.

I went into the bathroom and did as I said. My pulse was jumping in this erratic way that showed how excited I was for this…to have a roommate…a guy I'd met twenty-four hours earlier.

My new friend.

What the fuck was happening in my life? This wasn't like me.

But when I went back into the kitchen and saw Milo standing at the counter in a shirt and boxer briefs, happily chopping vegetables, I couldn't help smiling.

CHAPTER SEVEN

Milo

GIDEON WASN'T AWAKE when I got up the next morning. After dinner last night—a dinner where he'd liked my zucchini pizza—we'd gone to the hotel to get my things and check out. He had a bed in the spare room that honestly wasn't much better than the one at the hotel, but I was going to try really hard not to tell him that the next time I saw him. I didn't know if it would come off as rude.

He said he mostly worked days at the shop, but his hours could be random because it depended on appointments or walk-ins. Sometimes Freddy would message him when he was off, and Gideon would decide if he wanted to do the tattoo or not.

Oh, and when I couldn't get much sleep last night, I decided I wanted to start calling him Gideon. He was my friend and roommate now—*gah*, what if I sucked at the whole roommate thing? It was pretty obvious I would, but I really wanted to make this work with Gideon. If it didn't, I would move because I didn't feel right kicking him out of his apartment.

But I also just liked being his friend, and friends should call each other by their names, right? I felt I knew him well enough for that.

He had some random veggies in the fridge, thankfully, so I'd been able to make an omelet. I worried it might be rude to eat his food without asking, but Gideon had told me to make myself at home. And I would make sure I bought food to replace everything I took.

I cut enough to make him an omelet too, but he didn't wake up. I read a little bit, but he still slept. I paced…and waited…and waited…what felt like forever for either Gideon to get out of bed or for it to be late enough for me to call my mom in California.

As soon as my phone said ten—which was the perfect time to catch Mom before she left for work—I sat cross-legged on the couch.

"Well, if it isn't my favorite son calling me. Color me shocked."

"Mom…I've been gone like two days, and we talked yesterday."

"After you ignored me!"

"Because you wouldn't let me do what I needed to do!" I sighed. Sometimes she was a lot. She made me feel like a child, and there was nothing I hated more than that.

"Milo, you know I just worry."

"I do, but you have to let me make my mistakes and live my own life. I've made a plan, and I've thought it through." Well, the bookstore part. I didn't do much thinking when it came to living with Gideon. I just said yes because, well, because I wanted to. "I'm going to tell you what it is, and I want you to listen without criticizing. You need to accept the choices I've made."

There was a long silence on the phone, and I waited it out; finally, she said, "I'll try."

"I'm going to remodel the bookstore and—"

"That might take most of your savings! On a business you don't even know will be profitable and one that isn't something you even cared about until less than a week ago."

"You're already interrupting! And judging! I'm hanging up."

"No! I'm sorry, but…"

"I know. Do you think I'm stupid?"

She gasped. "No. You're one of the smartest people I know."

"Then act like it. I'm going to remodel the store, and I'm going to do the work I can on my own. It's not a huge remodel, and I'll be conservative in what I spend. I'm doing this because I want to, and it's what I think will be the best move for my business."

There was another pause, and I knew she was fighting the urge to tell me all the reasons I shouldn't move forward. But I was proud when she settled on, "Okay."

"And I've moved into the apartment upstairs."

"But the man lives there, doesn't he?"

"Yes." I closed my eyes, waiting for the world to explode, or at least my mom's head.

"You're living with a strange man you don't know?"

I pushed to my feet and walked over to the window. "I know him. Okay, so I don't know him super well, but I trust him."

"People trusted Ted Bundy too, and look what happened!"

"Gideon isn't a serial killer!"

"No one thought Ted Bundy was a serial killer either."

"Oh my God. Okay, so he might be a serial killer, but so could anyone I walk by on the street, or a guy I go out with…if I ever went out with guys. The point is, anyone can murder me, but I don't think Gideon will.

He's…nice. And funny. He didn't make me feel weird when I said I had to leave before the restaurant got loud. He wore flip-flops the first day, but when I complained, he wore sneakers the next. And he ate my vegetarian food and drives me around and—"

"Oh, Milo."

"Oh, Milo, what?" It was never a good thing when she said something like that.

"Do you have a crush on him? You need to be careful. I don't want you to get hurt. Do you even know if he's gay?"

"He's queer. He told me because the first time I saw him I told him I'm attracted to him and then asked him not to punch me. He also said he dated a guy who used to suck on his toes, but that's beside the point. I don't have a crush on him. Yes, he's very sexy, and I like to look at him—a lot—but I don't think he's noticed, and if he has, he hasn't been mean about it. He's my friend. And I don't have many of those, or any really, but I met Rachel too, and I like her a lot. I trust him. I haven't figured out why, but I do." I really, really didn't want her to ruin this for me. I didn't want her to make me doubt myself. "I'll be smart, and careful, and I won't think something silly like Gideon will be my boyfriend. I just want a friend."

"He would be lucky to have you as his boyfriend.

You're my favorite person in the world, and don't you forget it. Any man should feel honored to have you."

But she didn't think I would find one. She didn't have to say it for me to know, and I really couldn't blame her. I was okay with that, though I did want to have sex. A lot of it. Without the annoying sex noises. "I know." It wasn't a lie. I was a catch, whether people got me or not. "I'm going to call a service so I can get my bed moved out—the one here is really uncomfortable—and some of my other things shipped."

Mom knew me well enough not to ask why I didn't buy another one. "Okay…and keep me posted. If you need help, money or anything—"

"I need to do this on my own." Her breathing was slightly shaky. I'd made her sad, but I hadn't meant to. "I'm sorry."

"You don't have to apologize. I trust you, Milo, and I love you."

"I love you too, Mom." I ended the call.

"Sorry about the bed," Gideon said from behind me. I whipped around to face him. He was wearing nylon shorts and a T-shirt, his hair messy from sleep.

"I wasn't going to tell you! I didn't want to be rude."

"It's fine. It's an old bed." He nodded toward me with a half grin. "You're showing the whole town what you look like in your underwear."

"No one can see," I replied, but stepped away from the window. "I can try to wear shorts if it bothers you. I just really like to be in my underwear."

"You look good in them. I'm not complaining," he replied, making my face turn hot. That was extremely unexpected. But then Gideon reminded me of the kind of person who flirted with everyone. He was just friendly like that.

"I'll make you a veggie omelet for breakfast, and then I'm going to shower before starting on my to-do list."

"Hopefully you get dressed first." Gideon winked.

"That wasn't a funny joke."

He chuckled. "I suppose it wasn't. You don't have to cook me breakfast. I don't typically eat it."

"Gideon! You have to eat breakfast! It's important. You need to fuel your mind and body before you start the day." I went to the kitchen and pulled the eggs out. "We need to go grocery shopping. This is fun. I like having a roommate—probably just because it's you. I hope you don't start to annoy me too much."

He sat on one of the barstools. "I'll do my best not to. And I'll make dinner tonight if you're making breakfast."

I froze, a slightly panicked feeling surging through me. "Um…okay."

Gideon rested his arms on the counter and leaned in. "You don't want me to cook for you."

"I didn't say that." I whipped the eggs.

"You didn't have to. I can look up veggie shit."

"Oh my God. It's not veggie shit. That sounds gross. Please don't ever say that again."

"Fine, I see your point, but I can do it. I'll figure out something I can make for you."

I sighed. I hated that sometimes I was so picky about things. "It's not you... I don't know... It'll be fine. It's fine." Most of the time it was fine, but if I got in a certain mood, it might not be.

"If you really don't want me to, I won't," he replied, and I might have melted a little. I had no idea that was possible or that it would feel good. Melting insides sounded like a sickness one shouldn't want. "Or I can plan it, and if you change your mind, no biggie."

That...might work. It was perfect, actually. "We'll do that. I like that idea."

"Deal."

I turned the stove on to heat the skillet, then poured the eggs in. "Do you have any tattoos today?"

"I do. Three of them. They're all pretty small. I'm meeting Kris for lunch too."

"This is so bizarre! We're like a married couple!" I said

before smacking my hand over my lips. "I don't want to marry you."

"Ouch," Gideon replied. "You're always bustin' my balls."

"I'm not doing anything to your balls. I just wanted to make sure you knew I wasn't trying to say I'm in love with you or something. It's just funny how we're discussing our day while I cook for you."

"Hell, I can hardly get you to admit we're friends. Believe me, I don't think you're in love with me."

"Good."

"Okay." He grinned.

"You always smile at me. Not in a mocking way either. It's confusing. I wanted to ask you why you smiled at me yesterday too. Do you remember? When you were standing in the doorway, watching me at Conflicting Ink."

"I was probably thinking you're adorable, which is what I was thinking just now."

I put the veggies into the pan, and embarrassingly, felt my cock plumping some. Luckily, the counter blocked it.

"You were going to ask me something about Wilma?"

Shit. I'd forgotten to do that last night. I didn't look at him, just continued to make his food while I spoke. "I've been calling her Wilma Allen... I think because that's who she was in my head. I didn't even know about her until a week ago, and it's kind of like it was with you—you were Tattoo Guy until something inside me said I could call you Gideon—but that hasn't happened with her yet. And it might not ever because she's dead. That makes me sad because I want to know her or feel comfortable enough to call her Wilma or even Grandma. When I was talking to Rachel yesterday, she said Wilma Allen was like me. She didn't want to be called Ms. Allen, and now I'm worried that I'm disrespecting her by calling her by her last name. Maybe she didn't like it? I don't know Rachel well enough to ask her, so I thought I would ask you. Do you think she would care?"

There was a silence that felt as if it had stretched into a hundred years, so I turned the omelet and risked a glance at him. Gideon was watching me, his brows pulled slightly together, his head cocked just a bit. Not too much, or he'd look silly. He just looked really, really sexy, and maybe a little confused but curious.

"I think the most important thing to her would be your comfort. She wouldn't want you to call her a name you weren't ready to use. We used to talk a lot. I'd help her and Gene by working on things at their house or down in the bookstore. I knew her well enough to feel comfortable saying you can call her Wilma Allen if that's what you want. Also, that's pretty fucking cool that you care so much, that you would worry about using the last name of someone who has already passed away. I like you, Milo, and I'm glad we're friends."

I bit into my bottom lip, my chest and stomach ridiculously fluttery. "I like you, and I'm glad we're friends too."

"Good. Now, do you typically burn your omelets, or am I special?"

"Holy crap." I pulled the skillet off the stove. "I don't burn things. Ever."

"Eh, that's typically my luck. Thank you. For making it."

I plated the food and handed it over.

"Oh, I meant to ask you, did you call Gene yesterday? You never mentioned it."

I hadn't, and that was on purpose. "I chickened out. I was so excited about it, but then it just seemed really overwhelming. What if he doesn't want to talk to me? What if he's mad Wilma Allen left me the store? What if he tells me why she never had a relationship with Mom and it's really bad? What if he's not a nice man? He might be to you, but what if he's not to me?" These were the kind of thoughts I obsessed about sometimes.

"All those feelings are totally understandable. This is a

big thing. You never knew?"

I shook my head. "I didn't even know Mom was adopted."

"No one here knew either. Word travels, though, and once she passed, the news got out that she'd left the store to a grandson no one knew she had. I'm not sure how everyone found out it was your mom."

"I want to know the story, but I'm nervous to know it too."

"I can see that. Take your time. You don't have to rush, but like I said yesterday, Gene is a good man. He'll want to talk to you. He will love you because Wilma did."

The words *thank you* lingered on my tongue, but I struggled to set them free.

Gideon took a bite. Was it strange that I was watching him? The way his throat moved when he swallowed, and hoping for some indication that he liked it.

"I got food on my face or something?"

"*Have* food on my face, and no. And I don't have an eating kink either. There are a lot of unique kinks out there. I've read about them. But I don't think I have any, and if I did, it wouldn't be watching hot guys eat. I just wanted to see if you think it's good."

Gideon laughed and snorted and maybe sucked egg

up his nose. I couldn't tell. "You might be the greatest person I've ever met."

I bit my lip again. That was new…and annoying. I didn't get it. Well, I knew I liked him thinking I was great, but I wasn't sure why that made my smile try to take over my face.

"And yes, it's delicious."

I stayed there watching and chatting with him while he finished the omelet. It meant a lot to me that he liked it, but when he was finished, I forced myself to tell him, "I'm going to work now." I stepped around the counter.

He eyed me, his gaze raking me from head to toe, and…did he like me too? He said I was attractive. "Are you getting dressed first?"

"Oh shit. Yes. And I have to shower. Eep! I'm late."

"You don't have to be there at a specific time."

"I'm still late," I replied, then ran for my room. I gathered my things and headed to the bathroom. I hoped he didn't need it, since we had to share. I made it quick, cleaning up, getting dressed, and brushing my teeth, all in less than twenty minutes.

Gideon was in his room with the door closed when I came out, so I left. I would see him later…at work or at home because we lived together. So unusual to think.

I headed downstairs to my bookstore. I made phone

calls, setting up appointments for quotes and other odds and ends. From there I took measurements and made supply lists for the things I knew I could do myself. I was lucky that I had always been good with my hands. When I was younger, I used to watch videos online about building, then did what the videos taught, hoping it would make my dad relate to me more. It hadn't, and I was over him, but I kept on learning and making things. Mom had signed me up for classes so I could hone my building skills, not because she considered it as a career for me, but because even though she was overprotective, she also wanted me to be able to take care of myself in any way I might need to.

The whole day I was either thinking of Gideon or of Gene—Gideon because he was hot and my friend and he thought I was great, and Gene because he was Wilma Allen's lover, someone who could tell me so much about her.

I would call him. I'd known I would at some point, but I was pretty sure I suddenly wanted to do it now, like right that second. He'd even pushed Gideon out of my thoughts, and all I could think about was the man who had lived with her and loved her.

And maybe, if I didn't take advantage now, I would chicken out again.

Still, I didn't call Gene because…well, I didn't know why.

There was a knock on the glass door before it slid open. I looked over to see Rachel coming in with a mini-Rachel. Oh great. I was in a weird mood. I hoped Cammy was chill.

"We were in the neighborhood, so I thought we'd stop in and say hi," Rachel said as her daughter approached me.

"Hello, Milo," Cammy said.

I eyed her curiously. "Hello, Cammy."

"Mama usually likes me to say mister or missus, but she said not to with you."

Rachel was the best. "Yes, I hate it."

"Does it make you feel old?"

"It does, and it's stuffy. Do you like to read?" I found myself asking.

"I do. Mama and I read together every day. What's your favorite book?"

I named a few.

"I haven't heard of those."

"Maybe you'll read them one day. You're very calm."

"I know how to behave myself when I need to. Mama said to behave with you."

Rachel laughed. "Yeah, but you don't always listen."

"That's what kids do," Cammy replied, and I decided I liked her already.

"I was actually just thinking about calling you," I told Rachel. "Do you know Gene's address?"

"I do, and I like where this is going."

"Really? Thank God. I was worried it was one of my bad ideas, like where I do something and people don't like it."

"I jumped off my bed and sprained my ankle once. Mama said that was a bad idea," Cammy added.

"It was," I replied.

"I think Gene will like it," Rachel said.

"Can we get ice cream?" Cammy asked.

All three of us laughed. "Sure, baby girl." Rachel hugged her, then gave me the address.

"Bye, Milo! It was nice to meet you." I stiffened when Cammy hugged me.

"Nice to meet you too."

They waved and were on their way.

I mapped out directions and saw it was close enough to walk. I locked up and headed that way, the scent of the ocean and fish filling my senses.

I smiled at everyone I passed by. Downtown Little Beach was busy, and everyone offered a wave or grin in return. Some people stared and whispered, probably because they knew I was the mysterious grandson no one knew Wilma Allen had. I couldn't help wondering if this was the same route she'd walked, if this had been how she'd gotten to work or if she'd driven.

The house was on a quiet street, and it was small, with a short white picket fence. The home was painted white too, but had sky-blue shutters. *This isn't weird, this isn't weird, this isn't weird.*

I opened the gate and went through it, hoping they didn't have a dog who'd want to chew on my face even more than I did with my lip when Gideon said things that made me feel tingly.

The steps were slightly loose, which was a hazard, especially for someone who was likely old like Wilma Allen had been. I raised my hand and knocked, heard a deep voice from inside, and then the door opened to a man about my height, with gray hair and glasses.

"I can fix the loose boards on your porch for you. You might have kids who can…or someone else. And maybe it's something you could do yourself, but if not, I can." Shit. That had come out wrong. I should have introduced myself first. "I'm—"

"Milo?" he asked, a nostalgic sort of smile on his face.

"Yes," I replied, happiness bouncing around inside me. "I'm Milo."

"It's so good to finally meet you! You look a lot like her, my Wilma. Do you want to come in?"

I tried to take a step but couldn't move, wasn't ready to get that close with him yet. "No, I just wanted to meet you."

His brows pinched together, but he nodded.

"Did you know about my mom?"

"I did. Always. Wilma found you online. I'm not sure how, maybe from your mom. She used to look at your Instagram page."

Oh, wow… I couldn't piece together how to respond to that. "Why did she give Mom up?"

"It's a long story, and—"

I held up my hand, and he stopped. "Wait. I didn't mean to ask that. I'm not ready."

"That's fine. We can get to know each other first."

Gideon had been right. Gene was nice. "I want to talk to you more, but I don't think I can yet. I thought I would, but then I got nervous, and then I thought it was time again, but I just want to take it slowly."

"We can do that. Whatever you want, whenever you want. I…" Gene swiped at a few tears. "You remind me of her. I loved Wilma with all my heart. And she loved you too. I want to make sure you know that."

The need to cry built up inside me. That rarely happened, and I hated it when it did. "Thank you. I…I have to go."

Gene didn't stop me as I turned and walked away.

CHAPTER EIGHT
Gideon

K RIS AND ORLANDO were waiting for me at the Lighthouse when I arrived for lunch. They had a booth close to the one Milo and I had shared. I sat beside my brother and across from my best friend. "What's up, assholes?"

"I'm pretty sure you're the only one who takes things *in* the *out* door," Orlando teased. "Get it? What's *up assholes?*"

"Ha-ha," I replied, though I could see how I'd left myself open for the joke.

"Hey, don't knock it until you try it," Kris replied, which surprised me since he didn't make it public knowledge he was bi. I knew, of course, because I'd had his tongue down my throat all through high school, and Megan knew because that was the kind of relationship she and Kris had. They were open with each other and trusted each other, so he wouldn't keep that part of his identity from her. As far as I knew, no one else did, though.

"And you have?" Orlando asked.

"Wouldn't you like to know?" Kris waggled his brows.

"Not about you personally, and especially not about Snacks, but is this something I should be asking Heather to try? I don't want to miss out. Do you have a strap-on? I'm down to experiment with my wife. She likes it when she gets to be all bossy with me in the bedroom."

I whipped my head in Orlando's direction. "Um, too much fucking information, and don't call me Snacks."

"Why should gay guys get all the butt loving if it's that good?" Orlando teased with a playful gleam in his eyes.

I flipped him off, and both Orlando and Kris laughed. I gave my friend the finger too. "Fuck you both very much." I turned to Orlando. "And yes, you're missing out."

"Hmm. I'll have to let Heather know."

"You started this," I told Kris.

He shrugged. "And I'd do it again. It's fun."

Patsy was our waitress today. She brought over three sodas, so she'd probably already been by before I arrived. We ordered, and I kept it small since I'd had the omelet

Milo had made. Contrary to what my brother said, Snacks didn't fit me anymore.

"So, what's up with that guy the other day?" Kris asked.

"What guy? Does my little bro have a boyfriend?"

I rolled my eyes. "How old are you?"

"Young at heart, baby."

I ignored that comment. "What do you mean what's up with him?" I asked Kris.

"What's up with who? I still don't know who the guy is," Orlando said. "I'm feeling left out."

"Milo," I replied just as Kris said, "He just seemed a little strange."

Annoyance burned through me. "Don't call him that. He's not strange. He's just…Milo."

"Uh-oh," Kris said, just as my brother teased, "Whoa…you do have a boyfriend. Gid and Milo, sitting in a tree."

"Oh my God. Shut up. I don't have a boyfriend, and I know what the *uh-oh* means too. I don't like him in that way. I've known the guy for five minutes. He's cute as hell, but mostly he's just fun to be around. We're friends." And now I had to tell them he lived with me, which I suddenly wasn't looking forward to. "Seriously, though, don't call him things like that."

"Sorry. I didn't mean anything by it," Kris apologized, and I knew he meant it. The truth was, Milo *was* different, and I could see that, but that didn't make him weird or wrong. I didn't know if he had any kind of diagnosis, and honestly, I didn't care. He was just Milo who made me smile.

"He's Wilma's grandson," I updated my brother, who was nearly bouncing in his seat; it was killing him so much to be out of the loop.

"Oh shit. So not a dick?"

"Definitely not a dick. He's going to do a small remodel on the bookstore, actually. He wants to keep the current Little Beach charm, but update it some and make it a place people want to hang out. And so far, he doesn't plan on kicking me out of my shop or my apartment. In fact, he *movedinwithme*." I mumbled the last part as quickly as I could.

"So…wait…the guy you called cute…whom you defended…and swear you don't like because you've only known him for five minutes, is now your roommate?" Orlando asked.

"Yes. That covers it."

"You hate roommates," Kris said.

"I couldn't very well live in his apartment while he stayed at a hotel, could I?"

"As a renter you're protected by certain rights, so yes, you could. At least for a while."

"That's not what I was saying, and you know it." He was being purposefully obtuse.

"I think I need to meet him," Orlando said.

"He's basically your brother-in-law," Kris added.

As much as they annoyed me, I chuckled. "I hate you both."

"You should have a beach wedding," Kris went on.

"I've never met one of your boyfriends before. Usually you just go to the mainland to have all that butt sex you didn't tell me was so awesome."

"Wait, you and Heather don't…" Kris made a circle with the fingers on one hand and pushed his pointer in and out with the other.

"No, I mean, I've pitched, but like I said, we just haven't done the strap-on, me-receiving thing."

I rubbed a hand over my face and groaned. I was so screwed. Milo wouldn't know what to think about them, and I could understand why. Half the time, I couldn't decide what I thought about them either. "Fuck my life." They barked out a laugh as though they were hilarious. "You guys can't be like this when you meet him."

"Like what? I'm just me," Kris replied. "Isn't that what you said about him?"

"Milo can be *just him* because I like him. I don't like you."

"Gasp!"

"I think you might love Milo," Orlando joked.

"I think I might leave."

Orlando clapped a hand on my shoulder. "You know we're giving you shit, right?"

"Yeah." We'd always been like this with each other. I didn't expect them to stop now. That didn't mean it wasn't annoying.

"I get to be your best man, right?" Orlando added, and I couldn't help dissolving into laughter with them. They were idiots, but I loved them.

"Seriously, though…don't just randomly stop by my apartment or the bookstore to meet him."

"Cross my heart and hope to die," Orlando replied.

"Hardcore," Kris added.

Luckily, Patsy saved us by coming over with three plates in her arms. We ate and did our normal catching up. Mom and Dad were on a trip—they did a lot of traveling since retiring—and would be home soon. I wondered what they would think when they met Milo, which I had no reason to do. For all I knew, they wouldn't meet. When we saw each other, it was usually at their house instead of them stopping by my apartment.

We rotated which one of us paid, and it was my turn, so I took care of it before heading back to the shop. I tried to open the door at the bookstore, but it was locked. When I peeked inside, I didn't see Milo.

I had a butterfly tattoo on a nineteen-year-old woman and a tribal piece on a guy's bicep that afternoon. I kept finding myself looking toward the window, as if I would magically know if Milo was back next door. *It doesn't matter…why does it matter?* Maybe he broke me because I was being weird.

I finished a little after five and didn't stick around like I normally did. Walk-ins were pretty common, and I needed the cash, but I also wanted to see him.

I headed straight to the bookstore, and this time when I tried the door, it was unlocked.

I pushed it open just slightly and took a step inside. "Milo? You here?"

There was a clattering sound from behind the counter where the register was, and then his hair appeared, followed by his face peeking over. "Yes," he replied.

I frowned, walking over. "Is everything okay?" There wasn't a chair there, so he'd been sitting on the floor.

He looked at me as if I'd suddenly grown a second head. "Yeah, why wouldn't it be?"

"I don't know. You're just sitting on the floor, behind

the counter."

"Oh. I'm fine. I don't always like chairs, and sometimes I like smaller spaces, so I was hanging out here."

Okay, well, whatever floated his boat. "What ya doing?"

"First I was reading some of *Alice in Wonderland*. Rachel said I should. Then I drew this." He handed me a notebook. There was a sketch of the inside of the bookstore: where the café would be, seating areas, how he wanted to organize the shelves, everything neatly and perfectly labeled.

"Holy shit. Done many plans for remodels?" I couldn't have come up with this idea so quickly. I was decent at drawing, I needed to be for my job, but this was fantastic.

He frowned. "No. Why?"

I chuckled. "It's just really good."

"Oh, well, I can draw okay. I'm not the best, and I don't really like it or anything. I did take some design courses for fun, and I've done quite a bit of building—entry-level stuff. I'm good at learning quickly, and I used to watch a lot of YouTube videos. I want to be able to do whatever I need to do, ya know?"

I couldn't help looking at him, trying to find the words I needed, but they wouldn't come to me. He was just…so fucking cool. I didn't know how else to explain him.

"You're doing that weird smiling at me again," he added.

"Sorry."

His brows pulled together. "Don't be. It's a nice smile."

"I thought it was weird?"

"That too, but it also turns me on, and I don't know if that's a good thing since we're friends and roommates."

Welp, my dick took notice of that, blood heading for my groin. Not enough to get me all the way there, but I was sporting a little bit of a chub over the idea of turning him on. "So basically, smile at you all the time. Noted."

He rolled his eyes and stood. "You like to flirt with people."

I shrugged. "I do. I didn't get to do a lot of it growing up. I was in the closet until just before I left. I did a lot of flirting when I moved to Boston."

"You'll have to tell me about it sometime, but first I'd like to go grocery shopping and to tell you about my day."

I chuckled, almost teased him about him thinking he's more important, but I really cared more about his day than talking about my past anyway. "Let's do it, then.

We need to get some food in the house before you get hangry on me."

"You joke now, but you won't once you see it," he said playfully. I liked it when he joked around.

Milo picked up his bag and slung it over his shoulder. He locked up, and then we were in my truck, making our way to the one and only grocery store on Little Beach Island.

"Do you have a Costco?" he asked.

"Not here. On the mainland, of course."

"Maybe we can go sometime."

"Sure." He was quiet for a minute until I prodded, "So…your day?"

"Oh. I walked over to Gene's house. The second he opened the door, he knew who I was. And not just because I was a random new guy in town. I asked him. He said it's because I reminded him of Wilma Allen…and that I look like her…and she apparently stalked me on the internet, which clearly is a possibility with social media, but it still makes me second-guess my Instagram account. Probably not enough to delete it."

Color me surprised. "What? I'm shocked. I didn't expect you to be one of those guys."

"One of what guys? There are hot men on Instagram! I follow a lot of them. There are butts there, Gideon. Lots and lots of butts."

A loud laugh jumped out of my mouth so spontaneously, I nearly startled my own damn self. "And apparently you like butts."

"Doesn't everyone?"

"Good point. If they're smart, they do. Now the really important question is, do you show your ass on Instagram? If so, I'm gonna need that handle stat."

He laughed, then frowned. "Are you joking or not?"

"I'm one hundred percent not joking…unless that makes you uncomfortable because I would never want that…and I would never look at your naked ass without permission."

"Oh, well, if you ever want to, you can ask. It's not online, though. I'm not sure I'm brave enough to let strange men look at me naked."

But he would let me. *Stop it!* There was no denying I was attracted to him, but I really fucking valued his friendship already. I didn't have the best track record when it came to men, and I didn't want to fuck this up, so I needed to curb that line of thinking. "Maybe we should talk about Wilma and Gene again."

"Oh. Yes! I forgot. It was really cool talking to him. I only stayed a few minutes, and I didn't go inside. He didn't tell me much, but he would have. At first I thought

I wanted the whole story, but I don't think I'm ready. And it feels uncomfortable knowing before my own mom. It's heavy and feels like a lot. I don't know if that's just a *me* thing or not."

"No. I don't think it's a you thing," I said, reaching over and placing my hand on his nape. It wasn't the typical kind of affection for me to offer, and the second I did it, I almost jerked my hand back. Before I could, his gaze snapped to mine, and it was as if the static in the air sizzled and popped inside me. It was maybe the most ridiculous thing I had ever thought. I wasn't that kind of guy who thought stuff like feeling electricity between people and shit like that, but when he gave me a small smile, I couldn't help but return it.

"You have pretty eyes, but I really think you should look at the road now. My pulse is going a little too fast."

I pulled my hand back and faced the road.

"I don't always like to be touched if I don't know beforehand, but that was fine."

Shit. "I'm sorry."

"No, it's okay. I liked it."

Oh…well when he put it that way…

"Good." We were quiet until I parked and killed the engine.

"Thank you, Gideon. For being my friend," Milo

said.

"Nothing to thank me for."

I should be the one thanking him.

CHAPTER NINE

Milo

GIDEON AND I had been roommates for two weeks and one day. So far, he had only annoyed me once…maybe twice. He hadn't said if I'd annoyed him. I'd put a whiteboard on the fridge for us to use if we ran out of something—that way the other person knew before they made a plan to eat something they couldn't. Also if we went to the store without each other, we knew what we were out of.

I did take a car service a couple of times, and once I even went with Rachel. I didn't want Gideon to feel like he had to take care of me or anything, because he didn't, but as much as I liked Rachel, I wasn't a fan of the grocery store with her. It was much better with Gideon.

Other than the shopping trip, I had fun hanging out with her. Twice she'd even had Cammy with us. One of the times she was a little loud, but she was a kid, and I had to remind myself that was what they did.

Anyway, Gideon ate the last orange *and* all the strawberries and didn't put them on the list. I was hungry and planned to make a fruit salad, and I'd really wanted both, plus I didn't like fruit salad without strawberries. It was really frustrating that he hadn't put it on the list. There was a dry-erase marker attached and everything! I'd told him so when I'd gone down to Conflicting Ink to talk to him. He was working in the evening, and my whole night had been thrown off, but then I woke up the next day and he'd not only bought strawberries and oranges, he'd made the salad and had drawn a little hangry monster on a sticky note that I now kept in my wallet. So then I felt bad about being mad, and come to think of it, if I had annoyed him, it was probably that day. But at least his Milo Hangry Monster had been cute.

There was only one problem I hadn't shared with him…or maybe two. The first was that the more time I spent with him, the more physically attracted I was to him. I didn't love him or want to be his boyfriend or anything. We didn't know each other nearly well enough for that. I would probably be a handful as a boyfriend, and I'd accepted that it might not be in the cards for me. But he was really, really hot…and nice. And somehow being nice made him hotter.

It was weird.

My second issue was that I hadn't watched porn at all since I'd moved in. It was hard for me to have an orgasm without the visual stimulation. My hand on my dick felt good, but I wasn't really attracted to myself. Even though the sex noises bugged me, *seeing* sex or sexy people really did it for me, but I'd been so afraid he would walk in while I was jerking off to porn that I hadn't been able to make myself do it.

And I missed orgasms...a lot. It was making me grumpy, to the point that he might have to draw an ejaculation-starved monster next.

The good news was my bed and other items had arrived, so I slept better, but I was dying to come. My dick was very angry with me, and I couldn't blame him.

"I really like this color," Rachel said, looking at some paint samples I got. We were at the bookstore together. We'd cleared everything out, with Gideon's help, and put it in a storage unit. He also took me to get the supplies I would need for the counter in the café area and a few things like that.

"Do you think it would be rude if I asked Gideon to leave for a certain amount of time? Like just a couple of hours. I need to be able to know he won't come back. Even when he's at the shop, he makes trips upstairs at random times. I don't want to be a jerk…it's his apartment…but I really need some alone time."

She waggled her dark brows. "You find a hookup?"

"Oh no. I've never had sex with anyone else. I normally just do it with myself."

"Wait. What? You're a virgin? Do you want to be?"

"I'm twenty-four. What do you think?"

Rachel laughed. "Good point. Then why haven't you? You're hot, Milo. I can guarantee you could find a guy who would want to have sex with you."

I believed I could too, but I was picky. And I wanted to have sex with someone I trusted. I was worried a random stranger's kiss or touch or cum would gross me out. Like, how could I be okay with a stranger's spit in my mouth? What if they shot their load on me and I freaked out? I was okay with cum so far, but I'd only been around my own. There were too many possible disgusting things that could happen, and I didn't want to risk it. Plus, guys weren't breaking down my door or anything.

I thought this was one of those things that would make me look weird, so I didn't want to share it with her. "Veto."

"Huh?" She crossed her arms.

"I'm vetoing a discussion I don't want to have. I just want to talk about how I'd like to watch porn without the risk of him walking in on me. I'll be all in my head if I don't know, and it'll be too hard to have an orgasm." I didn't know why the thought of Gideon knowing I was watching porn embarrassed me. It was a normal, human thing. People wanted sex and pleasure, but I guessed I just wanted to be in control of whether he saw me jacking off to guys pounding each other.

"I love you so much," Rachel said with a smile.

"Why?" I frowned. "Because I like porn?"

"No, because I do. Does Gideon just walk into your bedroom without knocking?"

"No. Never."

"Then there you go."

"You don't know me at all. That doesn't help."

She laughed. "Okay, well, then no, I don't think it's rude. Just tell him you need a couple of hours to yourself, where you know he won't come home. Gideon's a cool guy. He'll respect that."

He would. I'd just already freaked out about the fruit, and I didn't want him to get sick of me. "Maybe I'll talk to him. For now, I need a distraction. Put on your goggles and hard hat."

"We're carrying wood. I don't need them."

"Safety first! No hard hat and goggles, no work."

"I don't love you anymore."

"I like you a lot. You're one of my first friends, but it's too early to love me anyway. I'm comfortable with the fact that it will come with time."

"Aw, Milo. I love you again. I'm sorry people suck. I'm happy to be your friend."

I smiled. "I'm happy to be your friend too…but Gideon is going to be my best friend, I think. I hope, at least. Is that okay? Don't tell him I told you."

I froze when she pulled me into a hug because…why? I didn't know what I did to prompt it, so I just stood there with my arms plastered to my sides. "Yes, that's fine. I absolutely approve of anything Milo and Gideon related."

"Perfect. I'm killin' this friend thing. That went really smoothly."

She laughed. "You totally are."

"Hard hat and goggles."

"Ugh. I changed my mind." But she put them on, and we got to work. She helped me haul some lumber and other items I'd need inside. I'd had to buy a couple of kinds of saws and kept a table inside and one outside to do projects on. Gideon had said I could borrow some tools from his family, but I didn't want to risk breaking something that didn't belong to me. Plus, I'd never even met them. He'd gone to his parents' house once when they came home from their trip, and he met his brother sometimes, but they never came to the apartment, and if they went to Conflicting Ink, I missed them.

I'd just started to frame out the U-shaped counter when Rachel asked, "Have you talked to Gene again?"

"Did Gideon tell you to ask me that?"

"No, but I'm taking it he's asked you."

"He asks me every couple of days." That was another annoying thing he did that I'd forgotten about earlier. "I went over once and fixed his stairs, but I didn't knock and he didn't come out. I left my cell number. He sent me a text to say *thank you*."

"Did you reply?"

"Yes! I'm not that clueless."

"But you fixed his stairs without asking or saying anything?"

"Well, I'd told him the first day we met that I could do it. He didn't say yes, but why would he care?"

"Good point, I guess."

"I've had two of those today. I have to go cut this board," I said, holding the one I'd just measured.

She followed me out back, where I kept the supplies behind the building. "You're a sweet man, Milo Copeland. Why don't you talk to him?"

"Veto. Two of those today too."

"Fine, I know how to take a hint."

We worked until about five, when she asked, "Do you want to go and get an ice cream? Don't tell Cammy I sometimes have dessert before dinner."

"I won't, and there will never be a time in my life when I turn down ice cream."

It was really hard not to go up and shower first, but I did my best to wipe the sawdust off and clean off in the bookstore bathroom. Then we walked down to the ice cream parlor, which was less than a block away. They had a huge, covered outdoor area. There were quite a few people, but it wasn't too overwhelming. Rachel got a cone, but I got a milkshake because I didn't like it when ice cream melted on my hand. We found a table outside and sat down. We were only there for a few minutes before a guy stepped up to the table and said, "I think you're my new brother-in-law."

"Huh?"

He chuckled, the sound familiar. "I'm Gideon's brother, Orlando. You're Milo, right?"

He held out his hand, but I stared at it for a moment. Why would he call me his brother-in-law? Unless he thought Gideon and I were dating? Go fictional me. "Yes, I'm Milo Copeland. Please don't call me Mr. Copeland. But Gideon and I aren't dating. Is that what you meant?"

He frowned slightly, but I could see he was trying to hold it back. Or maybe he didn't even realize he was doing it. People were like that sometimes; they thought things and didn't realize it showed on their faces. Orlando was wondering about me, thrown off by me too.

"No, I was kidding. I've been giving him shit, is all."

Was dating me something he would be teased about?

Orlando dropped his hand. Damn it. Why hadn't I shaken it? I wanted Gideon's brother to like me.

"It's good to finally meet you," Orlando added. "You're all the talk around Little Beach Island, especially from my brother. But he's made me swear not to stop by the bookstore or the apartment to meet you."

He laughed, but I didn't feel it. My stomach flipped uncomfortably. "Gideon doesn't want us to meet?" Was he embarrassed of me? He didn't seem like it. We went shopping together and sometimes went out to eat, but mostly we liked cooking at home.

"I don't think that's what he means," Rachel said just as Orlando replied, "Shit, no. Not at all. I suddenly feel like I'm screwing this up."

I was sure it wasn't him, but me. I wished I could veto this whole conversation.

Orlando forged on. "He probably thought I would say something stupid—and I'm pretty sure I did—but it's not that he doesn't want us to meet." His voice was soft and unsure, but for whatever reason, it just pissed me off. Or maybe *I* pissed *me* off because this was Gideon's brother and Gideon was my friend. I didn't want him to wonder why Gideon liked me. I didn't want Gideon to have been right when he didn't want us to be introduced to each other. "He says you're remodeling the bookstore and doing some of the work yourself."

"I'm capable. I'm not stupid," I snapped. My heart was beating too fast, my hearing a little echoey.

"I wasn't trying to imply you're stupid or incapable. I'm impressed. I couldn't do it. Gid is the one who's good with his hands." Orlando laughed uncomfortably and took a step back. He wanted a quick escape because I was a mess and I'd screwed all this up.

Rachel said, "Shit. I'm going to be late. We should head out, Milo." She was doing it to save me. That was the kind of thing friends did, and while I'd always wanted that, in that moment, I resented her for it because she'd *had* to try and save me. And I resented myself because she had to as well. I wasn't going to turn down the helping hand, though.

I fought to keep myself calm because Gideon was embarrassed of me and didn't want his brother to meet me, and he was right; I'd gotten this all wrong, and what if he didn't want to be friends with me after he found out? I didn't want to lose him.

"It was nice to meet you." I stood and forced myself to hold my hand out. Orlando took it, we shook, and then Rachel and I left.

"Don't tell Gideon," I told her when we reached the sidewalk.

"I won't. Hey, you wanna come have dinner at our house tonight? Or I can hang out at your place?"

I shook my head. "It's too much. I need to be alone right now."

We walked back in silence. Rachel hugged me goodbye at her car. I went upstairs and unlocked the door. Once inside, I took my shoes off and placed them in the stand. Then I removed my pants and hung them over the rack I'd put there for when I wasn't going straight to my room.

I'd totally screwed that up. Gideon had been right to be embarrassed of me.

CHAPTER TEN

Gideon

MY BROTHER WAS frowning at me when he arrived at Conflicting Ink. I tipped my head, silently telling him to follow me. I was pretty good at seeing when Orlando wanted to talk or was serious about something. We might not have a lot in common, but we were close and we got each other.

I headed into the supply room and started putting away the new delivery of ink we had gotten in earlier. I heard him say hi to Freddy before he stepped through the door with me. "So…I met Milo."

My fucking brother. I was sure he'd made a mess of things. Groaning, I dropped my head back. "What did you do?"

"I didn't mean to do anything! I was just joking with him, and I called him your husband. He got flustered and confused. Afterward I mentioned the work he was doing at the store, and he thought I saw him as too stupid or incapable. I don't know what happened, if I'm being honest. He left right away. I could tell he was upset, though. He's...not what I expected."

A flare of anger shot through my chest. "What is that supposed to mean?"

"Jesus, it doesn't mean anything. Simmer down."

He was right. I was overreacting. He hadn't said anything bad about Milo, and Milo wasn't what I had expected either.

"I just hope I didn't somehow offend him. I really wasn't trying to be a dick, but maybe I came off that way. The one thing I do know is that he doesn't have an appreciation for my sense of humor."

It was hard for me to sort through because while I was still learning Milo's quirks, even when I joked, or if he wasn't sure what to think of my sarcasm, he always told me. Even when he thought my jokes were dumb, he told me. He didn't leave the way Orlando said he had. "That's because your jokes are shit."

"Your boyfriend agrees with you."

"He's not my boyfriend."

"Yet." He waggled his eyebrows, but I ignored him. I was worried about Milo.

"Thanks for letting me know," I told him.

Orlando nodded and headed out like I'd hoped he would. I finished putting away the ink and then fucked around the shop. If Milo was anything like me, he would want to be alone for a little while. I hated feeling like people were up in my space when I was upset. I needed some time to myself before I wanted to be around others again.

But I was also nervous and pacing, and fuck, I just wanted to talk to him. "I'm going to head upstairs for a bit," I told Freddy, who was inking a customer.

"Cool, man. You comin' back?"

"Not sure."

"Okay." He didn't look at me, his concentration completely on the work he was doing. Freddy was incredible with color; I admired that talent in him.

When I went inside the apartment, I saw Milo's pants hanging on the rack. He wasn't joking when he said he hated wearing them at home. He never did. I wondered what he'd done in San Diego when he had company. But that was why he left them by the door—in case someone knocked and he needed to put them on. "Lo? You in here?"

"No!" he called from his bedroom, and I smiled.

I headed that way and gave a soft knock, even though he had to have known I was coming. "Then how did you answer me?"

"It's sarcasm. I do know what that is if you were wondering."

I frowned. Yeah, sometimes he struggled trying to determine if I was being sarcastic or not, but I hoped I never made him feel like I didn't think he understood it. "I'm coming in. Tell me now if you don't want me to."

When he didn't respond, I slid the door open slowly. His room was as clean as always. Three books were stacked on one nightstand, perfectly aligned, as if it was something he consistently made sure of, even though they weren't the same ones I'd seen there before.

That wasn't what held my attention, though. I sucked air through my teeth the moment my eyes found him because while I'd seen Milo without pants every day in the past couple of weeks, I hadn't seen him with no pants *or* shirt while lying on his bed, scowling cutely at me. His stomach was flat but not incredibly defined, his nipples light brown and pointed. His chest was slightly broader than his slim waist. He didn't have the kind of muscles you got in a gym or working manual labor all day, but they were distinct—the small ball in each bicep looking firmer on his crossed arms.

The happy trail that led below the band on his underwear was the same red as the hair on his head, but what I really loved were the freckles peppered all over his shoulders and likely down his back. I couldn't help wondering what they tasted like. *Stop that! You're not supposed to think about wanting to taste him. He's your friend, and he's upset.*

"You're looking at me weird," he said, tugging me from my appreciation of his body.

"I'm always doing something weird with you."

He frowned. "No, you're not."

"You're not scowling at me anymore." I went over and stood beside the bed. His hair was wet, like he'd just gotten out of the shower.

"I met your brother." He turned his head in the opposite direction.

"I heard. Apparently, you're not too happy about that…and maybe not with me either since you won't even look at me. Not sure what I did wrong, but I'd like to know, if you're willing to tell me." A minute of silence stretched between us, feeling heavy. "If he somehow offended you with the husband thing or anything else he said, that's just my brother being an idiot. He has a terrible sense of humor. I tell him so all the time."

"That threw me at first," he admitted, then sighed and repositioned himself so he was sitting crossed-legged. He sat like that often, I noticed. I joined him but on the edge of the bed, giving him his space. "I know I can't control my environment all the time. And that's fine. I'm used to it. I know how to deal with it, but I was a little off-balance because he was there, and the first thing he did was call me his brother-in-law. I wasn't sure what to think. Like...did I have more family I didn't know about? It took me a second to realize he was your brother, but by then I was already flustered, and then, when I told him we weren't dating, he said he just liked to give you shit, so I started to worry that dating me would be something to tease someone about."

Oh shit. That was the last thing I wanted him to think. "Hey, no. That wasn't what he meant, and it wouldn't be true."

"I know that now, and maybe logically I knew it then. I'm not sure, but at that moment, because I was already in my head, that was what it meant. And then he said you made him swear not to come by, and all I could think about was you being embarrassed of me, so I snapped at your brother when he asked about the remodel. I know people are surprised that I can do shit like that, but I can—and probably better than him or you. I felt bad afterward a little bit, but not totally because I really do know what I'm doing and—"

"Wait, wait, wait. Slow down. We'll work our way

through all that, but we need to address the whole embarrassed-of-you thing before we go any further. Where the hell did you get that idea? I'm not embarrassed of you, Lo."

"Why are you calling me that? This is the second time."

"I don't know. It just happened. Do you want me to stop?" When he grinned at me, I wondered what his smile tasted like.

"No. I like it. I give you permission to have a nickname for me."

"Thank you. Now, do you believe what I'm telling you?" Because if I did something to make him feel that way, I wanted to fix it. I wasn't embarrassed. There was no reason in the world to be ashamed of him.

"People have been before. My dad was. I used to be okay with it so I could keep people around, but I'm not anymore." He poked his finger into my chest with each word he spoke: "I. Don't. Deserve. That."

"I never thought you did." And good on him for knowing his worth. A lot of people didn't. Hell, I wasn't sure I did. "I promise you, I'm not embarrassed of you. That thought never even occurred to me."

"Then why didn't you want me to meet Orlando?"

"It's not that I didn't want you to; it's just, well, he

has a habit of opening his mouth and inserting his foot. I didn't want him to do that with you. And I also didn't want him to stop by and catch you in your underwear. I had a feeling he would do something stupid, which is exactly what he did, and I wanted to…"

He cocked his head, then shook it. "You can't do that. If we're going to be friends, you can't try to protect me from the world. Even if I screw up or freak out, you have to give me that. I can't be friends with someone who thinks I need them to shelter me from just the possibility of an uncomfortable situation. That means you're treating me differently than you would someone else, and I don't want that. Ever."

"I…" Didn't know what to say because he was right. And I respected the hell out of him for demanding it. "It won't happen again. You have my word." Fuck his father, whoever the hell that bastard was. I wanted to ask Milo about him but wasn't sure now was the time.

"Thank you. And there's a chance I might have overreacted a little, but I'm really strung tight. I haven't had an orgasm in weeks because of you."

My mouth dropped open. Milo simply reached out, hooked his finger under my chin, and closed it.

"You're going to have to lead me there because I'm not understanding how that's my fault."

"I need visual stimulation to have an orgasm, and I feel uncomfortable watching porn when you're in the next room. I tried once when you weren't home, but my brain kept telling me you could walk upstairs at any moment, so I couldn't get off. I asked Rachel if it would be rude to see if you can leave for a couple of hours and promise you won't come back. I think it'll help with my tension if I can come a few times."

Words were still lost on me, but my dick was definitely paying attention, thinking about Milo in here, jerking off or fucking himself while watching porn.

"Did I break you?" he asked, making me wonder how long I'd been quiet.

"You might have." I cleared my throat. "First, yes, you can ask me not to come home, and I won't. Second, you can watch porn while I'm in the next room. You literally haven't come since you moved in? I jerk it every night with you in the next room."

Now it was Milo's turn for his mouth to drop open, his eyes bugging out in a way that shouldn't be cute, but it was. "I wish I could watch."

Blood rushed to my groin, the ache of want making my head spin. "Wait. What? You can't jerk off when I'm home, but you want to watch me do it?" I was so lost.

"Confusing, huh? My brain is weird. You should try

living inside my head sometime."

I chuckled but couldn't get the thought of him jacking off out of my head—of the two of us jacking off together.

Milo grimaced, then shifted, and damned if my gaze didn't travel down to the prominent bulge beneath his underwear that hadn't been as big a few minutes before. "I'm hard."

"I can see that." My voice was an octave lower, deep and raspy.

"Oops?"

"I'm dealing with the same problem here."

"You are? I want to see! Sorry. That was rude. So was telling you I wished I could watch you masturbate. I hope I didn't make you uncomfortable. I would never do something against your will. Sometimes I open my mouth, and stuff just comes out."

"Jesus, Lo. You don't have to apologize for that. It's hot…thinking of us jerking off together."

"Together? I thought you didn't want to see me naked."

"Um…who said that?"

"Well, when we were talking about butts on Instagram, I said if you wanted to see me, just ask, but you didn't. I would have asked if you'd told me that…just sayin'."

Yep, totally hard now. Heat and desire surged through me, making my balls ache. His honesty was so damn refreshing. Even if I wasn't attracted to him, that would've turned me on.

My gaze found Milo, but he was looking at my crotch like he was trying to see through my jeans, and hell, we were so doing this. I didn't let myself contemplate if it was a bad idea or not.

"Can I see you naked?" I asked.

He bit into his lip, and fuck, I wanted to do it for him. I had to remind myself that wasn't what he was offering.

"Yes. Can I see you naked? And masturbating, please. Thank you."

"Yes," I replied, hoping like hell this wasn't a mistake, but wanting him too much to say no.

Milo didn't hesitate. He pushed up on his knees and tugged his underwear straight down and off before flopping down to his ass again. He was…goddamn, he was sexy. He kept himself manscaped—his red hair, which was darker there, neatly trimmed. Milo was fully erect, long and thick, the head slick with precum that leaked from his slit. Jesus, I wanted to taste him, wanted to lick him from his balls up to the crown and take him deep into my mouth.

"Gideon! You're staring and not stripping! Hurry! I want to see too."

"You're an impatient little thing, aren't you?"

"Wait? My dick is little? It doesn't seem like that from the porn I watch."

I chuckled while pulling my shirt off and tossing it to the chair. "No, it's not small. At all. That was just… I actually have no idea what that was. Note to self: don't call you little thing again."

"You're still not getting undressed fast enough."

"You only want me for my body," I teased, then stepped out of my sneakers and unbuttoned my pants. I didn't know why, but I thought he would be slightly shy for me to see him, which he clearly wasn't. Milo leaned back on his pillows, legs spread out while he cupped his sac.

"I like to play with my balls," he said.

"Well, it does feel good." I wondered how many men he'd done this with, how many times he'd jerked off or blown or fucked guys, when I had no business thinking about that or caring.

When I pulled my jeans and boxer briefs down my legs, he sucked in a sharp breath. "Holy shit."

"Extraordinary, isn't it?" I teased.

"Mine is longer."

"Way to boost a guy's ego, Lo."

"Oh. I'm sorry. Am I supposed to? Wow…that's a really hot cock…it's so…big…you have lots of…hair."

"First, I don't have lots. I just don't keep it quite as short as yours. And second, you don't seem very impressed." I hoped my playful tone showed through my words. I gave myself a slow, lazy stroke.

"I am…oh my God, I am. You're thicker than me. I kinda want to come right now. You have a really nice cock. I'm just…taking it all in…and trying to make myself believe this is really happening. Lie down next to me. Maybe it'll help if I can feel your body heat."

My dick jerked, liking that idea.

"Holy crap. That happened because of what I said, didn't it?" He leaned forward, his face so damn close to my erection I wasn't sure I would survive this encounter at all. When he blew on me, warm air ghosting around my dick, I groaned. "Not good?"

"Really fucking good. I thought we were jerking off?" If he wanted to do more, I was game, but I needed it to be what Milo wanted.

"No, we are. Sit down."

"Yes, sir."

He scooted over, and I sank down beside him. I had

to admit, he was right. This was better with the two of us lying beside each other.

"I have lube. Lots of it." Milo rolled over and pulled out two bottles, handing me one and keeping the other.

"Need two of them, huh?"

"It's cheaper to buy in bulk. But sometimes I don't use it in time, so that defeats the purpose."

I felt the laugh in my chest before I let it out through my lips. "You're an absolute delight, and I have never used those two words together before, so that should tell you something."

"And you're really hot. I like your cock. There's lots of veins. We should jerk off now."

"I'm down with that plan."

We both slicked up and set down the bottles. I hadn't just sat next to someone, jacking off with them, since I was in high school and Kris and I started fucking around. In some ways, it shouldn't be as hot as it was. I'd had a lot of sex, but damn, just watching Milo use his left hand to play with his balls while his other caressed his cock had my nerve endings spark a wild fire inside me.

"Fuck, you're so sexy," I told him.

"Wait. What? You said you're attracted to me, but you think I'm sexy?"

"Yes, and you stopped. Let me see you pleasure yourself, Lo."

"Oh…" He visibly trembled. "You don't have as much precum as me. You like to touch your head more. I can see it, see the way your thighs tighten when you do. You pay lots of attention there." Fuck…why was that so hot? Hearing him talk about watching me jerk? "This is so much better than porn." His hand sped up, and I groaned.

We were quiet for a moment, just lying there and jacking ourselves. It felt good as hell, but my fingers twitched to reach over and replace Milo's hand with mine, to play with his balls until he blew his load all over his stomach…or better yet, on me.

"Gideon?"

"Yeah?"

"It's okay if you say no, but I really want to touch your dick…jack you off, I mean."

"Christ." I almost shot at his question, which might have killed me. It shouldn't get me going that much just to hear someone say they wanted to give me a rub and tug.

"Just as friends…because I trust you. I'm not asking to be your boyfriend."

Something unfamiliar pierced my chest, a sort of pain I hadn't expected, but I didn't have time to think about that right then. "I'd like you to explain all that."

"Now?" His voice was loud, sharp.

"No, after, and yeah, but do I get to touch you too?"

"Yes. God yes. Touch me, please."

There wasn't a chance I'd say no.

CHAPTER ELEVEN

Milo

I WAS WORRIED I was dreaming, but I couldn't be, could I? I knew I'd made a fool of myself in front of Orlando and then came home to shower and pout, which led here. I didn't think I would have fallen asleep so that I'd be dreaming because I was too angry for that. But this was so, so good it had to be a fantasy because since when did I get gorgeous, naked men in my bed, telling me I was sexy? But then, this was Gideon, who was the nicest person I'd ever met. In such a short time, he'd become the best friend I ever had.

And God, he looked incredible naked. It was even better than I expected. I loved how muscular he was, the definition of his abs, and oh God, his cock was so thick. And now I was going to wrap my hand around it and jerk him off and… "Oh God." I shoved up so I was sitting.

"What happened? Is something wrong?" he asked,

panic clear in his voice.

"No. I just almost had my orgasm thinking about touching you, and I didn't want to because I haven't even done it yet…and you haven't touched me."

I smiled when his fingers danced over my shoulders. "We wouldn't want that, would we?"

"No, we wouldn't. I like it when you touch me."

"I like your freckles."

I grinned. "Thank you. I really want to get to the touching, though. I think I'm okay, but you should let me play around with your dick first so I for sure get the chance."

I was looking at his groin instead of his face, but somehow, I felt Gideon smile. "Okay."

Slowly, I reached my hand out. It was almost like I was outside my body, watching, but inside too, and the second my fingers fisted his erection and I felt the hot, hard length of him, I whimpered. If it were anyone other than Gideon, it would have been embarrassing, or maybe not because, whatever, I was just me.

I tried to hold him tight but not too tight. I wanted him to feel it but not to accidentally crush his cock. It was hard to do this with someone other than yourself. "Like this?" I asked, sliding my hand up and down.

"Yeah, that feels good. Just do it the way you would

with anyone."

"I haven't done this, or well, anything, with anyone other than myself."

Gideon stiffened. "You're a virgin?"

I stopped, looked at him probably like he was an idiot because, "Yes, how did you not know this?"

"I don't know, because you didn't tell me?"

"Gid! This is me!" He smiled. "What?"

"You called me Gid."

Oh...I had, hadn't I? "That's odd. I don't usually have that kind of nickname for people. I mean, you were Tattoo Guy, but that wasn't the same kind of nickname, and we didn't know each other. It was just my preconceived way to describe you, and it stuck. But you called me Lo, so I think I'll call you Gid; not all the time, but sometimes. If you don't hate it. If you do, tell me. If not, can we get back to me masturbating you?"

"Yes, as long as you don't ever say *masturbating you* again."

I loved that he trusted me, that Gid clearly had questions but didn't make us stop or push them on me, making me feel like he didn't trust me to make decisions for myself.

I ran my hand up and down him again, savored the feel of him against my palm.

"You can squeeze a little tighter if you want."

"Okay. I'm gonna play with your head the way you like."

"Jesus, Lo. You might kill me."

"Please don't die. I might never have this chance again."

He chuckled, but I didn't know what was so funny about me killing the first guy who let me touch his cock. I played with his crown, rubbed my hand over it and down his shaft. He was breathing heavily, his chest rising and falling…

"I know I said this before, but you're really, really sexy, Gid."

"So are you." He rested his hand on my thigh, making my dick twitch. I almost felt like my balls might pop; they were so full, which wasn't a pleasant image. "You flinched. What's wrong?"

"I just had an uncomfortable vision of my balls exploding and cum covering the room."

"Ouch." I reached with my other hand and teased his sac. "Fuck yeah…like that. You feel so good."

Oh God, he was doing the sex talk and…so far, I didn't care. It didn't bother me at all.

"You're so hard, but your skin is so soft. It feels awesome. I mean, I know what a dick feels like because I touched mine all the time before moving here, but it's not the same with someone else. Whoa…you're leaking a ton of precum now." I swiped it with my thumb, and, huh, Gideon's fluid wasn't so bad. That was a good sign. "Every time I stroke up, your thighs tighten…and I like your tattoos…and I hate tattoos, so that's just strange."

"I want to touch you too." Gideon's hand slid up my leg, back down, then up again. "I want to make you come, Lo. Will you let me make you come?"

"Yes. Absolutely."

"Lie down again."

I did as he said. He was the expert here. Gideon rolled onto his side, facing me. My hand was still on his cock, but I wasn't moving it, and then… "Fuck…*fuck*." My eyes rolled back when he wrapped a tight fist around the base of my shaft and slid up. "I'm not going to last long."

"That's okay."

"This is *amazing*." The urge to close my eyes was there, but I wanted them open too. I wanted to watch Gideon touching me. Pleasure pooled in my groin, shooting off like fireworks from there, exploding all through my body. "How can it feel so different to have someone else touch you than it does with yourself?"

"Maybe I'm just that good," he said playfully.

"Could be. I don't have it in me to argue.

Um…tighter, please…and a little faster."

"You don't have to be afraid to tell me what you want."

I rolled onto my back, and when Gideon changed positions, using his other hand to cup my balls, playing with them and rubbing my taint, I realized I'd let go of him, that I was just lying back and taking the pleasure he gave me.

"Okay…that's good…pull them some. I like that." He did, and I almost surged off the bed. "Yes! Like that."

"Bossy, aren't you?"

"Please make me come." I thrust into his fist. This was maybe the best moment of my life. My whole body was sensitive, but I felt safe…safe and cared for because it was Gideon and he was my friend. I could say anything to him, and he didn't judge me or make me feel like there was something wrong with me.

And so far, it seemed like he enjoyed touching me too, so that was a plus.

"I can't wait to see you shoot. Can't wait to see the look on your face when I make you blow your load all over yourself. That's it, fuck my hand."

"That's not annoying… Why isn't that annoying?"

"Huh?" He stopped.

"Don't stop!" I shouted, and he laughed. Gideon

jerked me again, his tight fist around my dick, and I did what he said, fucked into him, making my world splinter apart. My whole body got tingly and light and like maybe I might float off the bed. When he pulled on my balls again, I couldn't hold back. I arched off the bed and yelled out. I didn't even know what I said, but if I were watching me in porn, I'd hate me.

Cum splattered on my stomach and chest. Somehow it felt even better than usual, maybe because it was Gid who'd made me do it.

When I looked over, he was smiling at me, with some of my jizz on his hand, and it didn't seem to bother him. I wondered if his would bother me. "I don't know if I can move, but I really want to do that to you now. Also, that was the best moment of my life. I'm going to jerk you off now, and then I'll die afterward."

"I'm all yours," he said. That was just sex talk. I knew it, but it made me feel warm inside. Gideon lay down, and I rolled to my side, looking down at him while I took him in my hand again. I caressed him like I did before, paying a lot of attention to his glans. He moved like I did, small pumps of his hips, sharp breaths from his lungs, which made pride surge through me. I couldn't believe it was me making him feel that way.

"I might not like your cum. I don't like…fluids, most

of the time. Mine is okay, so maybe yours will be too. I used to struggle with lube too, but that's okay now. Maybe because it helps get me toward the pleasure part?"

"Maybe," he replied. "You can stop right before I finish if you want, and I can take over."

"No!" I rushed out. "I want to try. Maybe we should kiss. Do you think we should kiss?"

"I think we should kiss."

"Hopefully your saliva is okay. Sorry, I have a lot of quirks." Ugh. I was even annoying myself right now.

"Come 'ere, Lo. If you don't like it, pull back."

He went to touch the back of my head, and I tensed up. "No, don't! On my body it's okay, but I really don't want my cum in my hair." *Please don't let me be messing this up.*

"Okay." He nodded, and I leaned in on my own. I pressed my lips to his, and oh…this was nice so far, even though we weren't doing anything. "Relax."

Telling someone to relax usually had the opposite effect, but it didn't with Gideon. I did, melting into him. My tongue was definitely in his mouth, and I wasn't grossed out at all. It was…oh shit, was I getting hard again?

Our lips moved together. He let me explore his mouth, and I did the same for him. I liked Gideon's spit...a lot. Kissing wasn't nearly as gross as it sometimes looked. When he slid his tongue into my mouth again, I liked that too.

I made a noise, and he ate it down. I didn't realize I'd stopped stroking until he wrapped his hand over mine and guided me. For the first time in my life, I was making out, naked with another man, touching him and pleasuring him after he'd made me jizz all over the place.

I never wanted it to end, but it was only a few minutes later that Gideon pulled back and said, "I'm gonna come. If you don't want my load on you, back up." He pulled his hand off so I could remove mine, but...I didn't want to. I wanted to try because, again, this was Gideon, and his care made everything so much easier. I kept going, kept stroking him, watched as his back bowed off the bed the way mine had and he spurted white strings up his chest, hot splatters of it hitting my hand, and...so *not* gross. It was the hottest thing I'd ever seen.

The second he was done, I grabbed my own cock, stroking myself to my second orgasm. This time, my load landed *on* Gideon, on his stomach and in his pubes and on his cock.

"Wow." I dropped onto my back. "That was incredible."

"I'd say so. You came twice."

"It's been a while." We lay there for a moment, both of us quiet. My brain started spinning some, and my body felt gross and sticky. "Don't leave...or move. Just...I'll be right back." I ran to the bathroom, where I wet a washcloth and cleaned myself. After throwing it into the hamper, I got another one wet and went back to my room, where Gideon was still lying naked and covered in cum and tattoos. I started to wipe him up.

"I can do it."

"I want to." He lay back while I cleaned him, wiping all the sticky mess from his stomach, the dark hair at his groin, and his soft cock... How was this happening? And I liked it, this feeling of taking care of him. It wasn't often I felt as though I was taking care of someone, spoiling them and giving them what they needed. It was strangely powerful.

When I finished, I put the rag in the hamper and sat down naked beside him again.

My eyes were drawn to his nipple piercings, so I reached out and fingered one. I wondered what it would be like to lash my tongue over them.

"Are you okay to talk about the virgin thing?" Gideon asked.

"Yes, though I'm not sure what you want me to say. I

don't have a lot of friends...no real ones except you and Rachel. I've never had a boyfriend. I refuse to pay for sex. I've met a few guys on apps, but when we spoke, they weren't really interested. I think they thought I was odd."

"I think I hate them."

I rolled my eyes. "You don't know them."

"I can still hate them."

"I guess." I shrugged. "I mean, I probably would have changed my mind if they didn't because I can't have sex with someone I don't trust. And I definitely couldn't have their tongue and saliva in my mouth or their cum on me. I wasn't even sure I'd like yours. People in porn sweat so much, and I'm really weirded out about sweating with someone. When you think about it, sex is really gross, and doing that with a random person...or letting them inside your body or being in theirs?" I shivered. "I just...I need to know someone. I need to trust them and feel comfortable with them, and I've never had that until you."

Surprise seized me when he sat up, leaned in, and kissed me again, slowly and lazily. Gideon's tongue swept my mouth, and mine did the same to him. All too soon, he pulled away.

"Am I good at kissing?" I asked.

"Very."

"And you liked having orgasms with me?"

He grinned. "Oh yeah."

This was maybe the most perfect situation in the world. "Do you want to do it again? Not now because I came twice, but I was thinking…if you enjoy it, maybe we can keep doing it. I want to experiment with all kinds of sex. I'm especially interested in blow jobs and fucking, though I don't think I can let you come in my mouth, and I would probably need to fuck you first because I'm iffy on having someone else inside my body. I might be able to since it's you." I worried Gideon would think I was in love with him, that he would be stuck with me and that would make him say no. It was important to me that he knew this was just for the orgasms.

He stared at me for a second like he wasn't sure what to say. Panic clung to me, weighing me down. "You don't have to. It's fine if you want to say no…or, if we do it and I'm not good or you're bored of me, you can tell me and we'll stop. If you suck, I'll tell you too."

"I have no doubt you will."

I relaxed. It was so nice having someone who knew me and accepted me, who didn't care that I might tell him he wasn't good at something. "Friendship first because I don't have many of those, and no worries, I don't want to be your boyfriend or anything. I know I said that before, but it's true. I just really want to have sex. A lot of it. And you might be my only chance."

"Um...thanks?"

I rolled my eyes. "You know that's not what I meant. I told you first I find you attractive, and I said you could see me naked. I just don't want you to think I'm like, in love with you or something. You're my best friend...and we're really good at it, Gideon. We're bestie goals, but I'm also really interested in your cock."

He barked out a loud laugh, which made me relax some. "So basically, I'm getting a lot of sex with an incredibly attractive man who I also happen to like spending time with? Where do I sign up?"

"We don't have to put the deal in writing or anything. If you'd like a contract, I can write one up, though."

His mouth came down on mine again. Gideon must really like kissing. "I would love to help you explore sex."

Happiness ballooned in my chest, but then... "Wait. Will you be having sex with other people? Because then I'll be thinking about that like...what if you swallow their cum and I don't know, and you come home and I kiss you?"

"I won't be having sex with anyone else until we're done."

"Me neither." Obviously. "We should shake on it."

"We should kiss on it instead."

I liked that idea. And when Gideon took my mouth, pushing me down to my back and lying on top of me…I came again.

It was awesome.

CHAPTER TWELVE

Gideon

A WEEK HAD gone by. Milo and I had jerked each other off almost every day, sometimes twice a day. Once he just wanted to watch me jack myself while he took care of himself because he didn't feel like being touched, or, as he put it, *peopling*, and another time he was *too pissed for orgasms* because of a phone call with his mom. I didn't know what had happened, but it was clear to me she wanted to know what was going on in Milo's life and also to have a say in it.

We hadn't gone any further yet. I was following his lead, but like him, I was looking forward to blow jobs and fucking. If it never happened, I'd be okay with that too. I just liked spending time with Milo—that was the most important thing, no matter how good orgasms felt with him. And they did.

I rolled over, pulled on some underwear, and got out

of bed. One trip through the apartment told me Milo was already at the bookstore for the day. He was making great progress. I wished I could stay and help him, but it was a mandatory family beach day.

I showered and got ready before heading to the bookstore. The door was unlocked, so I slipped inside to see Milo on a ladder, using a gun to nail a board to the back wall.

I watched him for a second. He was good with his hands and building, and that had surprised me. I hated that it had. As much as I tried not to, I was human and had my own preconceived ideas about people. It was something I actively worked not to do, even more now that I'd met him.

When he finished, he climbed down and noticed me. "Goggles and hard hat, please."

"I'm not working or even close to you."

"Gideon!"

"Fine, fine." There was a table beside me with extras, so I put them on. "It's looking really good in here."

"Thank you. I feel like I'm behind, and then I had three uneven cuts this morning, which I don't typically do. I think I stayed up too late making you come. I try to get a solid eight hours."

"Oops?" I teased, and he laughed.

"It was fun. And I could have gotten up later, but that would have just frustrated me in other ways, so it is what it is."

"I'd stay and help if I could. I used to fix things for Gene and Wilma pretty often."

"You missed the porch stairs," he said without a hint of humor in his voice.

"So you've told me. I didn't do work for them they didn't ask me to do."

His eyes widened behind his goggles. "Was that rude of me?"

"No." I shook my head. "You're fine. Wanna take the day off and head home with me?" I hadn't meant to ask, but now that I had, I was glad.

"Why would I want to do that?"

I tried not to frown, but I wasn't sure I succeeded. "I don't know. I just thought you might want to take the day off, is all." And at some point, unless he moved, he would meet my family. It was hard not to see everyone in Little Beach. But the truth was, I just wanted to hang out with him. My family was great, we loved each other, but I still always felt like the oddball with them. It would have been nice to be around someone who…hell, I never felt that around Milo, did I? Like I didn't belong.

"Oh. Well, thank you, but no, thanks. I have my own

personal things to do today."

"Have fun with your personal shit, I guess." My words came out harsher than I'd meant, and the fact that they had was disconcerting. Why the hell was I annoyed?

"You're mad at me, and I'm really confused about why. You invited me somewhere, and I said no, thank you."

"Fuck." I tried to run a hand through my hair but just knocked the hat off. "I'm not mad at you. I'm just being an idiot. Ignore me."

Milo cocked his head, his eyes slightly squinty as he studied me. "Did you *want* me to come with you for some reason?"

"No," I lied. Because even if I did, why should he rearrange his day for me? Especially for no good reason.

"Okay. I can, if you want, because we're friends, and that's what friends do for each other."

I shook my head. "You're fine, Lo. You have shit to do, so you can do it. Maybe I didn't get enough sleep either—that, or you drained my brain out of my balls somehow. I'm not sure I've come on such a consistent basis in my life."

He grinned. "Orgasms alone have always been great, but orgasms with someone else are fucking awesome."

I laughed. "I'm gonna head out. I'll see you at home

tonight."

"I'll cook dinner."

"But then it won't have meat."

"I can use the tofu…?"

"No. God no. That's disgusting. I like a lot of what you make, but I'll never eat tofu again. It nearly killed me."

Milo rolled his eyes. "And people think *I'm* dramatic." He pointed to my feet. "You're wearing the torture devices again."

"*You* are dramatic, and *I'm* going to the beach."

"I don't care. Your poor toes. And those aren't safe to wear here. Get out!"

I laughed. "I'm going, I'm going."

I was in my truck heading toward my parents' house before I realized I was still smiling.

"WHAT'S NEW WITH you?" Kris asked. "You've been keeping to yourself a lot lately." We were sitting in the backyard, which led to Mom and Dad's private section of the beach. Kris and Meg often ended up at my family get-togethers. Our parents had been close all our lives, which was likely part of how we'd fallen into being best friends. We grew up spending birthdays together and hanging out while our families had. His mom and dad had moved a few years back. They were tired of living on the island and actually headed for the mountains.

"I always kind of keep to myself." Well, not totally. We got together, went out to a meal or had drinks, but his life was closer to how Orlando lived now—working Monday through Friday, nine to five, and the whole marriage, mortgage, saving-for-retirement thing. I wasn't there yet. Though I had a feeling Milo already put money back for retirement. It seemed like the kind of thing he would do. He might have his quirks, but he also had his shit together.

"But even more so lately. Meg mentioned you haven't been by in a while."

"Yeah, I guess so. I've been hanging out with Milo a lot."

"What's going on with you two?" I looked over to see Mom talking with Heather and Megan. She reached over and rubbed Heather's six-month-pregnant belly. Dad and Orlando were by the grill, no doubt talking law and cases and all that shit I had zero interest in but they loved so much. I returned my attention to Kris.

"Nothing, really. We're just friends—good friends, but that's it."

"That was fast. You don't typically call people good

friends that quickly. In fact, until him, I think I was your only good friend." The two of us laughed. "Do you have much in common? You seem an unlikely pair."

I shrugged. I wasn't sure it really mattered what we had in common or how unlikely we were. Sometimes people just fit in your life, and strangely, Milo fit in mine. "I don't know, Kris. He's a vegetarian, with an accounting degree, who has no ink and hates it when I wear flip-flops. He makes lists and schedules and puts reminders in his phone. Also, don't eat all the fruit and not put it on the shopping list, or you'll have one angry Milo." I chuckled, having to work to bite back my smile. "But he makes me laugh and makes me look at the world differently. I like spending time with him." I liked having orgasms with him too, but Kris didn't need to know that.

In a confusing way I still couldn't sort through, I felt more comfortable, more like myself sitting around talking with Milo than I did with my own family, and hell, my own brother and my best friend. Relationships were so fucking layered. I loved Kris, and Orlando was the best brother a guy could ask for. We all gave each other shit and had each other's backs. I knew they would do anything for me and I would for them, but when I was with them, I didn't feel the… How did I even put it into words? The calmness? Contentment? Happiness? I felt when I was with Milo.

I traced circles on the extra-long picnic table we sat at before looking at Kris when he didn't respond. "What?" I asked.

"Nothing."

"Aw, how's my little bro doing?" Orlando gave me a noogie because apparently we were ten.

I glanced over to see Mom, Dad, Heather, and Meg approaching too. "Why couldn't I have been an only child?" I asked.

"I'm older, though, so if there was only one, it would be me. I'm the cooler Barlow brother anyway," Orlando replied.

"I don't know how I'm going to handle two kids when the baby comes. At least the new one won't require as much attention as this one." Heather pointed to Orlando, making everyone laugh.

He wrapped his arms around her. "You love me just the way I am. Don't pretend you don't."

Dad and Mom put plates down on the table. Orlando sat beside me, and Heather next to him. Megan and my parents joined Kris on the other side.

We all dug in. There was chicken, potato salad, and grilled corn on the cob.

"How's the shop?" Mom asked. Typically, Dad didn't

even try. It wasn't that he didn't care, but it wasn't something he would ever think about. With him and Orlando, they were into the same things, so it was automatic. Yeah, there were things all three of us did together—we grew up camping and fishing and building things—but when it came to those everyday conversations, Dad and Orlando had always had more to talk about than Dad and I did.

"It's going well. Business is steady enough. It could be better, but I'm getting by."

"Yeah, it'll be tough—a tattoo parlor on the island. The good thing is, even though we're not a major vacation destination, we do get some tourists, and I'm sure that helps," Dad said.

"It does."

"I'm not sure how sustainable it is in the long run, but—"

"Lando," Mom said, using his nickname to differentiate him from my brother, and I silently thanked her. I wasn't in the mood to hear how my business would likely fail. We'd talked that to death if you asked me.

"You're right, dear. I'm sure it will be fine," Dad replied. "Oh, Orlando, remind me to talk to you later about a client. I'd like your advice."

My brother nodded. I busied myself by taking a bite

of my food.

"Your brother tells us you've made friends with Wilma's grandson. I can't believe we never knew that Beverly was her daughter. I'm sure that was so difficult for her." Mom shook her head as if to reinforce what a tragedy that was.

"Yeah, definitely. Milo's working through understanding it himself."

"And," Mom started—well, shit. I knew this was coming and wasn't even sure why I hadn't told them about Milo—"I had to hear through the Little Beach Gossip Line that he's living with you. Gideon, why wouldn't you tell us that?" Mom turned to Orlando. "You too."

My brother held his hands up. "Don't look at me. It's not my business to tell."

Mom gave her attention to Kris next, who said, "I plead the fifth. Gid is my best friend. I can't incriminate him."

"In what, you jackass?" Orlando asked.

"Hey, I'm sticking up for Gideon, unlike you, who can't keep your mouth shut. You're the one who cornered Milo," Kris teased.

"Cornered? What does that mean?" Dad asked.

"Nothing," I said. Was it time to go home yet? I took

a bite of potato salad to stall. "Just like I told everyone else, it's his apartment. He has more of a right to it than I do. But yeah, we're friends. He's a good guy."

"I heard he's also…homosexual. Are the two of you…?" Mom asked tentatively.

I sighed. "You can say gay, and you don't have to let the words drag out before you say it. Yeah, he's gay, but we're just like the straights; we don't all have to want each other because we share the same orientation."

My words must have come out sharper than I'd intended because Orlando nudged me and Dad said, "Hey, you know she didn't mean anything by it. We love and support you and treat you no differently from your brother. If he didn't have Heather and suddenly lived with a woman, your mom would ask the same thing."

He was right; she would. I mumbled an apology, and Mom added, "I just want you to be happy. I want you to have someone. And even though the two of you are just friends, you could have invited him today."

I nodded without telling her that I had and Milo hadn't wanted to come.

It was quiet for a moment, slightly awkward while everyone ate. It was Megan who broke the silence. "We have news. Kris and I are going to have a baby."

"Oh my God!" Mom shrieked. "Two little ones to

love on?" She hugged Megan while Heather, Orlando, and I got up to do the same. The conversation steered from me to the babies while we finished eating.

I was happy for Kris, for Meg too, of course, but it also made me feel stagnant. Like everyone was moving forward without me.

After our stomachs settled, I tilted my head toward the ocean. "Race you there," I told Orlando and Kris.

My brother started running before we were ready, Kris and I right behind, calling him a cheater.

We stumbled into the ocean when a thought hit me out of the blue—I wondered if Milo liked to swim.

CHAPTER THIRTEEN

Milo

I STOOD ON the porch of Gene's house, the house he'd shared with Wilma Allen, my biological grandmother. My toes hit the doorstep, and I wondered how Gideon's feet were doing. He hadn't worn the flip-flops in weeks, but he had today when he went to his parents' house. He might have to get used to wearing them again. I should make sure to tell him that he didn't have to do that, that he didn't have to worry about me, because him skipping them for my benefit could make having the annoying thing between his toes even worse.

This is not the time to think about Gideon, I told myself, shutting those thoughts down. I didn't know why I was putting this off. I wanted to know about Wilma Allen. It was part of the reason I'd come to Little Beach, yet I continued to make excuses. That wasn't like me, and I was tired of it being me, so after making sure to get at least a half day's work in, I'd gone home, showered, and walked over.

Now I just needed to knock.

The door opened before I had the chance, and there he was, Gene, the man who had loved my grandmother.

"The steps are holding up," was the first thing I said. "Sorry again for fixing them without asking. It was a hazard, and at your age, not very safe."

Gene chuckled. "Most things aren't very safe at my age. I'm older than your grandmother."

Crap. That was probably rude. People didn't like to be reminded of their ages. "Would you like to invite me in?" I asked.

"Of course." Gene stepped aside. "Come in."

I went into the house. It was clean and homey, if slightly cluttered for my taste. I didn't like a lot of extra stuff, like knickknacks. The furniture was older but in good shape. My mom would hate it, but she was picky in a different way than I was. I wondered if Wilma Allen had been as well.

"Are you my biological grandfather?" My brain told me it was maybe not the best way to ask and that I should work up to it, but I wasn't always good at listening to those thoughts reminding me how I should act or react. Most of the time, I just did what felt right.

"I wish I could say I was, but no, I'm not."

"Oh." I walked through the living room, looking at photos on the walls of Gene with Wilma Allen. "Did you know my biological grandfather?"

"No. Are you thirsty? I have tea and orange juice."

"Orange juice is for breakfast. Tea, please. Unsweet."

Gene grinned.

"What?"

"Wilma hated sugar in her tea too."

"Oh," I said again. It was becoming my favorite word lately. It seemed like Wilma Allen and I had a lot in common…well, two things. So far, we had two things in common.

"I'll be right back."

He disappeared into the kitchen. When he was gone, I plucked a photo of Wilma Allen on the beach off the wall. She was beautiful. Her hair was like milk chocolate the way Mom's was. They had the same smile, but where Mom's face was clear, Wilma Allen had freckles like me.

"I can put it back," I told Gene when he came back into the room.

"It's fine. You can look at whatever you want. It would make Wilma happy."

I took the glass from him. "My mom is very upset with her. She didn't want to come… She never wanted to stay in Little Beach or to come back. I didn't understand it until I heard about Wilma Allen."

He nodded, sad understanding in his eyes. "She's entitled to her feelings. I'm sure it's hard for her to understand. But Wilma loved her. She has always loved Beverly more than anything in this world. Life is complicated sometimes."

"Can you tell me why? Why she gave Mom away?" I thought about my mom, how protective of me she was, how she'd chosen me over her husband. Sometimes she pushed too hard and wanted too much control, but I'd always known she loved me because of it.

"It wasn't like that. Well, I guess that's what she did, but it wasn't what she wanted to do. All she wanted was what was best for your mom."

I took a drink of the tea, looked down at the photo again. "Will you tell me? The story? I want…I want to feel close to her, even if she's not here, but it's hard for me because I don't know or understand her. In my head she's the person who hurt my mom, but she's also the person who gave me a bookstore and watched me online, and she wouldn't do that if she didn't care."

"She cared very much." Gene walked slowly over to the couch and sat down. I took the armchair across from him, putting my drink on the table beside me. "Wilma was seventeen when your mom was born—sixteen when she got pregnant. Back then, people didn't do those things. Her family was poor, and she hadn't yet finished school. She couldn't take care of herself, much less a baby. Her parents would have disowned her. They nearly did just because she'd gotten pregnant."

That all made sense. My mom was sixty. She'd had me at thirty-six. It hadn't been a planned pregnancy because she hadn't thought she wanted kids. My father hadn't either. She'd been on birth control, but apparently I was an eager swimmer, which was really gross to think about, so I nipped those thoughts in the bud. But Wilma had been seventy-seven when she died, and all those years ago, I couldn't imagine it was acceptable for a sixteen-year-old to be pregnant.

When I couldn't find any words, Gene continued. "Wilma was…God, she was perfect. I loved her, but she was a little quirky. Times were different, and they didn't understand people like they do now. Anything unique meant wrong, and even if it had been appropriate for Wilma to have a baby at her age, her parents made her believe she wouldn't be a good mother, that it wasn't good for the baby. So, before she started to show, her parents sent her away. She went to live with an aunt. In the meantime, they arranged the adoption with the

Meyers, a local family on the island. They were good people, and she knew they would be good parents to Beverly.

"She stayed away for years—finished school living with her aunt, went to college, which she had to fight for the right to do. But when Wilma set her mind to something, there wasn't anything she couldn't do. She was determined to prove to the world that she was unstoppable, and she was." He wiped a tear away, his hand shaking.

"When did she come back?"

"Your mama was fifteen at the time. Wilma was so damn proud of her. Said she was smart and strong and didn't take anyone's shit."

I laughed. "She's still all those things."

"Beverly was happy, and she'd had a good life. Legally, Wilma wasn't supposed to say she was Beverly's mom, and she felt she didn't have the right either. They'd raised Beverly and given her the life Wilma didn't think she could. But this is Little Beach, so of course they saw each other a lot. Wilma used to work at the library, and your mom was always there, studying or checking out books. They'd get to talking about literature. It made her happy, seeing her daughter grow, but it broke her heart not to be able to tell her. As much as she wanted to, that wasn't fair to the Meyers."

I nodded, still trying to figure out how to wrap my head around all this.

"She was so happy when your mom told her she'd gotten into Stanford. It was her happiest times, she said, being close to her daughter. And then when Beverly's parents died in the car accident, she found the papers. She confronted Wilma. She was hurt and angry that Wilma had been there and never told her. I think part of it was the pain of losing her adoptive parents too."

"It's almost like she lost three parents at once," I said.

I could see Mom looking at it that way. And I knew she would struggle to understand Wilma giving her up. To her, that meant she didn't care. I got that because I often saw things in black and white the same way, but it was something I worked to change. The world was full of shades of gray. And listening to Gene, I could see the sorrow and regret in his features and knew it was Wilma's emotions living on in him.

"Did Wilma tell her the truth? What happened?"

He shook his head. "She regretted it. I think, even though she was doing what was best for Beverly, she always hated herself for it. She felt like she'd given up, so no, she didn't, because she thought Beverly was right to hate her for her decision."

I knew the rest. Mom left Little Beach after that and never came back.

My chest ached. The whole thing was a tragedy.

Poor Mom.

Poor Wilma.

"What about her father?"

"He was a sailor. Wilma loved him and thought he loved her, but he left when he found out she was pregnant."

Like my father, only he left when I was twelve.

My chest was heavy, this deep melancholy weighing my bones down. "I think I need to go."

"Thank you for coming."

I stood and reached out to hand him the photo.

"You can keep it if you'd like."

I looked down at it, at Wilma, because that was who she was to me now. I didn't need the Allen. "Yes. Thank you. Do you mind if I come back? For more stories and photos? I can also fix whatever you need around the house, and at tax time, I can do those too."

He chuckled. "I'd like that, Milo. You don't have to do my taxes, but I might take you up on the other part. Gideon helps too."

Gideon. I missed him, which confused me, and I wanted to share this with him.

Gene walked me to the door. I held the photo close to my chest the entire time.

The whole walk back to the apartment, I hoped Gideon would be there to talk to.

CHAPTER FOURTEEN
Gideon

"Gideon? Are you home? I'd really like to talk to you," I heard from the living room. I'd just gotten out of the shower and changed after the day with my family.

"Yeah, I'm here." I headed toward the living room just as he finished taking off his pants and laying them over the rack, with his back to me. "I came in at the perfect time," I teased.

"Because you like my butt? Or am I missing something?"

"Because I like your butt."

"Thank you. Yours is nice too. And your chest. I like it when you don't wear a shirt. I mean, I like it when you're naked, and you're still attractive clothed too, but shirtless is more realistic for day-to-day living."

I leaned against the counter, smiling at him. It was

impossible to be in a bad mood around Milo. "Are you saying you'd like me to go shirtless when I'm at home?"

"Yes. Please. Thank you. As long as the timing is appropriate, at least."

I snickered before walking over to him and cupping his cheek. "You only like me for my body and my mad orgasm skills."

"Is there a problem with that?" he asked, his tone and gaze serious.

"I...you little shit." I pinched his ass when he started laughing.

"Ouch! Stop. And that was a good one. I definitely had you going." I pulled him close. Milo rubbed his thumb against my nipple. "I never thought piercings and tattoos would be sexy."

"That's because you never met me before."

"You're very conceited."

"Only when I know I'm right."

"I need to show you something." He pulled away, changing the subject. He could flip the switch like that when he wanted to, but other times he was hyperfocused on things.

Milo grabbed something from the rack that I hadn't seen and handed it over. It was a photo of Wilma when she was younger, wearing a black bathing suit. I'd seen it before, on the wall of Gene's house.

"You went over?"

"I did. Can I tell you about it?"

My chest tingled with the knowledge that he wanted to. I liked when Milo shared things with me, liked hearing about his day and what was on his mind. It made me feel important.

"Yes." I took his hand and pulled him to the couch. Milo followed easily. We sat down, and he immediately shifted to sit cross-legged.

"Gene told me the story about Wilma placing my mom up for adoption."

I noticed he'd only used her first name and not both, which meant he'd had a shift inside him when it came to Wilma. It was the same as when he'd called me Gideon instead of Tattoo Guy.

My fingers twitched to reach out and touch him, to pull him close and comfort him, but I wasn't sure if I should. Milo had made it clear we were friends with benefits, and that was what I wanted too…I thought. Or hell, who the fuck knew? It just felt different to jokingly hold him when we were teasing than to do it now. It felt too boyfriendy.

"I'm here if you want to share that."

"I already told you I did, silly. I'm just sorting my

thoughts so everything doesn't try to come out at once."

I nodded, letting him do his thing. The seconds turned to minutes before he finally said, "She got pregnant with my mom when she was sixteen."

I listened with rapt attention while he shared the story. Wilma meeting a sailor, getting pregnant, her parents almost disowning her, then forcing her away to have Beverly and the adoption; Beverly's reaction when she found out.

His neck was bent, his gaze angled down, his voice soft. When he finished, Milo swiped at his face, rubbing the stray tear into his skin.

"It's all really, really sad, isn't it?" he asked.

"Yeah, it is. How are you feeling?"

He shrugged.

"Was that another of my dumb questions?" I hoped to pull a smile from him. Milo's smiles were like winning the lottery.

"No. I liked that one."

"Come 'ere." It didn't matter if it felt like crossing an imaginary line I'd drawn for whatever the hell reason I'd drawn it.

I gently grabbed Milo's arm, and just like when we'd walked to the couch, he let me lead him. I leaned back, pulling him with me until I lay down with him on top of me. He rested between my legs, my arms around him, his cheek pressed to my chest, skin to skin.

"I wish you could have met her," I told him, brushing my finger back and forth over his bicep.

"I do too. I want to know everything about her."

"Gene will share. I can too. I have my stories about her." His smooth face nuzzled my pec. I willed my cock not to get hard because now wasn't the time. "Are you going to tell your mom?"

"Yes, but she's tricky. She's the most stubborn person I know. When she has an idea in her head, it's hard to make her see anything else. I have to do it in the right way at the right time, but I'm not always good at that, so we'll see."

I kissed the top of his head. "You'll figure it out," I said, then found myself asking, "Do you want kids?"

"No, I don't think so. Most of the time they're hard to deal with, but I like other people's sometimes. Cammy is cool when she's not too hyper. Do you?"

"No, I don't think so. I like other people's too. Heather is pregnant. Megan just announced she is too."

"Does that make you feel lonely?"

His question sucked the wind out of me. How did he know? "Yes."

"Things like that make me lonely sometimes. Not

enough to change me, though."

I kissed the top of his head again, was going to talk to him more about my family, but he said, "This is nice. I've never done this before either."

"Lucky me."

He lifted his head so he could look me in the eye. "I think you're very good at getting men into bed. You're all flirty and generous with the compliments. You should teach me to do that."

I rolled my eyes. "I wasn't trying to fuck you when I said that. I'm being serious, but it's good to see you have respect for my game. I've never had trouble getting laid when I wanted unless it was because I was here, and there were no men who swung my way."

"I don't know why anyone wouldn't want to have sex with guys. They're so fucking hot!"

I laughed. "Yeah, well, women are beautiful, and straight men likely don't understand why we don't want to bang them."

"Good point. Also, I won't want to talk about Wilma anymore tonight so I'm not sad. Tell me more about your day."

I huffed out a humorless laugh. "Real talk?"

"Do I ever want or do anything else?"

I felt like I was smiling, even though I wasn't. It was

the most foreign feeling, like Milo had injected happiness inside me. "Good point. I was being a big baby and feeling sorry for myself, and then I came home and talked to you, and it all feels really fucking trivial."

"It might be, but that doesn't mean you're not allowed to feel it. I read a lot about people and emotions because it's so damn confusing. Even if it's not logical, feelings are valid."

"I…" I thought maybe Milo Copeland was my favorite person in the world. "You understand people more than you think."

"Are you flirting with me again?" His lips curled playfully, a spark of humor dancing in his eyes.

"Am I really that good if you have to ask?"

"Are you stalling? I think you're stalling."

When we laughed, our bodies vibrated together, making his joy echo inside me. "It's silly. I just…sometimes I feel like I don't fit in my family. My dad and Orlando are lawyers, and I'm a tattoo artist."

He frowned. "What's wrong with that? You're good at what you do, and your job makes people happy."

"Shit. I've never looked at it that way before, that what I do makes people happy." Which was ridiculous really; of course it did. They came to me with something they cared enough about to permanently put on their bodies.

"I'm very good at this. Who knew? What else do you have for me?" He rested his arms on my chest, his stomach on my groin, watching and waiting.

"I think I've created a monster." But I loved it. "I'm not sure how to explain it. My dad doesn't talk to me like he does with Orlando. He loves me and supports me, but we don't share the same kind of bond that he does with my brother. I'm not even sure if he knows it. Like we discussed, I don't want kids, which makes my mom sad, even though she already has a grandbaby on the way, and now Meg is pregnant, so it's almost like another. I feel like I stand out when I'm with them and like they wish I were someone else, and holy shit, I sound ridiculous. I'm going to stop talking now."

I expected him to laugh, but he didn't. "I know what it's like to feel like you don't fit, like people would rather you were someone else. That's not something anyone else has to understand because it comes from inside you. I think…I think people worry too much about everyone being the same, or like, *their* feelings are the only *right* feelings, ya know? Like however I feel has to be how you feel, or it's wrong or stupid. But really, we're all unique, and most emotions, experiences, thoughts, being left out or not, or lonely or not, or how we grieve or not—

whatever the situation—those can't be wrong because they're part of being human, and no two experiences are the same. So…it's not ridiculous, and thank you for trusting me. When you feel like you don't fit, just know you fit with me. I'm not sure if that helps or not. I do that with you. If I've said something awkward or someone looks at me strangely, I just think about what it's like to be with you," Milo said.

It wasn't until he added, "Did I say something wrong?" that I realized I hadn't replied, that I'd just sat there looking at him, my heart beating so hard, I thought maybe it wanted to jump out of my chest and crash through his.

He thought about me, and that helped. When he felt alone or upset, he imagined what it was like with me. How could I do that for someone? "No. You said something perfect."

"Wow…there's a first time for everything." We laughed, and as we did, our bodies moved together. My cock took notice of the sexy man on top of me, hardening against him.

"Oh," Milo said. "I think your penis wants to come out and play. Mine does too."

I cupped his face between my hands. "You're the craziest person I've ever met. My dick is definitely interested, but I was wondering how yours might feel about playing in my mouth."

I swear his eyes glossed over at the question. "You want to blow me?"

"I do."

"Yes, please. Let's do that right now. I'd like you to suck my cock."

"God, you're fun. Sit up."

He did, tugging off his shirt as he went. "Take your clothes off too. I want Naked Gideon."

"Naked Gideon coming right up." I stood and pulled my shorts and underwear down, kicking out of them. My dick was already achingly hard. I gave it a slow stroke as Milo licked his lips.

"I don't know how I lived my whole life without having sex. Can I blow you too?"

"One hundred percent yes." I knelt in front of him, tugged his underwear off. Milo's cock bounced against his stomach, hard and leaking, his balls so tight and full.

"You have such a pretty dick." I wrapped a hand around his hot length, and Milo hissed.

"Yours is too. I like it a lot. I think I'll compare all cocks to yours from now on."

Discomfort tied me up, squeezed a hand tightly around my throat. I didn't ever want Milo to be with anyone but me. "None of them will be as good."

"No," he said breathlessly as I leaned in and circled my tongue around his glans. "Oh fuck! I won't last very long."

"That's okay. I'll take that as a compliment for my cock-sucking skills."

"Really, it's probably just because I've never had a blow job before."

"Always busting my balls, Lo." I nuzzled his short pubes. He'd clearly cut them again recently. I inhaled deeply, pulling in the musky smell of him.

"Whoa! What are you doing? I didn't shower! I'm probably sweaty down there."

I smiled into his groin. "I don't care. In fact, I'd rather you are. It's sexy as fuck. But of course, if you want me to stop, I will. Just know I think it's hot."

"Oh." Sometimes that felt like it was his favorite word. "Don't stop, then."

I breathed him in again before pulling him forward so his ass hung off the edge of the couch. My tongue lapped at his balls. I loved the salty taste of his skin, the scent of his arousal, the way his breathing picked up, sharp sounds falling from his lips.

"Can you, um…suck them, please?"

"Yes. We know how your nuts love attention."

"They do…very much. Fuck! Gid…" The last part he said when I pulled his sac into my mouth, sucking and loving on him.

I rubbed up and down his shaft as I enjoyed his body. Each sound out of him fueled me, made me want to give him more because there was nothing like witnessing Milo take his pleasure.

Our gazes met when I used my tongue on his crown, teasing his slit and tasting his precum. His eyes rolled back, and his cock twitched. He definitely wasn't going to last long.

I kissed the tip of his erection, and he gave me a small smile. "Thank you."

"For blowing you?"

"For liking me."

My heart punched at my chest again, swelled so big I wasn't sure I could contain the damn thing. I was determined to make this the best head anyone had ever received, so I pushed those thoughts aside.

"I'm very good at this." I winked, then took him into my mouth, deep into the back of my throat, opening it for him and not stopping until my nose was in his neat nest of hair.

"Gideon…oh God…wow…suck me…I'm sex-talking, but I can't help it, and…wow…I already said that, didn't I? But wow."

I pulled off, then swallowed him down again, using my hand sometimes too when I focused on his crown. One of Milo's hands was fisted into the arm of the couch, the other on the cushion before he let go and buried it in my hair. He pulled, making it burn, but I wasn't sure he knew he was doing it.

I just kept sucking him, savoring his taste and feel and letting each of his *wows* dissolve into me. It was the sexiest moment of my life.

When he snapped his hips, ramming his cock down my throat, I gagged.

"Oh my God! I'm sorry! They do that in porn!"

"You can fuck my mouth, Lo. I just didn't expect it. Choking on dick can be sexy. Do it. You can lead the way."

A sunburst of desire bloomed in his gaze, his hand tightening in my hair before he did as I said. Milo thrust his hips, taking his pleasure, taking pleasure from me in a way I was happy to give, and it wasn't long before I saw the difference in him, before his eyes glossed over and he got a loopy smile on his face.

"I'm going to…if you don't want it… Wait, do you swallow because if not…" He tried to pull off, but I didn't let him, bobbed my head in his lap and hoped it showed him I wanted to taste his load. Wanted to swallow it all down and have his flavor in my mouth all night long.

"I'm coming… Gid, I'm gonna…" He didn't have the chance to finish before the hot splash of his cum flooded my mouth. I let it slide down my throat, took the next spurt hungrily, while he used me to unload in, still pulling my hair. "Oh my God," he breathed. "I said that already, didn't I?"

"A few times." I was aching myself, my balls tight and full of my desire for him.

"I want to go to sleep, but I'm also hungry, and I really want to try to blow you too."

"You don't have to."

"I want to. Can you stand up? I think that would be hot."

I had to say I agreed with him. I pushed to my feet, my dick bobbing in front of his face.

"I don't know if you can fuck my mouth like I did yours. And remember, I don't want to swallow. I have to work up to that. Maybe you can come on my chest, and then I'll taste it. I should have tasted it before, but—"

"Shh. You're fine, Lo. I promise you, whatever you do to me, I'm going to love. We haven't tried the coming-on-you thing. Are you sure you'll be okay with it?"

He nodded, leaned in, and gave my cock a quick swipe with his tongue. He didn't say anything before doing it again, then pulling the head into his mouth. "That's not so bad."

"Thanks?"

"I'm sorry. I'm ruining this. I want to do it. I want to real bad. I actually dreamed about doing it, but it's just a lot."

"Then you don't have to. Or you can try later."

I attempted to pull away, but he stopped me with a hand on my hip. "No! I want it, want you. I want to make you feel good the way you do me, and…well, even though my brain is a mess, I've always been really interested in sucking cock. I'm going to start on your balls."

I looked down at him while he did, while he first gave quick lashes of his tongue, then slower ones. I held the side of his head gently, caressing him, hoping he took it as the form of comfort I meant it as.

When he moved up to my cock again, he started at the base, licking his way up, and damned if it didn't make my knees weak because it was him.

"Fuck, that's good. So damn good."

He smiled, kissed the head of my dick the way I'd done to him, then sucked it into his mouth. As ridiculous as it sounded, I trembled. It was the best feeling I ever had in my life.

"Your mouth is incredible." With my words, he took me deeper, using his hand in unison, jerking me and sucking me. It wasn't technically the best blow job I'd ever had, but it was Milo, and he wanted it so bad it made every sensation a million times better.

Milo didn't deep throat me, didn't even try, and I didn't care because he had my cock in his mouth. He'd trusted me to be the first to give him this, and I would forever be grateful for this moment.

"Yeah, like that," I said when he sucked harder, stroked faster. "Jesus, I could get used to your mouth. Are you going to let me? Are you going to keep sucking me off when we want to come together?"

He groaned, the feeling making satisfaction vibrate through me.

When he pulled off and whispered, "I like the way you taste…the feel of you on my tongue," my orgasm beat down the fucking door that was barely holding it back.

"Shit. I'm gonna come." I pulled back, went to wrap a hand around my cock and angle it away from his face, but Milo licked his palm and swatted mine away. He grabbed me with the pressure he knew I liked and stroked me just a few times before my balls drew up and I spurted, ribbons of cum hitting him in the neck and chest, running down his skin in a way that made me shoot a third time.

He looked at me, all wide eyes and swollen lips, painted with my load, and said, "Was it good? Even though I can't swallow?"

For a moment I was struck speechless. How could he not realize after how hard I'd come? "Swallowing my load doesn't matter. Remember, this isn't porn, and everyone likes something different. That was the best blow job of my life."

"I doubt that."

"Stop calling me a liar." I leaned in and kissed his cheek so he didn't get the taste of himself on his tongue. "You look hot with my cum on you."

"I *feel* hot with your cum on me…like I'm really sexy."

"You are."

He dipped his finger into my jizz, licked it, and gagged. "No. I'm sorry. That's disgusting. I can't do it! Like ever."

I laughed because it really didn't fucking matter. I just liked him. "Contrary to what some people might want others to believe, swallowing isn't a prerequisite for good head. I'll just paint you with it every time instead."

He nodded. "Speaking of eating things, I'm hungry. I know I said I'd cook dinner, but I thought you might want to make eggplant parmesan with me."

"I can do that, but I'm still a firm believer that it would be better with chicken." The meals he made were actually really good, but I liked to give him shit. I was pretty sure Milo knew that.

"You complain, but you always eat." He stood. "I don't like meat."

"You like my meat." I waggled my eyebrows and grabbed my cock.

"Oh my God. That was bad. Really, really bad." But he was chuckling. "Let's stay naked. We should double the time we wash our hands, though."

"Yeah, but you have an apron. I don't." He had one because he cooked in his underwear so often.

"Oh. I forgot to tell you I got you one, just in case."

He went to his room and came back with an apron that matched his, saying: *Don't ask me what I'm wearing under this.*

"I ordered it from the shop in California where I got mine." Milo tossed it over. "Come on, Gid. I should have eaten a half hour ago. Good thing I had a blow job. I'm too happy to get hangry."

"Suck Milo's cock every day. Got it." I joined him in the kitchen, and we got to work.

CHAPTER FIFTEEN

Milo

WE HAD GRADUATED past hand jobs, and while they'd felt really good, now that I'd had a dick in my mouth, that was always how I wanted to make Gideon come. We'd spent the last two weeks sucking each other off every chance we got. I admit it was usually me who prompted all the oral stimulation, but when a guy goes twenty-four years without having a mouth on his dick, it's a little exciting when it happens and said mouth lives with you and is very willing. I still didn't understand how Gideon could be okay with eating my cum, but he was, so I wasn't going to complain.

I'd gotten quite a bit done at the bookstore. It should actually be finished in a couple of weeks, and I couldn't wait. Today I had workers out doing some of the jobs I couldn't. I'd already been downstairs three times, but I was trying to force myself to leave them alone. Of course,

Gideon was sleeping in. I didn't know any twenty-six-year-old who slept until ten or eleven most days, but since his shop didn't open until noon and it was downstairs, it made sense that he could.

But I was *bored,* and if I was bored, I wouldn't be able to hold back my need to micromanage the workers downstairs. It was a thing. I wasn't afraid to admit my flaws.

I thought about calling Rachel to see if she wanted to hang out, but instead I found myself sliding Gideon's bedroom door open. He was asleep in his underwear, the blankets kicked down so they hung half off the bed in a way that would make me crazy. "Gideon," I whispered. When he didn't budge, I cleared my throat. Nothing. How in the hell did he not wake up? I took a step back, planning on sneaking out of his room, but again, *bored.* So I resorted to a totally fake cough and squeezed his name in there. *Cough, Gideon, cough.*

His eyes slowly fluttered open.

"Oh, you're awake."

"I wonder how that could have happened?"

I shrugged. "Beats me," I said, flopping onto his bed. "I'm antsy…and when I'm antsy, I bug people."

"There's a joke in there somewhere, but I'm too tired to find it. *Ant*sy. *Bug* people. Get it?"

"It's so adorable when you try to be funny." It was one of my favorite things about him.

"Evidently you think I failed." He wrapped an arm around me and pulled me close. "Let's go back to bed."

"*Gideon.* No. I can't. And you have morning breath."

He pushed up onto his elbows and looked down at me. I was on my back, watching him. "At least I know I'll never get a big head while you're around."

Shit. I'd offended him. Why was it so hard to figure out what to say sometimes? I just wanted to tell the truth. But Gideon was my favorite person. I didn't want to ever hurt him. "I'm sorry. I didn't mean to make you feel bad."

"You didn't. I'm kidding, Lo." He nuzzled my neck. "Wanna fool around? I'll brush my teeth first. Even take a quick shower if you think I need it."

I chuckled, my dick already getting hard. "It's odd, but I kind of like your sweat. I never would have expected that. And I always want to fool around, but if we're home, I won't be able to concentrate without going downstairs, and I think the workers hate me. I micromanage."

"No! You? I'd have never guessed."

"I sense sarcasm. Stop being mean to me."

"You told me I have bad breath!"

"I said morning breath. There's a difference." I can't explain what happened next, how we got from there to rolling around, tickling and wrestling with each other, but we did. I should one hundred percent hate this, but I was laughing so hard, my stomach hurt, and my chest felt weirdly full, like someone was using a pump to blow it up in a way that should be uncomfortable but was just...right.

He rolled on top of me, had me on my back while he straddled my hips. Gideon held my wrists down. My dick was erection city at the moment. Him resting his ass against it didn't help the situation—at all. "Do you want to go to the beach?" he asked, staring down at me, his burned-honey eyes taking me in. He was so hot, and not for the first time, I wondered what he was doing here with me.

"Yes," I replied, more breathless than I should be. Gideon smiled while brushing his thumb over the pulse in my right wrist.

The air around us felt weird...different...confusing.

Buzzzzz! My heart jumped with the sound of my phone going off in my pocket. "Oh my God. That scared me."

"Ignore it."

"What if it's the guys downstairs and they need my

help?" I managed to tug it out of my pocket without Gideon getting off me…which I liked, because I wanted Gideon on top of me. Like maybe we could find a way to live that way and do everything that way. *Excuse us, we're stuck together because he's my best friend and it feels good.*

"It's my mom," I said but still answered. "Hello, Mother."

Gideon collapsed on the bed beside me.

"You haven't called me in a week! I'm always the one who has to call you. I just like to know you're okay, Milo."

I sighed. I knew she did, and now that I understood things with Wilma, maybe that was part of the reason. Still, I couldn't help wondering if she would do this if I were someone else. "I'll try harder. Things have been really busy."

"Have you seen Gene again?"

"Yes." I'd told her we were spending time together. I'd asked her once if she wanted to know the story, and she said no, so I hadn't asked again. Plus, I thought that might be the kind of thing you did in person, but I didn't know. "Are you having your coffee before work?" I knew she was, but I wanted to change the subject.

"I am. I miss talking to you in the mornings. What are you doing?"

"I was wrestling in bed with Gideon. In a little while we're going to the beach."

"Ah fuck," Gideon whispered.

Mom was silent, too silent for her...

"We weren't having sex! I wouldn't have answered if that were the case. And we haven't done that yet. Not all the way, at least."

"Sweet Jesus," Gideon said. For a second I thought he was mad at me, but he just buried his face in my chest, his shoulders vibrating like he was holding back laughter.

"The two of you are a couple?"

"No. We're just friends. People do that, Mom. It's just a thing." Granted, I hadn't hooked up with friends before, but most people did, and why not? If Gideon and I were an example, this was something everyone should be doing. It was perfect, and we had so much fun together.

"Is that what you want?"

"Yes to both—I want to be friends with him *and* have sex with him. I told you, Mom, he's my best friend." We went through this every time we talked, though usually minus the sex stuff.

She sighed, and I knew without seeing her that she was biting her tongue so she didn't say something she knew I wouldn't like. "I don't want you to get hurt."

"Gideon would never hurt me." He wouldn't. I knew

that to the marrow of my bones. He lifted his head then and gave me a smile I couldn't read before kissing my chest. I wished I didn't have a shirt on so we were skin to skin.

"It happens all the time, Milo. Even if he doesn't mean to, that doesn't mean he won't."

"If it happens all the time, then it's an experience I should have, right? It's a part of life. You can't protect me forever."

"I can try," Mom said sadly. "I think I'd like to come out there."

"No!" I rushed out. I realized how that sounded and added, "I'm not trying to upset you, but I just… I'm trying to stand on my own. Maybe after the bookstore is complete and things settle down."

The silence stretched between us before Mom said, "I need to get ready for work. I love you, Milo."

"I love you too." I ended the call.

"You okay?" Gideon asked.

"Yeah. She's sad, and I don't want to make her feel that way, but I need to do this, and if she comes here, she'll take over. I got my micromanaging from her."

Gideon nodded, and somehow I knew he understood. "Thank you for trusting me. And I wouldn't ever hurt you on purpose. I promise."

He couldn't promise not to do it at all. Life didn't work that way. "I promise not to hurt you on purpose either."

Gideon pushed up on his elbows again, his chin resting in one of his hands. "Deal. Now let me go shower so I can take my best friend to the beach."

"And brush your teeth!" I called when he got out of bed.

"I hate you!" he yelled back.

No, he didn't. Even I knew that.

CHAPTER SIXTEEN

Gideon

I BRUSHED MY teeth and took a quick shower. I tried not to think about Milo's conversation with his mom. The last thing I ever wanted to do was hurt him. He meant…hell, he meant more to me than I ever would have expected. More than maybe he should.

When I finished, Milo was waiting for me. "I made you a smoothie for breakfast. Is that enough?"

"You didn't have to make me anything, Lo. I don't want you to feel like you have to do shit like that for me."

"I don't. I like to. What do you think of my sandals? Flip-flops with nothing between my toes! Just a strap over the top of my foot. You should invest in some."

"But my flip-flops don't bother me. Just you."

"I'm kidding. I don't want you to worry about wearing them, remember? Let's go. We can stop in at the bookstore on our way." He'd set a pair of shorts by the door and now slipped his sandals off to pull them on before stepping into them again.

"Yeah, but do we really have to check on them?"

"Yes, Gid. Yes, we do." He hefted a bag on his shoulders. "I got towels and sunscreen and hats for both of us in case we need them. I wish we had a beach umbrella. Do you have a beach umbrella? It's good to be prepared."

Milo always was. Even though we hadn't gone to the beach together yet, I'd learned that he needed to be the one to get everything set up when we went out, otherwise he would stress out about something being forgotten. "I do, actually. And a beach blanket. They're downstairs."

We picked up the beach umbrella from one of the extra storage rooms in Conflicting Ink. I tried to get Milo not to stop in at the store, but it didn't work. It took us twenty minutes to get out of there because he had to check everything to make sure it was being done properly.

We were close enough to the beach to walk. I hefted the umbrella over my shoulder, and Milo carried the bag. Luckily, it wasn't an incredibly busy day. The sand was littered with families, groups of people, single people, but not as crazy as it could be where it was hard to find a spot.

"If we were in California, we'd be screwed," Milo said as he laid the blanket out.

"Do you miss it?" I shoved the end of the umbrella into the sand.

"I miss my mom. I know she's a lot, but she's the only person in my life who's always been in my corner."

"That's good. I'm glad you have her."

He nodded, and we sat down. "Take off your shirt. I'll put sunscreen on you, and you can do me."

I swear it was like my dick had ears, holding out for any time Milo let out some kind of innuendo. *Do him? Yes, please!*

I did as he said while he pulled the bottle from our bag, and then he began to rub it on my shoulders and back. "When did you know you like tattoos?"

"I was always interested in them. I thought guys who had them were hot. All my teenage porn involved men with ink."

"Do you wish I had tattoos?"

"What? No. Absolutely not. I like you the way you are."

"That's good because I don't know if I could handle it. If I ever decide I want one, I'll come to you."

"Deal."

"They're hot…on you…and your piercings. Especially the ones in your nipples. I like to flick them with my tongue."

Heat spread through my groin. "Stop giving me a boner in public."

He gasped, looking over my shoulder. "You're hard?"

"No, but I will be if you keep talking about sucking things on me."

"Ugh. Fine. Turn around so I can do your front."

I did, cocking a brow at him. "You know I can do this myself, right?"

"Yes, but I like touching you."

I liked him touching me too. He rubbed sunscreen on my torso and arms, but I drew the line at my legs. I could do that myself. I returned the favor, adding the lotion to his front, back, then his cheeks, nose, and forehead. "We wouldn't want this pretty face to burn."

Damned if he didn't blush.

"Did you go to the beach often in California?" I asked when we lay beside each other on our sides.

"When I was younger. It's weird to go alone or with your mom as an adult."

I didn't understand why Milo didn't have friends. There was no one I liked spending time with more.

"There were people, Gideon," he said, reading my thoughts. "It wasn't like I was completely lonely; just…no one who lasted or that I connected with. No one that my brain would call a true friend because I knew that

I'd be too much for them. And honestly, I was okay with that. People are difficult. You're not, though…or Rachel. It just clicked. I've never experienced that before."

We had clicked, hadn't we? "That's because I'm awesome."

"Why don't you have a boyfriend?" His eyes didn't meet mine when he asked, but I couldn't pull my gaze away from him.

Jesus, it twisted me up when he said things like that to me. Made me realize I wanted things that weren't on the table, that he didn't see us ever being more. "You asking me out?" I teased.

His eyes snapped to mine. "God no, I would never do that."

"Sometimes I think you hate me." My smile must have told him I was joking because he buried his face in his hands and laughed.

"I'm sorry. I'm the worst. I didn't mean… I wasn't saying…"

"It's fine, Lo." He didn't have to explain himself. He wanted friendship and sex. There␣was nothing wrong with that. I quite liked our arrangement, though sometimes I wondered if I'd be okay with the boyfriend thing too.

"So why don't you have one?"

"Well, I'm not sure you've noticed, but Little Beach is sincerely lacking in queer, eligible men."

"Good point. Did you have one before?"

"When I lived here as a teenager, or when I moved to the city?"

"Both. Everything. I want to know everything about you."

I didn't think there was anything I wouldn't share with him either. "I was dating someone for about a year and a half before I moved back home. I thought it was serious, and we'd discussed monogamy and supposedly were on the same page. But I found out he'd been cheating on me almost our whole relationship."

"Why would someone ever cheat on you?"

"Right? It makes no sense. I'm a catch."

"Did you love him?" Milo traced circles on the blanket with the tip of his finger.

"No. I liked him a lot, though. I thought there was a chance I could love him. It wasn't meant to be."

"Have you ever been in love?"

I sighed, unsure how to answer. "That's a difficult question. You know Kris? We've been best friends our whole lives. When we were teenagers, we started to experiment with each other. He was the first person I ever told I'm gay."

"Is he bi?"

"Yes, and while his wife knows, it's not something he shares with many people, so that needs to stay between us." I trusted Milo with the secret, and I knew Kris trusted my judgment and would be okay with Milo knowing. "But yeah…I loved him, and that got confusing because he was my best friend and I didn't know if the love came from there or if I was really *in* love with him. Eventually I decided it was the latter, but Kris didn't feel the same. For him, it was friends with benefits. It was tough because he felt bad, like he'd let me down, because he hurt me and didn't see me the same way. But he couldn't help how he felt—or didn't feel, I guess."

"Is that why you left?"

"Part of the reason. I always wanted to experience life off the island, though. I didn't think I would come back."

"Is it awkward between the two of you?" he asked next, and I shook my head.

"No. He's my best friend." I nudged him. "Well, one of them. I have two now."

Milo bit his bottom lip and grinned. It did something to my insides, twisted me up in a good way. "Did you have sex?"

"It depends on what you consider sex. We jerked each other off, gave each other head, and of course a little frottage, but we didn't actually fuck."

He looked away, rolled to his back. "Do you still? Love him, I mean?"

"I love him, but as a friend, like family. I'm not *in* love with him anymore. I realize now that it's better this way. Kris and I aren't a match, and I don't want to be. I don't think I'm lucky in love. Maybe it's not for me."

"I don't believe that—love not being for you. If there's anyone who deserves it, it's you."

My heart felt like it somehow got softer, maybe just for him. He was so damn sweet. Milo made me want to be everything he thought I was. "I'm going to kiss you now," I told him.

"In public?"

"Is that okay with you?"

When he nodded, I leaned down slowly, so fucking slowly, drawing it out for both of us—

"Milo!"

He scrambled up, popping me in the face with his head. "Shit." I grabbed my nose. My eyes immediately started watering as pain pulsed through my face.

"Oh my God! I'm so sorry! I didn't mean... I wasn't..."

"Hi, Milo!" Rachel's daughter, Cammy, slid to a stop, kicking sand up onto our blanket, her mom right behind her.

"Sorry. I think we maybe interrupted something?" Rachel said.

"Gid, are you okay?" Milo pushed my hands away and studied my nose. "It's really red."

"It really hurts."

"I'll get you some ice."

"I'm fine," I replied.

"I'm so sorry," the words fell from his lips again, making me feel bad that he was so upset.

"Lo, I'm good. I promise." I kissed the tip of his nose, as if he'd been the one to get hurt, hoping he wouldn't mind since we had an audience.

I felt Rachel's eyes on us. I wasn't sure how much Milo might have told her about us, but when I glanced up, she was definitely curious.

"What ya doing?" Cammy asked.

"Hanging out with Gideon," Milo replied. "You don't have too much energy today, do you?"

"*Milo.*"

"*Cammy.*"

"Mama did my hair. Do you like it?" It was in cornrows with beads at the bottom.

"I do. It looks good. I like these." Milo pointed to the bottom of her braids. He was good with kids. I wondered if he realized it. Cammy clearly adored him.

"Why did Gideon kiss your nose? And why was he so close to your face when I got here? Is he your boyfriend?"

Milo's jaw dropped open.

Rachel laughed. "Sweetheart, don't be nosy," she told her daughter. "Milo, feel free to answer."

She winked at me.

"No. Gideon isn't my boyfriend. We're just—"

"Really close friends!" I cut him off quickly, hoping he wasn't going to say we were having sex.

He turned to me and lowered his voice. "I wasn't going to say it."

"Just wanted to make sure."

He gave his attention back to them. "We're bestie goals. Do you guys want to hang out with us?"

It was the second time he'd used the term to describe us. It was cute and perfectly Milo.

"Yes!" both Rachel and Cammy replied. As much as I liked them, I was slightly disappointed in their answer.

Before they sat down, Milo made me get up so he could shake the sand off the blanket. The four of us hung out for a bit. I didn't realize Cammy was around Milo as much as she obviously was, which became clear from their conversations about the park and books and ice cream. Rachel and Milo had a similar relationship to mine and

Milo's—but without the sex, of course. They teased each other and talked about everything and anything. She complained about the hard hat and goggles he made anyone who went in the bookstore wear.

It was fun watching him with them, and I wondered if it could ever be like this with Kris and Meg or Heather and Orlando. I wanted them to know Milo the way I did, to see how fun he was and why I liked him so much.

Eventually we made it to the ocean and swam for a bit before heading back to relax on the blanket.

"I'm going to put my first book order in soon. I want to get some of the newest titles," Milo said.

"We should plan a big grand opening event for the store," Rachel replied. "It'll be ready in a few weeks, right?"

"Yeah, but I hate parties."

"It would be good for business, though," Rachel replied, and while she was right, I didn't want to push Milo.

"What do you think?" he asked me because of fucking course he did.

"I think Rachel has a point, but I also think you need to do what feels right for you and what you feel comfortable with." He didn't like a lot of loud people, especially if he was inside. Other noises didn't seem to bother him as much since he was fine with the equipment for building.

"Will you plan it?" Milo asked Rachel. "And be there?"

"Of course. I'll help however I can, but I agree with Gideon—if you don't want to, don't do it."

He shook his head. "No, I think it's smart. Plus, I need to get to know more people in town. I'm going to invite Gene." He turned to me. "Will you tell your family about it?"

"Of course."

My chest felt full when he reached over, took my hand, and didn't let go.

CHAPTER SEVENTEEN

Milo

THE NEXT COUPLE of weeks flew by. I was busy at the bookstore. Rachel was there with me a lot, and when Gideon wasn't at the tattoo parlor, he helped too.

Gideon… I smiled at the thought of him. He seemed almost perfect in every way. He did frustrating things sometimes, like he still forgot to put items on the shopping list, he slept in when I was bored, and oh my God, I fell asleep for a little while in his room after we blew each other one time and I realized he *snores*. Usually I went to my room, or he went to his after we made each other come, so I'd never heard it before. I kept earplugs with me all the time so I'd have them if needed. I put some in his room too in case I ever fell asleep in there again.

But even the frustrating stuff felt *endearing*. Like, how could I think things I hated were a tiny bit cute when he did them? It didn't make any sense at all. I was pretty sure that having orgasms with someone short-circuited your brain.

What Gideon and I had felt like more than just friendship and orgasms, but I wondered if that was me reading the situation wrong. Even that time he'd teased about me asking him out, I thought he'd been joking, but I was always so careful to show him that I wasn't misunderstanding what we were. I didn't want him to call it off because I was getting too clingy.

The bookstore was finished, and this evening we were having our grand opening celebration. Rachel had worked so hard putting it together, and I wanted to be happy about it—that's what friends did—but really, I just wanted to throw up. It felt like a party, and I wasn't very big on parties. They were close to the top of my list of things I hated.

I flopped down on my bed, wishing I didn't have to go.

"Are you okay?" Gideon asked from my doorway.

"I don't want to put my pants on."

"You'll definitely draw a lot of attention if you don't."

I sighed, and Gideon came over to sit beside me. "I think maybe this wasn't a good idea. A lot of people will want to meet me at once. I'll have to talk to all of them and answer questions, and…it's a lot." But I didn't want it to be a lot. I wanted to be able to do it. I didn't want anything to hold me back.

"Lo…if it's too much, then don't go. Rachel can handle it. I'll help her. And if you head down and it's overwhelming, then come home and I'll deal with it. You worked so hard getting Little Beach Books remodeled, working on the new site and social media and stuff, that I would love for you to be able to enjoy your accomplishment. If you need me, I'll be there to help. I don't read very much, and I know I'm not as smart as you, but…"

Was he kidding me? "You're smart. Especially about life. There are lots of ways to be smart. And you're kind. And everyone likes you. It helps, knowing I have my best friend with me." He nodded, rubbed his thumb over his bottom lip, looking deep in thought. "What?"

"We're bestie goals, right? Do you want to try and go? Or do you want me to make an excuse for you? I can say you're sick."

I loved that he was willing to do that. Mostly, I didn't want people to make excuses for me. I didn't want to be treated with kid gloves, something my mom often did. But on the other hand, she was also so strong-willed that she pushed me at times when I didn't want to be pushed. Gideon didn't. He left it up to me, and that helped. "I want to enjoy this. I deserve to enjoy this. I worked really fucking hard."

"Damn right you did. Have I told you how hot it is when you say fuck?"

I grinned. "Like if I said…can I fuck your mouth later?"

A deep growl pulled up from his chest and slipped out. Maybe sex talk wasn't so bad… I still wasn't sure about doing it the way they did in porn.

"Please fuck my mouth later."

"If you're lucky." I winked, trying to be flirty and hoping I didn't look like an idiot. Really, I was the lucky one.

I stood, but Gideon grabbed my wrist and pulled me back toward him until I was between his legs. It was warm today, but I wanted to look nice, so I wore a short-sleeved button-up shirt and a bow tie. He ran his big hands up and down my thighs. "I'm really proud of you, Milo, and I just… Thanks for letting me tag along for the ride."

My skin flushed too hot, and not in a sexual way either. The fire inside me burned, all the heat congregating in my chest. Didn't he know there wouldn't be a ride without him? Didn't he know how much he meant to me? "You don't look it, but you're very sweet."

He laughed. "As long as it doesn't show, my reputation will stay intact. Let's go."

Gideon took my hand and held it until we reached the rack by the door where I'd hung my pants earlier. But once I put them on, he didn't seek out my hand again, and it made me wonder how I was supposed to act around him tonight. I'd held his hand at the beach, but…this was different. His family would be there, and he might not want them to know he was having sex with me—or blow jobs and jerking off with me. Did that count as sex? I figured it did because not everyone liked penetrating or to be penetrated.

Now that the question squeezed its way into my thoughts, it was all I could think about. I'd already made a fool of myself in front of Orlando. What if I did it tonight and embarrassed Gideon? What if he wanted to keep our sex a secret, and I kissed him or touched him or craved him holding me? He'd said he would be there for me, and I believed him. Gideon didn't lie to me, but he was also so kind he might do something just for me even though it wasn't what he wanted.

My breathing sped up, and Gideon stopped us just before we walked around to the front of the building. "Are you okay?" he asked.

"Yes." It wasn't true, but I wanted to be okay. I wanted this night to be perfect.

He cupped my cheek, brushed his thumb beneath my eye, and kissed my forehead. "You got this."

I nodded, but I was thinking…do I, though? I was glad he had faith in me because I didn't.

Rachel was already in the bookstore. Her family would be coming with Cammy. The doors opened at six p.m. because she thought a short evening event would be nice. We'd put out new tables on the cobblestone walkway, and Gideon and I had put up fairy lights on the lattice overhang.

"I still can't get over this place," Gid said. He walked to the café area, ran his hand over the blue countertop. We had a beachy theme going throughout the place, with lots of white and light blues and coral.

"You've seen it before."

"I can still admire it." He winked, and my stomach got oddly fluttery.

Rachel was all business. "We should set the food out before everyone arrives." She knew how to get shit done. I adored that about her.

We had a bunch of finger foods, some vegetarian and some not, though I wouldn't be eating anyway. I didn't like to grab meals off the same plate other people did. It weirded me out.

We organized it three times, the first Rachel not liking how we set it out, the second I didn't, and the third way we both finally agreed. Gideon stood back and did his thing because he didn't care.

There was a knock on the glass, and it was Autumn, a local who sometimes helped Rachel out with Cammy if her parents were busy. She had experience as a barista, so I'd hired her for the café.

Eventually, Gideon said, "It's six. You want me to unlock the doors?"

I nodded without looking at him. When Gideon walked past me, he kissed my cheek, and it helped, which was just plain stupid. How could a kiss soothe me?

When the bell jingled, I tensed up briefly before exhaling a deep breath and straightening my spine. "Hi, welcome to Little Beach—oh geez. It's just you, Gene."

The older man chuckled. "Not happy to see me?"

"No! That's not it. I just thought it was someone I didn't know, and I had to get my nerves up to greet you."

Sometimes I didn't make sense even to myself. I would mostly be fine working at the store every day, but this was a planned event where I had to entertain, and that seemed entirely different.

"You're about to get your second chance," Gid said just before two people and two kids walked in. I assumed they were a family.

"Hello. Welcome to Little Beach Books. We're so glad you guys stopped by. I'm the new owner, Milo Copeland, but please don't call me Mr. Copeland." There. That wasn't so bad.

"It's so nice to meet you!" the woman said. "We were glad to hear you'd be reopening. We missed this place. Your grandmother was a special woman."

Please don't ask about Mom or the adoption, please don't ask about Mom or the adoption.

"Thank you. Gene has been sharing stories with me. They were—"

"Partners," Gideon cut me off.

Partners. Right. I should use that word. Lovers might make the kids get embarrassed.

"Feel free to have a look around," I added. When they walked away, I asked, "Do I have to greet everyone like that?"

"No, sweets. You're fine. I'll greet people," Rachel said.

"Oh, thank God. I'm already over it."

Gideon chuckled.

People filtered in and out over the next half hour, and it wasn't so bad. Autumn was kept busy making coffee, and Rachel did a lot of the talking, though people would approach me from time to time.

At one point a gentleman who looked about thirty came in and asked, "Do you have *The Street Vendor's Son* by Wilder Welles?"

I was fairly certain my eyeballs nearly popped out. "Oh my God! Yes. I love that book!"

And it was a queer book too. Maybe Gideon hadn't been as alone as he thought here.

"Come with me. I'll show you." I led him over and plucked the book off the shelf for him, and then we walked together to the register, where I began to ring up his order. "Have you read it?" I asked.

Gideon was close, and I saw him watching us. I gave him a thumbs-up.

"No, but I've heard great things." He grinned at me. Well, he seemed nice.

"I'm Milo Copeland."

"Nelson. Nice to meet you."

"You too."

"Do you plan on having a book club? If so, I'd like to join."

This was so exciting! I loved making new friends. "Yes, I do. My best friend—well, one of them—got me to read *Alice in Wonderland*. I wasn't a fan. The movie was weird too, so I'd likely be picky on the selections, but it's definitely on my list."

"I'll have to come back and get information on it, then."

"I hope you do."

He gave me what seemed like a shy wave, then slipped out.

"Gideon! Did you see that? He was nice. Do you know him?"

He was frowning. "No, I've never seen him before in my life. Tourist, maybe."

"He said he wanted to join the book club, so I think he must be new here."

Gideon crossed his arms.

"What's wrong?"

"I love what you've done with the place!" a woman interrupted us. "Your grandmother was lovely. We didn't know…about her and Beverly."

"Neither did Beverly."

"Oh…" she replied. I thought she might not have liked my answer, but I didn't care.

Gideon threaded his arm through mine, and wow, that felt nice. My pulse immediately slowed down.

"If you'll excuse us," he told her.

More people approached us from there. It was slightly overwhelming—all the attention and questions—but luckily no one tried to touch me.

Gideon stayed glued to my side. We were by the table as he picked up a mini sandwich when I heard, "What's up, Snacks?" in a voice I recognized as his brother's. I looked up to see Orlando with a pretty woman who had a round pregnant belly; then Kris, and the woman who must be his wife, Megan, and then two older people who were clearly Gideon's parents.

Nausea immediately went to war with my body, attacking my gut fiercely and brutally. Gideon was my best friend. I wanted his family to like me. I didn't want them to wonder why he would want to hang out with someone like me.

Don't fuck this up, don't fuck this up, don't fuck this up.

"I really hate it when you call me that," Gideon told him. Of course, at the same time, about ten more people showed up. We stepped out of the way of the food, and he turned to me. "I had a thing about sneaking snacks when I was a kid. The whole hand-in-the-cookie-jar thing? That was me."

"Oh…well, that's okay. You have a great body. Even if you didn't, that would be okay. I think as a society we put too much emphasis on physical attributes and how much someone weighs." I looked at Orlando. "Not that you're doing that. I wasn't trying to insinuate that's something you do. I just…" *Shut up! That's what you need to do—shut up.*

"Thank you for defending my honor." Gideon rested his hand on the back of my neck, caressing my nape in what I knew was support. "Also, did you hear that? I have a great body," he told his brother. Before anyone could say anything—and by anyone, I meant me—Gideon continued. "Mom, Dad, Heather, this is Milo. Lo, you met my idiot brother, and Kris and Meg at the Lighthouse, but this is Heather, my dad who's also Orlando, and my mom, Annemarie."

"It's lovely to meet you, Milo. Gideon has told us so much about you," Annemarie said. I saw all their gazes flitter toward Gideon's hand on my neck, so I stepped away from him.

"Thank you. It's, um, good to meet you too." I gave my attention to Heather. "Do you know if you're having a girl or a boy?" Well, that they could tell. Whoever the baby was, they would let their parents know one day if they were correct.

"A boy," she replied.

"Does he have a name yet?"

"Jacob."

"Hello, baby Jacob," I said softly, keeping my distance and not touching her. I'd heard about people who touched pregnant women's bellies, which was rude to do without permission. Even I knew that. I felt everyone's hot stares on me, which just made me feel like I was overheating. Was that weird? To want to include their baby that way? "I'm sorry, I didn't ask if that was okay."

"You don't have to be sorry. That was very sweet. Now he'll recognize your voice when he's born, and he'll remember you're the first person who thought to say hello to him." Heather's smile relaxed me some.

I looked at Gideon, who winked at me. He reached his hand out, like he was going to touch me again, but then pulled back. I tried not to frown, wondering if I'd already done something wrong.

CHAPTER EIGHTEEN

Gideon

MILO AND I hadn't discussed how we would act around my family, but I had to admit, it dented my confidence some when he'd pulled away. And that didn't count the guy who had definitely been interested. I'd never met him before, but I'd already decided I didn't like him. I had to remind myself we were just friends, friends who liked to have sex with each other, but friends all the same. Technically, he was right to step out of my hold. The last thing we needed was my family getting ideas about us—more ideas.

"What did you do before you moved to the island?" my dad asked him. College was important to him. It was always one of the first questions he asked. While he never said it to me, I knew he was disappointed I didn't get a degree, but I truly didn't believe higher education was for everyone. It wasn't a standard of how smart or accomplished you were.

"Oh, I was in finance. I started college at sixteen. I graduated with a master's at twenty-two from Franklin University before going to work at my mother's firm."

Holy...*sixteen*? "Really? You never told me that." Now I rubbed the back of my own neck in reassurance, which was fucking crazy.

"I guess we never talked about degrees. What's yours in?" Milo asked.

"I didn't finish college," I replied, feeling insecure about that for the first time in my life.

"Oh, I didn't know that about you either."

Does it matter? a quiet voice in my head asked, but this was Milo. He didn't care about things like that.

"You and Gid hit it off quickly," Kris said.

"We did. He's...well, he's my best friend. I know he's yours too, so I didn't mean he wasn't, especially because you've known each other your whole lives." Milo's slightly panicked gaze darted my way. I wanted to comfort him, to kiss his temple and tell him to breathe because he was doing fine, but I also didn't want to cross the line he'd drawn when he'd stepped away from me.

"We can share him." Kris put an arm around my shoulders and pulled me close before *he* pressed a kiss to my forehead. That wasn't odd for us, but I saw the flash of uncertainty in Milo's eyes before he took a step backward.

"Ew, I don't know where your lips have been," I joked.

"Hey now," Meg said.

"Oops, sorry. You know I love you. It's your questionable taste in men that has me concerned," I teased, making everyone except Milo laugh. The urge to ask him if he was okay sat on the tip of my tongue, but I also didn't want to seem like I was coddling him. I hated that myself and knew he had strong feelings about it.

A loud group of teenagers came in, likely for the free food and coffee. They were laughing and talking, their voices carrying high above the already chatty room.

Mom asked Milo a few questions about the store and the area he'd lived in California. It was only a couple of minutes later that Nadine Anderson approached him to talk about having book club meetings at the store—what the fuck was it with everyone and book clubs? And then Janet Hughes overheard and pulled his attention away about her knitting group meeting there too.

A young man I didn't recognize asked him about a job. My family all talked around him about the changes in the store.

I could sense his tension going higher. Each time

someone spoke to him, his replies were quicker, choppier. Even to my own ears the room was getting louder, and that was before a baby suddenly started crying.

He flinched when someone bumped into him.

"Lo?" I said softly, but he shook his head, clearly not wanting me to make a big deal of it.

He wrung his hands together, then rubbed one over his chest, massaging over his heart. People approached, and he smiled and spoke, but it wasn't the smile I'd gotten used to from him. It didn't reach his eyes and light up the whole goddamned room.

No one else seemed to notice, but no one else knew him the way I did. He was trying to hold it together. I didn't know what to do to help him, and again, I didn't want to cross the line, didn't want him to feel like I thought he needed saving.

There was a crashing noise, and he startled. I looked over to see that somehow, the punch bowl had been knocked off the table.

"You'll have to…um…I have to go." Milo rushed toward it. I glanced quickly at my family to see concerned looks on Mom's, Orlando's, and Heather's faces.

"I'm gonna help him." My heart thumped too rapidly against my chest as I made my way to him. Rachel was there too. Milo's movements were rushed and clunky as he tried to clean up the mess. "Mingle. We'll take care of this," I told her, and she nodded, then started trying to distract people.

"Lo?" I knelt beside him. He was bent down on the floor, red punch on his knees. He had his eyes closed, looking down, and was rocking back and forth. "Milo?" I rested my hand on his nape again, hoping it was okay.

"I can't. I'm sorry. I can't…I can't…I can't…" he kept saying over and over.

"Hey, we're good. You're good. Let's get you outta here." A shadow fell over us, and I looked up to see Orlando.

"I'll grab a mop and help you guys get this cleaned up."

"Thank you. He got punch on his pants, and I have the key, so I'm going to take him upstairs." It was a weak excuse. I could just hand it over to him, and hell, he lived there, so he would have his own, but it was all I could think of on the fly.

"That's cool. I got this." Orlando smiled. I sent a silent thanks to my brother as I nudged Milo to his feet.

He didn't speak, but his breaths were quick, short, his body tight.

I didn't want to be too obvious, so I grabbed his hand, laced our fingers together, and plastered a fake smile on my face as I led Milo to the back exit, upstairs, and inside.

When we were safely behind the closed door, I wrapped my arms around him, breathed in his hair, and kissed his temple. He shook, his body trembling so hard that mine vibrated with him. "It's just us. We're good, Lo. You're good." I'd never wanted to comfort someone more in my life. I wasn't sure if I should or even how to do that. Who the fuck was I, really? A friend who gave him orgasms?

"I'm sorry."

"Hey, what are you apologizing for? You don't have any reason to be sorry."

"Because I was two seconds away from freaking out? I shouldn't have done that. It was too loud. I should have used my earplugs. And too many people. They were all asking me questions and touching me and bumping into me and…" I tensed up, wondering if I shouldn't be touching him since he didn't seem to like it in this situation, but then he buried his face in my neck. "I wanted to be okay. I want your family to like me and not wonder why you're friends with me."

"They like you. Hell, did you see my dad's eyes light up when you talked about your degree? You might be his new favorite. They're not going to wonder why I like someone who's kind, funny, smart…totally hot."

He didn't laugh the way I hoped he would. "My pants are bugging me…and they have punch on them. I can't. I need to get them off. I don't like to be sticky."

Milo pulled back and went for the button, but I put a hand on him. "Can I?"

He nodded slowly, so I knelt and unfastened them. I took one of his shoes off, then the other. One sock, then the other, setting them by his clothes rack. I tugged his pants down next, helping him out of them, then laid them in their place too.

I looked up at him, and he was staring down at me. "You confuse me even more than other people do."

I frowned. "Well, that doesn't sound good."

"It is."

I stood. Kissed him, but slowly, without tongue.

"Will you go back downstairs, please?" Milo said. "I don't want to need you. It's important that I handle things on my own. And I trust you to make sure the party goes okay."

I didn't want to leave at all, but I replied, "Of course."

"Can you tell your family I have a headache? I understand if you don't want to lie, but I kinda do now, so you're not."

I agreed, then reached for the door, stopping with my

back to him. "You know…it's okay to need someone sometimes, Milo. It's okay to want to stand on your own too, but needing someone doesn't make you weak. It's not unique to you."

He didn't reply, so I walked out and made my way back downstairs. Orlando had gotten the mess cleaned up, and Rachel was at the register while people made purchases.

"Where's your friend?" Mom asked when I joined them again.

"He had a headache. I had to let him in the apartment." The looks on their faces made it clear they didn't believe me. "He's fine," I said, my tone sharp and defensive.

"We know," Mom replied.

I made eye contact with my brother, again trying to silently thank him, and he winked at me.

"This is new," Kris said.

"What's new?"

"Seeing you with a boyfriend."

"I know, right?" Meg concurred.

"You guys are so cute!" Heather added.

Ugh. Fuck my life. I knew this would happen. "He's not my boyfriend." The words detonated a truth bomb inside my chest. Holy shit. I wanted Milo to be my boyfriend. I was disappointed that he wasn't, and I wasn't sure he wanted to be. This was different from when Orlando and Kris had teased me about him before. We were closer now, and yeah, I wanted to claim that title from the man who made it a point to tell everyone we were only friends. "Don't say that to him or tease him about it, okay? We're just friends."

"Embarrassed of you, is he?" Kris joked, ignoring my second sentence completely.

"Ha-ha, fucker," I countered. "I'm gonna help Rachel at the register." Because I'd rather do that than walk around, trying to entertain.

I did, and my family left not long later. It was almost three hours before the last person left the store. I sighed, leaning against the counter. "That was a lot."

"How's Milo?" Rachel asked.

I shrugged. "Not sure." But I wanted to know. I was slightly bummed he'd sent me away. I understood it, but I was bummed all the same.

"Go ahead and go upstairs. I'll take care of things down here and lock up."

Relief flooded my veins. "Thank you. I owe you."

The apartment was dark and quiet when I got upstairs. Milo's pants were gone from their spot by the door. He would have put them in the washer. It didn't surprise me that he couldn't leave the mess until morning.

I lingered in front of his bedroom door, but forced myself not to go in. He'd asked for space, so I'd give it to him.

I went straight for the bathroom instead, taking a quick shower, then headed into my room in just a towel. When I turned on the light, there was a lump under the blankets and a familiar head of auburn hair on the pillows.

He'd gone into my room to sleep.

He'd never done that on his own. He'd crashed after orgasms, but not this. I liked it. I liked it too much.

With a smile on my face, I removed my towel, turned the light off, and climbed into bed, wrapping my arm around his waist to go to sleep.

CHAPTER NINETEEN

Milo

I WOKE UP as soon as Gideon turned on the light, but tried not to move. I liked my bed better. It was more comfortable and easier to sleep in. His wasn't like the hotel's had been, but still, it wasn't mine. I'd climbed into it because I wanted to be close to him, and I wasn't sure how I felt about that...or if he'd wonder what I was doing since we hadn't just blown each other.

I smiled when his lips pressed gently against my shoulder. Gideon's kisses were the best. He was affectionate and seemed to like being affectionate with me. I never thought I'd be the type who liked cuddling—my space meant too much to me—but I liked cuddling with Gideon. That was probably a bad sign. I worried my feelings for him were growing too much.

"Did it go okay?" I asked quietly. Stupid freak-out. I got so mad at my brain sometimes.

"It did. Mom said she'd love for you to come over with me sometime."

My heart punched against my chest so hard I thought it might fall out and land in Gideon's hand, which was holding mine. A lot of the time I didn't care what people thought of me; what was the point? I couldn't change it. But Gid's family weren't just anyone. They were his, and he was mine—well, not *mine*, but sometimes it felt like he was. "They didn't notice anything weird?"

"Lo."

I rolled over toward him. His room faced the front street, so there was a soft glow from the lights outside. "Gid, I'm neurodivergent. I don't always behave like everyone else. That's okay. It feels like placating me if you act any differently."

He sighed. "They didn't say anything. But if they did, it wouldn't change how I feel about you."

I nodded.

His hand slid down to my ass. I was in nothing but my underwear, and he pulled me close, which immediately made my dick start to wake up. He grinned. "You get hard at the drop of a hat."

"It's our favorite saying," I teased. He was right, though. I really liked sex stuff and wanted to do as much of it as possible. I also really liked Gideon, maybe more than I should. He'd made me feel cared for tonight, and not in an overbearing way or one that belittled me, but one that made me feel important to him. I copied his movement, sliding my hand down to rest on the curve of his butt cheek. "You're naked."

"Maybe I was hopeful there would be a sexy man in my bed."

"Or you just took a shower."

"I did not," Gideon replied. He kissed the tip of my nose, and I was pretty sure my cheeks turned red. It was perfectly intimate. He'd had my cock in his mouth, yet that action felt almost more personal. I craved getting even more personal with him.

"I like being best friends with you."

Gideon's head rose slowly, his gaze angled down at me. For a moment, I feared he was going to change his mind, that he would ask if I was okay from earlier, but he didn't. He just said, "I like you too."

"Can I have sex with you, please? Penetrative sex," I clarified, surprising myself. "I want to feel you, to be connected to you that way, like we're a part of each other. Also, I enjoy orgasms." His breath puffed against my face when he chuckled, the scent of mint toothpaste filling my senses.

"You're insatiable."

"I have a lot to make up for."

"Yes," Gideon replied before pressing his lips against mine. We kissed for a while, tongues dipping into each other's mouths. I didn't think about the gross aspects of it with Gideon anymore, that we were sharing intimate fluids with each other. I just thought that maybe I wouldn't ever be okay with anyone's but his. Eventually, he climbed on top of me, kissed his way down my neck, my chest, my stomach, before pulling my briefs off and sucking my cock into his mouth.

My hips shot off the bed, my dick fucking into his throat. "Don't! You can't do that, or I'll come in your mouth." And I didn't want that. I wanted to shoot my load inside him…well, inside a condom, inside him.

"Always so quick to blow your load." There was a playful lilt to his voice. I recognized so many of Gideon's tells now, the little things unique to him, like how to tell when he was kidding or what each of his smiles meant.

"I last a lot longer than I did in the beginning."

He nuzzled my groin but didn't suck me. "I have so much fun with you."

I smiled, unable to hold back the sunburst of happiness inside me. "I have fun with you too. Now, I would like to have fun with your butt."

Gideon laughed, knelt over me, and pressed a quick

kiss to my lips. "My butt is all yours." He flopped onto his back, though, and I was okay with that. I lashed my tongue over his right nipple piercing, then his left. I loved the way the cool metal felt against my tongue. "You have a pierced-nipple kink. I knew you'd want those first."

I also knew what to do with those. I'd never had my dick inside someone before, so I was nervous. "I've watched a ton of porn, as you know, but I want you to talk me through it. I don't want to hurt you, but I want to do it all myself too. It would probably be really hot to see your fingers in your ass, though. We'll save that for another day."

"You're full of surprises. Grab the lube and a condom from my nightstand."

I opened the drawer and pulled out the lube first, then the small, square package, which I set on the table.

"Do you want me to lie like this? You can open me up while you kiss me, or if you want, I can roll onto my stomach, and you can just focus on my ass."

"Yes, please. I want it all." I would soak up any moment I could have with Gideon and hold on to them forever.

"I can handle that. Lube up your fingers and get started."

I did as Gideon said. He spread his legs, held them

back for me, and I knelt between them. I didn't use my tongue to kiss him, instead licking at the piercing in his nipple while I rubbed his hole with a slick finger. "Like this?"

"Yeah, God yeah. You can press a little harder, rub circles around my rim, then push a finger in whenever you're ready."

I appreciated him instructing me this time. I wanted to do a good job, needed Gid to like everything I did to him.

I moved to his other nipple, nipping at the metal bar with my teeth while massaging his hole. He smelled like soap from his shower, the scent of his skin turning me on even more. I buried my face in his neck, nibbled there too, my dick hard and leaking, so hungry for his hole.

With the tip of my finger, I pushed inside. Gideon's arms wrapped around me, pulling me close while I slid my digit in and out. My mouth went to work on his neck, tasting and sucking on his skin.

We rutted together, cocks dragging against one another, as I concentrated on his body, the way it felt relaxed but still somehow thrummed with pleasure. His hole was hot inside. I wasn't sure I could ever handle it on my dick. When I pushed a second finger into him, he arched toward me and said my name in a sexy, lust-filled tone. "Lo…fuck, just like that."

Sparks ignited deep within me, flaring brighter and shooting out further with each one. His ass felt so good, his skin tasted so perfect. I had to have every single part of him, my desire strengthening the suction from my mouth.

"Fuck…*fuck*."

I pulled back. "Sorry." Holy crap. I'd bitten him.

"A little teeth is good, but not too much."

"Got it." I went to his mouth instead, feeding him my tongue, tasting him, and how had I ever lived in a world where I hadn't had the privilege of kissing Gideon? How had I survived it? Been happy in it? I was ridiculously close to blowing my load, so I pulled back. "I want to see it now." I flicked on the lamp as Gideon turned to his belly, then pushed up on his hands and knees. I added more lube just in case, leaned close, and looked at his hole that was slightly open from my fingers. "I can't believe you're going to let me inside there. It's a really nice hole."

"Aw, he likes you too. I can't wait to feel your cock stretching me out." The thing was, I knew Gideon usually liked to top more. He said he was vers and bottomed, but if he could choose, he leaned toward topping. Somehow, though, I knew that if we kept being friends who had sex, forever, and I never let him fuck me, Gideon would be okay with that. It was the kind of man he was.

I leaned forward and kissed his ass cheek. "I'm going to try and let you do it to me one day too."

"I don't need it."

"Maybe I do." Maybe I needed Gid to have me that way.

"Come on, Lo, fuck me."

I started with two fingers, watching as they slipped inside him, his tight, wrinkled pucker straining around them. "This is so hot…and kind of interesting, the way our bodies adjust to accept each other."

He laughed. "Oh, baby, talk the human body to me in bed."

I playfully smacked his ass. "Be nice—whoa. Your hole twitched around me when I did that."

Gideon looked back over his shoulder. "You're the most ridiculous person I've ever met. Your balls look like they're going to pop, and you're taking your sweet time to study my body before you fuck me."

He had a point. "Right, then." I couldn't help but focus on him, though, as I added a third finger. He was so tight, but each thrust helped loosen him. "I want to watch when I fuck you." My dick jerked. "Oh Jesus, yes. I'd like to see my cock slide in and out of you, see how you take me, and how each time I move, your body reacts. You show me what you like that way. It's in how your muscles tighten and how you tremble and..." Wait. Was I dirty-talking? I certainly hadn't meant to, but I was pretty sure I was.

"Christ, that was hot."

"Was it? I was sitting here trying to figure out if that was sex talk or not."

"So much sex talk. Fuck me, Lo. Take my ass."

Yeah, that was so much better in real life than porn. I pulled my fingers out of his body, fumbled with shaky hands until I got the condom open and rolled down my shaft.

Once I was lubed too, I moved in closer, kneeling behind him, cock pointed toward his ass like it was saying, *This way!* My tip was just pressed against his open hole when I said, "Gid?"

"Yeah?"

"Thank you."

He looked back at me and smiled. "You're welcome." It was the most perfect thing he could say. I knew he wanted to tell me I didn't have to thank him for this, but he didn't because in my mind I did, and he was respecting that.

I pushed forward slowly and... "Oh God. Sweet Jesus. You're so hot. So tight. I used to hate sex talk, and now I can't stop because oh my God, I might die…Gid…wow."

He laughed, which made his body vibrate, shooting pleasure right toward my balls. "Holy fuck." My eyes rolled back. I kept pushing in, savoring how his body took me until my groin met his ass. "I can't move."

"Eventually, you need to."

"Can I just live here forever?"

"Not sure that's realistic."

"I thought I was supposed to be the serious one out of the two of us."

Gideon pumped lube into his hand and began to stroke himself. "Fuck me."

I wasn't going to deny him that. I pulled back before snapping my hips forward over and over again. My body was buzzing, like I would explode, pleasure and happiness shooting around inside me. Every slide of our bodies made me feel like the luckiest man alive, like I had something no one else did, and it was glorious and perfect and really made me want to blow my load.

It was…strange and different, feeling myself *inside* someone, knowing I was in his body, but there was also nothing in the world like it. Gideon and I were a part of each other, connected intimately in a similar way to how I felt connected to him in my head, like this was just a thing that was always supposed to happen, an extension of the bond we shared.

"Gid..."

"I'm almost there, Lo. Fuck me harder. Make me come calling out your name."

Um...yes, please. I grabbed his hips, slammed into him harder and quicker. *"Oh God, yes!"* Like my words hit some kind of magic button, Gideon's ass tightened around me, spasmed while his breathing picked up the way it did when he came all over me.

"Milo...so good." His back curled, his breathing sharp as I knew each contraction was him shooting onto his hand and the bed.

I had done that.

With my body.

Tingles shot up my spine as my balls let loose. I spurted, my orgasm overtaking me and making me fill the condom.

We collapsed to the bed then, me on Gideon's back, and I knew he was lying in the mess. I rolled him over, leaned against his chest, letting his cum make us stick together. "Sex is the best thing I've ever experienced."

He kissed the top of my head. "We're good together."

"We are." I didn't know what I would ever do if I lost Gideon's friendship.

CHAPTER TWENTY

Gideon

MILO FUCKED ME twice more over the next week, and both those times we fell asleep together in his bed. I didn't really care where we had sex or where we passed out afterward, and since I knew he did, I just automatically went there. The thing was, those weren't the only nights I slept with him. Another time we'd been in there talking, and then he'd just turned out the lights and we went to bed. Last night, after we played chess—something he was trying to teach me, but I was shit at—he'd stood and said, "I would like you to sleep in my room tonight, but I'm too tired for sex." When I hadn't replied right away because I'd been surprised, he'd revised it to, "l would like you to sleep in my room tonight, please."

He hadn't needed to attach the nicety on the end. I would have done it regardless. In fact, I wasn't sure there was anything in the whole damn world I wouldn't do for Milo, and that was…unexpected? Concerning? Fucking awesome? I hadn't landed on the answer yet, just knew it was true.

I was meeting Kris for an early lunch today before I headed to the shop. My first tattoo appointment wasn't until one.

When I got to the Lighthouse, my friend was already there, sitting in a booth. He waved me over, and I slid in across from him. "How's life?" he asked.

"I can't complain." *Don't mind me, I'm just having an internal freak-out because I'll do anything for Milo and I'm struggling to admit to myself what that means.* "How's Meg?"

"The morning sickness is killing her. I don't know why in the fuck they even call it morning sickness when it can happen all day, which it's starting to do for her. It breaks my heart to see her puking her guts up every day or being constantly nauseous."

"Goddamn, that sucks. What does her doc say?" I took a drink from the glass of water set on the table in front of me.

"Some women just get hyperemesis, I guess. They said everything is okay with the baby. They might put her on this medication they say is safe during pregnancy. It's just weird because at first it was only in the morning, but this past week it's all day." Kris rubbed a hand over his face in clear frustration and worry.

"Sorry, man. Let me know if there's anything I can do."

"I will."

The waitress approached and took our orders. I got a big-ass fucking burger. It wasn't that I didn't eat meat anymore, but sometimes it was just easier to have whatever Milo was having.

"How's Milo doing?" he asked, and damned if a stupid smile didn't pull my cheeks back almost to my ears. Kris chuckled. "Yeah, I thought so."

"Thought so, what?" I pretended not to know what he was talking about.

"You like him."

I shrugged because there was no reason to deny it. Even if I wanted to, Kris would see through my lies. "Yeah, I do. He's…" Hell, I didn't even know how to explain Milo. "He just makes life better," was the only answer I could come up with.

"Yeah, Meg does too. Not the same as what you felt for me, is it?"

I wasn't surprised Kris went there. He could be pretty blunt. I respected him for it. "Nope, though I realized that a long time ago. Maybe in a different world we could have been more, but we're better as friends."

Kris nodded. "He's crazy about you too. He watches you like he's in awe of you, like there's nothing you can't do."

I laughed. "Oh, he knows there's plenty I can't do. He's trying to teach me chess, and it's a mess." We shared a chuckle, which turned into a groan from me. I leaned back against the seat. "I wanna be with him for real." But I wasn't sure that was something Milo would want.

"I'm pretty sure you already are."

"Nah, not really. He was on the phone with his mom, and she flat-out asked him. He said I wasn't, that I would never be his boyfriend."

Kris frowned. "Ouch. He said that in front of you?"

I thought about the time I'd invited him home with me and he'd asked why he would do that. "He's honest. Sometimes he says things and doesn't realize how they make others feel. He's not trying to be hurtful; things just don't process the same for him."

"Still...maybe you should talk to him."

"What? You mean be an adult about the situation? Why would I want to do a crazy thing like that?"

Before he opened his mouth, I could see the serious gaze Kris sent my way. "Because then you might be happy, and I don't think you realize you can have that—or that you deserve it."

My chest got heavy, like each word had packed more and more weight on it. Jesus, I wasn't sure how to respond to that. Kris had never said something like that to me before. It wasn't true, was it? "I have no reason to feel that way."

"People don't have to have a reason to feel a lot of things. Sometimes we just do. It's how we work, some predisposition or whatever the fuck in our DNA. It just is what it is. Look at that 'cursed love' tattoo on your chest. You feel that way, don't you?" He pointed where those words were inked into my skin.

In some ways I did. In my twenty-six years, there'd been only two people I'd actually wanted more than just fucking with. One had been Kris, who didn't feel the same; the other had been an asshole who was cheating on me. Two people before Milo, at least. I didn't think I could handle losing him, and it would be a whole lot harder to just be friends with him afterward, the way I was with Kris. Milo was special, like he occupied this hidden space inside my chest that hadn't been there until he discovered it.

"Here you boys go," Patsy broke up our conversation, setting plates in front of us. Thank God for that, because

I wasn't sure how in the world I would have responded to him.

Kris took a bite of his food before pointing at me with his fork. "Nice hickey, by the way."

I lifted the neck on my shirt to try and cover it. "Shut up."

When he laughed, I couldn't help but join in.

CHAPTER TWENTY-ONE

Milo

AS IF HE had a beacon attached to him, I looked up from the stack of books on the counter just as Gideon walked by out front. He had his hands stuffed into his pockets and didn't turn my way, but still my heart pounded. Just seeing him made me feel like maybe I was having a heart attack or something, the funny feeling he brought to my chest growing every day.

I wasn't stupid; I knew I had a crush on him. It wasn't my first crush. This one just happened to be with one of the most important people to me in the world, one I just happened to be having sex with, and a person I was incredibly afraid of losing. I worried it was more than a crush too. That was part of the reason I always stressed we were best friends. We were, of course, but it was to remind myself not to think Gideon was more to me, and also, so he didn't think I saw us as something more than we were.

This whole arrangement felt too good to be true, which meant it likely was. The urge to go next door and talk to him banged around inside me like it thought it could push me there from the inside, but we had customers in the store. Autumn was in the café area, where a few people were working away on their laptops, and she could probably watch things, but…why did I need to go see Gideon? I'd just left him snuggled in my bed a few hours ago.

My bed.

Gideon slept in my bed.

Ugh. Crushes sucked.

The bell over the door jingled. "Hi, welcome to—oh, it's just you."

"Gee, don't be too happy to see me," Rachel said.

"Sorry. I'm almost always happy to see you, but I also don't need to greet you like you're a customer."

"Good point."

I stacked the books on a cart and wheeled them over to the window display I was setting up in front for summer reads. Gideon let me use some of his beach towels, and we'd gone to the dollar store for buckets and shovels and other goodies to make it look really cute.

I sighed.

"What's wrong, sweets?" Rachel asked.

I almost bit back a reply, but what was the purpose of having friends if I didn't actually use them for the things friends were meant to do? "I'll probably never have a boyfriend," I admitted. Before, it had really only been the lack of sex that bothered me. Now I was having orgasms with someone, and I realized I wanted more. I didn't even know if I'd ever be able to have sex with anyone else because it was a long shot that I'd ever find someone I trusted the way I did Gideon.

He would be the best boyfriend.

"Why do you say that?" she asked while I organized books.

"Because I know me." A lot of people couldn't handle me, and I couldn't handle a lot of people, so that made my odds pretty dismal.

She was quiet, contemplative for a moment, before saying, "Gideon likes you."

I tried not to get too excited, tried not to hope she was right. "Gideon is a nice person, who's also my friend and likes to have sex with me."

Her mouth dropped open, and she did an awesome dying-fish impersonation. "Wait. Slow your roll there, buddy. You're having sex with Gideon?"

I studied the shelves. "This is all wrong. It looks ridiculous. I think I need to rearrange it."

"Nope. Sorry. Absolutely not. You don't get to drop a bomb like that and then go about your merry business. I mean, I knew the two of you were close, and there was the whole hand-holding incident…and he touches you a lot…oh, and God, the way he looks at you."

"Huh?" I stopped what I was doing. "Gideon looks at me in a special way? And is there something wrong with me having sex with him?"

"Of course there's nothing wrong with screwing him. You deserve to get yours, and I swoon over the way he looks at you. It's the way we all hope someone will stare at us."

That caught my attention. "What way? How does he look at me?"

She smiled. "It's a cross between him wanting to eat you alive and—"

"Gross. That doesn't sound good at all."

Rachel waggled her sculpted black brows. "Oh, but it is."

Realization hit me. "Like he wants to have sex with me?"

She glanced around, and I realized I might have said that too loudly. "Like he might die if he doesn't have sex with you right then and there."

I thought maybe Rachel had an active imagination. "I look at Gideon all the time, and I don't notice him wanting to rip my clothes off in the middle of the bookstore. Also, that doesn't mean he wants to be my boyfriend. It means he enjoys my penis."

"Whoa, you top him?"

"Rachel!"

She held her hands up. "Sorry! You're right, not my business. But you didn't let me finish. He looks at you like...I don't know, like sometimes he can't believe you're real."

I shook my head. "Probably because he thinks I'm weird."

"That's not what I mean." I knew that, but I kept my mouth shut. "Gideon stares at you like he's lucky to even be in your orbit, Milo, like if you leave a room, you're going to take everything good with you. Like maybe he doesn't know how he ever survived without you."

My stomach suddenly decided it was time to compete in a gymnastics event, flipping over and over again. "People don't really look at others that way. It's book stuff, fantasy, romantic movies."

"Well, your love interest is Gideon."

We chuckled together, and I really, really wanted to look at Gideon to see if she was right. Maybe I'd somehow missed it, but I didn't believe it was true. I'd drive myself crazy until I knew for sure, though. "Can you finish this, please?"

"Um…yeah, sure. Where are you going?"

"To stare at Gideon." My gaze flicked toward the counter. "Someone's heading over to check out too."

"Gee, thanks, Milo. Just let me do all your work for you." Her voice was soft and teasing, and while hugs weren't my favorite thing, I suddenly wanted to hug Rachel. So I did. Quickly. Then backed away as if she could give me cooties.

"I'll be right back."

This was maybe the dumbest thing I'd ever done, but I'd also spent my life being very careful. I didn't do a lot of stupid things, so I deserved to do one now.

I left the store and went directly to Conflicting Ink. We really needed to bust part of a wall down and put in a door between us.

Gideon's brown eyes shot toward me when I stepped inside. I watched, trying to see if he wanted to eat me alive or thought he was lucky, but I didn't see that at all. Just surprise.

"Hey, what's up?" he asked while tattooing a man's shoulder blade.

"Nothing. I just came to see you."

He grinned. I squinted my eyes, but it looked like a normal smile to me. "You can pull up a chair if you want. This is Colton. His wife is from Little Beach, and they come back every summer for vacation. Colton, this is my friend Milo."

"Nice to meet you," Colton said.

"You too." I wanted to tell him I wished he could leave so Gideon and I could be alone, but I knew better than to say that.

"I always get ink from Gideon while I'm in town," he said, but I just stared at Gid. He wasn't watching me, instead paying attention to what he was doing, which I supposed was a good thing. He was putting ink permanently in someone's skin and all.

"Everyone says Gideon is the best at what he does. If I ever got a tattoo, I'd want him to do it."

Gideon tilted his head just a little, one side of his mouth kicking up. "I'd have my feelings hurt if you didn't."

"Oh, I wouldn't ever want to hurt your feelings."

"I know." He winked. "I'm giving you shit."

And Rachel was crazy. Gideon most certainly did not want to eat me alive or eye me as if we were two characters in a romance novel. I crossed my arms. I shouldn't have gotten my hopes up.

"What's wrong?" he asked, before dipping the tattoo machine into ink. I'd researched tattooing because I was interested in what Gideon did. Before, I'd always thought it was a gun, but they preferred the term *machine*.

I thought maybe you wanted to be my boyfriend?

"Nothing. I should go back to work." I put the chair back and walked out.

The second I was in the bookstore, I said, "Gideon *so* doesn't want to eat me."

Autumn dropped a coffee mug, which shattered on the floor. Oops. I should be more careful who was around and how loudly I spoke. Luckily, it was only her and Rachel close by.

I grabbed the broom and dustpan, but Autumn said she could do it. I leaned over the counter just as Rachel said, "You were there for five minutes."

"And he didn't look at me any special way."

She dropped her head back as if I was exhausting her. Well, I was exhausted too. She'd started this. "Talk to him, Milo. You're the most honest person I know. Talk to Gideon and tell him how you feel."

She had a point. I could do that, couldn't I? But what if I tried, and all it did was chase Gideon away?

CHAPTER TWENTY-TWO
Gideon

I WAS BOOKED solid all day. I didn't see Milo again, but he hadn't left my mind. Something had been off when he'd come by earlier. It was killing me not to know what it was. The timing was suspicious as fuck, considering I'd just been talking about him to Kris earlier. He wouldn't have said anything to Milo, but could someone have overheard? Did someone mention opening night or say something about the two of us and it had upset him? I was driving myself crazy trying to figure it out.

It was nine when I finished at the shop. Freddy was still there, working on a piece. "See you tomorrow." I waved on my way out.

"You too," he called back.

I went next door first. I wasn't sure if Milo was closing, which they did at nine, or if Rachel had gone in. I saw him inside but didn't notice Autumn or anyone else.

I tried the door, and it was unlocked, so I went in, just as he was finishing up sweeping. "Hey, you." I pushed my hands into my pockets and leaned against the counter, close to him.

"You're nervous, or you're thinking about something. Those are the only times you keep your hands in your pockets."

Well, shit, I didn't even know that about myself, but it didn't surprise me that Milo did. "I've been worried about you all day." I looked around. "Are we alone?" It felt like he had something important to say, and that stupid fucking negative voice in my head kept telling me that meant this was over.

He nodded, then blurted out, "Rachel said you look at me like you want to eat me alive. I figured that could be just because of the sex we have, but then she also said you seem lucky to be in my orbit, and something about how when I walk out of a room, everything good leaves with me, which is crazy talk. I don't know how I could be that special, but then I was curious, and I wanted to see, but you just appeared normal to me. Then I was sad because…well, because I feel lucky to be in your orbit every time I'm around you, and when I'm not with you, sometimes it feels like I'm not complete."

I pushed off the counter, unable to believe I was hearing what I thought I was hearing.

Milo continued. "My brain knows that's the most ridiculous thing in the world. How can I not be complete without you? We're separate people. We don't need each other. I lived my whole life just fine before you, but it's all different now. I want to be your boyfriend and for you to sleep in my bed every night—not yours anymore, but you've been better about that. But we're best friends, and I don't want to lose you, and you can't possibly want the same things with me. Not when I'm…me."

I took a couple of steps closer to him. Just as he tried to speak again, I put my finger to his lips. "Shhh." I couldn't believe I hadn't burst out of my skin. I hadn't expected this—to want him or for him to want me.

"Did you wash your hands?" he asked, and I lowered my arm.

"After my last tattoo, yes, but not after cleaning up. Sorry."

"It's okay."

I cupped his cheek, then slid my hand to his nape so I could tug him forward and press a soft kiss to his lips. "I do want to eat you alive. It kills me how much I want you, but it's not just the sex, Lo. You make me happy in a way I didn't know I needed. I *do* feel lucky to be in your world. Sometimes it scares me how much."

"Orbit."

"Close enough. I'm telling you I want you to be my boyfriend, and *that's* what you focus on?"

His smile lit up the whole damn island. "Really?"

"Yes."

"But what about our friendship?"

"Maybe that'll make us even better together," I replied, even though I knew that wasn't what he meant. It was a valid concern.

"If we break up, I don't want you to decide you don't want to be friends with me anymore."

He was maybe the sweetest man in the world, and I didn't think he knew it. "I hope we don't break up, but I can't promise we won't. Relationships don't work that way." He could be the one who decided he wanted it to be over. "But what I can promise you is that I'll always want to be friends with you."

"Like you are with *Kris*," he said, emphasizing the name in an exaggerated way.

"Milo Copeland...are you jealous of my other best friend?"

"Yes," he admitted. "It's part of why I felt weird at opening night, but I didn't want to tell you."

I plucked the broom from his hand and leaned it against the counter before tugging him against me. I kissed his neck. Milo dropped his head back and groaned. "You don't have to be jealous. It's not him I want."

"It's me," he replied.

"So fucking much."

Our mouths crushed together. He pushed his tongue directly between my lips, and I let him. Milo's dick was hard against mine, our arms tight around each other, our bodies rutting together as we pulled at each other's clothes. Not off, unfortunately, because we were in the middle of the bookstore, which was what made me stop.

"I want to fuck you, boyfriend," Milo said, and goddamned if my whole body didn't sizzle with need.

"Let's go upstairs."

"I don't want to wait. I just want to let go and do it, like we want each other so much, we can't take the time to go upstairs."

"You and your goddamned porn," I said, but my dick was definitely into the idea.

Milo didn't respond. He grabbed my wrist and tugged me with him, stopping by the register to grab his bag. He led me to the bathroom, which was right off the main part of the store.

"Really?" My dick twitched. I was *so* down with this, but I didn't think he would be.

"Stay away from the toilets." We kissed our way inside.

His back hit the wall, and I pressed him against it. That seemed to fuel him on more. I slid my thigh between his legs, and Milo instinctively rode it while my tongue plunged into his mouth. "I'm taking it you have supplies in the bag?" I asked.

"Yes. I decided since we're having sex, I should always be prepared. Also, will you give me a hickey like I did you?"

I growled into his shoulder. "Fuck yes." I wanted to give him everything. I kissed him there, then licked his neck before sucking skin into my mouth.

"Gid. Oh my Gooooood." His nails dug into my shoulder before his hand slid up and into my hair. I wished we were already naked, that his hot skin was against mine. He gasped, panted, still rubbing on my thigh like he could get off this way. Honestly, he probably could.

I sucked harder, wondered if he could feel the blood rushing to the surface, wanted him to wear my mark proudly.

I pulled back when his hands traveled to my ass, trying to get underneath my jeans. "You're all purple." My lips pressed to the hickey with a soft kiss.

"Good. Can I fuck you now?"

"Hell yes."

We were frantic with our clothes after that, ripping them off. When I went to drop mine to the floor, Milo grabbed them. "Don't you dare!" He laid them across the top of the shelves he'd put in for toilet paper and other supplies.

Milo opened his bag, which was there too, and pulled out a small container of lube and a condom.

"Over here." I stood in front of the sink, ass out, holding on to the cool porcelain and looking into the mirror.

"Awesome idea. We can watch each other this way, but I can look down to see my dick in your ass too. That's my most favorite thing."

"Don't ever change."

Our gazes met, his so soft, so open, it damn near stole my breath. "Thank you." Milo kissed my shoulder. I spread my legs, felt his lube-slicked finger at my hole. He drew circles around it, then pressed the tip inside. "I still can't believe you let me do this to you."

He fucked me with one, then two fingers, our gazes locked in the mirror the whole time. He would lean forward to kiss my shoulder or neck, wrap an arm around me to play with my nipple piercings or to stroke my aching erection.

"Give me your cock. I want to come with your dick in my ass," I told him. Milo trembled.

When his fingers were gone, I missed the feel of him inside me. Milo fumbled with the condom and lube, pressed his forehead to my shoulder as he pushed at my rim.

"Look at me. I want you to hold my gaze when you enter me."

He did, no hesitation, no embarrassment, and smiled.

Milo worked his way into me slowly, stretching my hole out to fit him. I loved the burn, the feel of him. Loved getting fucked in ways I never had before, because this was him.

When his groin met my ass, we breathed out together.

It was all over after that.

He lost himself inside me, pulling back and slamming his hips forward again and again. We weren't quiet, Milo saying my name and telling me how good my ass felt. I told him to fuck me harder, and he mumbled about how much he loved sex talk.

My hands were sweaty, my grip sliding off the sink. I reached for it again and knocked the container of soap to the floor. We stumbled some, hitting the shelf, a bottle of air freshener falling with a *clank*.

"Oh God. This is so good," he gasped out before his

teeth dug into my shoulder.

"Fuck!"

"I'm sorry."

"Don't. It's good. Do it again."

Milo did, biting me while I took my dick in hand with fast, tight strokes.

"You gotta come, Gid. I love it when your ass spasms around me…when you make my balls spill into you."

Aaaaaand, that was hot as hell. He was good at this. My vision went blurry, hand still jerking. When Milo pinched my nipple, it was all over, my balls drawing tight, ropes of cum spurting all over the sink.

Seconds later, he succumbed to his orgasm as well. "Gideon, Gideon, Gideon," fell from his lips while his cock jerked inside me. "I like being your boyfriend," he said breathlessly.

"I like it too."

We kissed again, somehow stumbling and knocking more things over while laughing and touching. We cleaned each other up, then the space, got dressed, and washed our hands. I opened the door, signaling for Milo to go out first, and he did, heading into the store—and stopped dead in his tracks. I ran into the back of him, then held on so he didn't fall.

"Mom?" he questioned.

My gaze darted up, and yes, there was a woman standing there in the middle of the bookstore.

"You forgot to put the closed sign up or lock the door," was all she said seconds before her tight stare landed on me.

CHAPTER TWENTY-THREE

Milo

I LOOKED BACK at the bathroom door, then at Mom, and my face caught fire, embarrassment feeling like it was burning the flesh off it.

I'd just had sex…in the bathroom…when Mom was in my bookstore, the store anyone else could have come into because we'd forgotten to lock the door.

Did she know? Did we smell like sex, or had she heard us? Because we hadn't been quiet. Now that I knew what it was like to have sex, I understood why people were so loud about it.

"Hi. Ms. Copeland. I'm Gideon. It's nice to finally meet you." He stepped forward and held his hand out for Mom. She looked at it but didn't move, which confirmed she likely knew what we'd been doing in there.

"Oh God. We washed our hands, Mom." It was super embarrassing, but what was the point in trying to hide it?

"Milo!" Mom gasped in unison with Gideon's, "Ah, shit."

"Well, we did. I didn't want you to think we would have sex and then come out here dirty. Also, Gideon didn't have his fingers in—"

"We're so sorry this happened!" Gideon cut me off.

"That was crude, Milo."

"It was honest. You know I'm always honest." I didn't know why she expected me to be any different now. Just because it had to do with sex? "What are you doing here?"

She flinched, and while I sometimes struggled to read other people, I didn't when it came to Mom.

"I didn't mean for that to sound like I'm not happy to see you, because I am. I'm just surprised, is all."

"Clearly," she replied. "You said you and Mr...."

"Barlow," Gideon filled in. "But please, call me Gideon."

"You said you and Mr. Barlow were just friends," she finished.

"You did that on purpose. You know I don't like it when people call me something I'm uncomfortable with. Why would you do it to Gideon?" She was being rude to him for no reason. He didn't deserve that.

"It's fine, Lo," Gideon soothed.

"No." I shook my head. "It's not." I turned to Mom,

and I could see the regret in her eyes. I could also see the steel will she had trying to take over. "We were just friends, but now we're friends and boyfriends—that's a lot of uses of the word *friends*, but we're both. That's what we decided." I reached over and grabbed Gideon's hand, but his arm was slightly stiff. I frowned. Looked at him. "Did you change your mind?" Leave it to me to only get a boyfriend for two seconds.

"What? No. I want to be with you. I'm just trying to tread carefully in a delicate situation." Gideon gave his attention to my mom. "I, um…I'm sorry we had to meet this way, but your son, he's very important to me and—"

"Then maybe don't have sex with him in public." Mom gave him a look that had scared many people before him.

"I'm the one who took him to the bathroom," I said.

"I understand your concern, but frankly, where Milo and I choose to do anything has nothing to do with you."

Oh shit. I should have known Gideon wouldn't back down to her. It was the kind of man he was.

"Milo is my son."

"Milo is a grown man," Gideon countered.

"Milo is right here and doesn't appreciate being spoken about as if he isn't or doesn't have any say himself," I added.

"I'd like to talk with you alone," she said to me, but I shook my head.

"Not if it has to do with Gideon. He's my boyfriend. I know that comes as a surprise to you, and you probably didn't think I would ever have this, but—"

"I didn't think that. Do you really believe there's anything I want more than your happiness?" Mom's voice was softer, more vulnerable than usual.

"No, I know you want me happy." But she still didn't think I would ever find someone. *I* didn't think I would ever find someone either.

"It's okay," Gideon told me. "I'll go for a walk. I'm sure the two of you have some catching up to do."

It was late, and I just wanted to go upstairs and climb into bed with him, but I knew he was right.

Gideon leaned in, kissing my cheek before his mouth trailed close to my ear. His voice was low when he said, "She can stay with us if you want. Your choice." I nodded, missing his touch when he let go of me. "I have my key. I'll lock the door behind me."

When he was gone, Mom said, "Oh, Milo."

"He's very cute, isn't he?"

She bit back a small smile. Mom was tough as nails. She wasn't afraid of anyone, and people feared her, but I didn't.

She walked over to one of the small café tables, and I took the seat across from her. "It's beautiful, your store. You did a good job with it."

My pride in Little Beach Books swelled to the surface again. "Thank you. It means a lot to me. I like it here. It's the first time in my life I feel like I have something that's mine."

Mom sighed. Her gaze turned down to her hands, which were locked together on the tabletop. "I just worry about you. It's normal, you know? For parents to fret about their child. You think it's just because you're on the autism spectrum, but it's not."

"Yes, but you do it *more* because I'm neurodivergent. And I know I'm different. I'm okay with that. I like being me. I like how things make sense to me."

"I don't want you to get hurt."

"Everyone gets hurt. Everyone gets their heart broken. I know that Gideon might break mine. Odds are he will. He might get to the point where the things he thinks are cute become annoying."

"Then he doesn't deserve you."

I shrugged. "That's not the point. I still deserve that experience. I'm twenty-four, and I've never had a boyfriend. I've never had my heart broken. I never even had sex until Gideon, and—"

She held up her hand. "I don't need the details."

"I wasn't going to share them." Silence sucked us in for a moment before I said, "If I knew the future, if I knew Gideon would shatter my world and there was nothing I could do to change it, I would still be with him. Not because I'm a glutton for punishment, but because I don't want my life to be so carefully curated with *what-ifs* that I don't live. And that's tough for me. My brain, logic, tell me that's stupid, but sometimes *in here* wins out." I rubbed a hand over my chest. "And I want it to win with this."

She swiped her thumb beneath her eye, catching a single tear. "You were always braver than me. It took me years to trust your father, and then I finally did and he left me. The only reason I'm thankful for that experience is because I have you. I would never risk it again, and while I understand where you're coming from, I don't want that for you. It's my job to protect you."

"No, it's not. It's my job to protect me."

"You don't really know this man, Milo. Don't you think it's interesting that he befriended you straight away? Invited you to move in? Oh, and he just so happens to need you so he can keep his business."

"Do you think someone can't like me just for me? Am I not good enough? Do I not deserve that because I don't see the world the same way other people do?"

"No. I would never mean that. You're the light of my life. You're the best person I know, and you deserve every happiness in life, but you also have to be careful. There are a lot of bad people in the world, people who would use others. I'm just telling you to be careful because Gideon has something to gain by being with you. If I ever chose to date, I would have to be mindful of the same thing—of people wanting my money or the business I built."

I pulled back, closed my eyes. Logic told me she was right. Not that I didn't trust Gideon, but there *were* bad people in the world, people who used others; yet my heart knew he wasn't one of them. "Gideon and I might not last, but he wouldn't do that. He wouldn't use me that way."

"I hope you're right."

I hoped I was too. "I missed you," I admitted.

"I missed you too, so much it hurt." Mom wasn't the type to speak her true feelings that way, to admit her vulnerabilities to others, but I had always known I was one of the people she trusted.

"I'm glad you're here."

"Me too." She reached across the table and squeezed my hand. "The hickey is a bit much, don't you think?"

I tried to cover it.

"Wrong side."

I'd completely forgotten he'd given it to me. I smiled. "Oh, Milo, what am I going to do with you?"

"Can we talk about how I have a really hot boyfriend?"

"No, I'm too old, and that's weird. Plus, I don't like all the tattoos…and the piercings. Honestly, why would he do that to his face?"

"I like his face."

"I'm sure you do. Promise me you won't do that to your body."

"I'll do no such thing," I teased, even though I had no plans of getting tattoos or piercings…I didn't think.

"I thought you wanted me to like him?"

"I do." And I knew she would try, for me. But I also knew my mom well enough to know it wouldn't be easy. She couldn't flip a switch inside her that way. She was suspicious of Gideon, and it would take a lot to change that. "He makes me happy. I might love him. How can you tell? Did you love Dad?"

She wrung her hands together.

"I didn't mean to make you uncomfortable."

"I know, and yes, I did. I probably loved him before I trusted him, certainly before I dated him. There's no one way to tell. One day you'll just feel different...or you'll look at him and it'll hit you how your world wouldn't feel complete without him. You'll recognize it when the time is right."

I felt like that sometimes, like my world wasn't complete without him. I'd told him as much. "I'm sorry Dad hurt you. I'm sorry that it was because of me, and—"

"No. It wasn't because of you. It was because of *him*."

Maybe that was it, maybe she thought Gideon would leave me since Dad left her because of me. She could tell me all day long I wasn't the reason, but we both knew I was. He wanted his son to be the kind of person I never could be.

"Do you still love him?" I'd never asked her that question, but I'd always wondered. Did she regret it, choosing me? Did she never date again because she had lost the one man she had loved?

"I love what we could have been if he'd been a better man."

I picked at one of my fingernails on my left hand. "You really won't ever let yourself love someone again?"

"No," she answered honestly. "I'm not really built that way."

I supposed she wasn't, and I'd known that before I asked. "Wilma—"

"I don't want to talk about her."

"But it wasn't what you think."

"I can't, Milo. Not right now, okay? Maybe not ever. What's the point? It's all in the past. She's gone, so dissecting it changes nothing."

There was no getting around it, no pushing her. It would only make her run further away. "How long will you be here?"

"I don't know."

"Do you want to stay with me and Gideon tonight? But not every day. I love you and all, but…you know."

She rolled her eyes, but a smile curled her lips. "Yes, I know. I heard. And I thought you would never ask."

CHAPTER TWENTY-FOUR

Gideon

BEVERLY COPELAND WANTED me to die a slow, painful death. She didn't say that, but she didn't have to. She wasn't even rude to me. She tried to be extra nice, likely for Milo's sake, but I saw the daggers in her eyes when she didn't know I was looking.

She hated me.

She hated me because she thought I would hurt Milo.

Part of me couldn't even be mad at her for that. She loved him and wanted what was best for him. On the surface, it could very much look like I was using him. I had reasons to use him. He owned the building where I lived and worked. So yeah, I got it. Still, a week later, the death glares were becoming a bit much. At least she'd only stayed in the apartment for the one night and was now at a hotel. Milo had told her, *"I know I said you couldn't, but you're welcome to stay, Mom. Just know we have a lot of sex,"* which was likely another reason she wanted to set me on fire and watch me burn.

I'd slept in later than Milo, which I often did. We both had the day off. I'd lain in bed for a while, thinking about Beverly and Milo, when he finally came in and launched himself onto the bed. "I'm nervous to see your family today."

"Why?" I fingered a lock of his hair. He was… Christ, he was so fucking beautiful. I had no idea what he was doing with me.

"I don't want to say the wrong thing or do the wrong thing, especially now that we're boyfriends. I already made a fool of myself last time."

"No, you didn't."

"I was there."

I chuckled. "I was too."

"Gideon…it won't do either of us any good to pretend. I know I don't always act like everyone else. Denying it doesn't make it less true. Also, it pisses me off more than being hungry and when I can't have orgasms with you."

This time it was a loud, belly-deep laugh that fell from my lips. "That last one is new."

"Sex is new. Don't change the subject."

I sighed. "Whatever happens, we'll deal with it together. How's that?"

He grinned, and damned if it didn't feel like his happiness filled me with my own. "You're perfect—okay, not all the parts of you, but you're the perfect boyfriend."

"One good thing, being with you means I'll never have to worry about being too conceited." He could bust my balls and compliment me at the same time.

"Shit, I'm sorry. Did that hurt your feelings? I was just telling the truth."

"No, I'm kidding." I didn't kiss his lips because I knew he didn't like it before teeth were brushed in the morning. So I pressed my mouth to his forehead and then rolled out of bed.

We showered together, then got dressed for a day at my parents' house. To be honest, I was slightly worried about it too. Not because I thought Milo would do something wrong, but because I'd never had a boyfriend around my family. I'd never had good luck with men at all. I was afraid I would do something stupid and lose Milo, and then the other people I loved would be entangled in it. At least they didn't know about me and Kris, and they'd never met my asshole ex.

Milo packed a bag with beach towels and some other things. We stopped at the door for him to put his pants on, along with his shoes. A robe now hung close by, which was what he wore over his underwear when his mom was over.

Speaking of his mom, we were picking her up so she could go with us to meet my family.

Things were suddenly taking off at Mach speed.

Beverly was waiting outside when we pulled up at the hotel. Milo tried to get out of the passenger seat, but she told him to stay put and climbed into the back cab. I was wondering how this whole experience would go. If she made it obvious she didn't think I was good enough for Milo, Mom would lose her shit. In some ways, she couldn't be more different from my family—she was city and wealthy and it showed—but in others, she was more like them than me.

"Aren't the hotel beds horrible?" Milo asked her.

"They're not bad. I've slept on worse."

"Mom stayed in a hostel before she could move into the dorms at school. She found a job, working her way through college on her own." Pride beamed from his smile.

"Wow, that couldn't have been easy." My gaze flicked to her in the rearview mirror, but she wasn't looking.

"I did what had to be done, is all," Beverly replied.

It didn't take long to get anywhere on Little Beach Island, but Milo's nerves were obvious. He fidgeted more with every minute that went by. When we pulled up in front of my family home, I rested my hand on his nape and pulled him close, my forehead against his. "We'll be fine, Lo. I promise," I said softly.

"Okay," he replied, and I pressed a quick kiss to the tip of his nose. When we pulled apart, I couldn't stop from darting a quick look to Beverly, who was watching us, head slightly cocked, eyes studying.

"Rach will be a few minutes late," Milo said as he got out and pulled the bag over his shoulder. The three of us met on their side of the truck.

"Tell her she can just come around back when they get here."

Milo shot off a text before automatically taking my hand and entwining our fingers together. For someone who'd never had a boyfriend before, he'd fallen easily into the relationship.

We walked around the side of the house. My parents had decorated with a luau theme, which meant Mom had forced Dad to help her. She loved to do things like that when she entertained.

There were tiki torches, drinks in pineapples, leis on the table as well as hanging from a tall hook stuck in the sand. They'd pulled out the second picnic table too.

No one had seen us yet, and Milo plucked a yellow lei

from the stand and put it over my head. "What color should I wear?" he asked, and my pulse ridiculously fluttered over such a simple question. I didn't know how he could make everything feel so fresh and new.

"Green."

He frowned.

"Blue?"

"Deal."

I laughed, because of course he would ask me what color while knowing which ones he wouldn't wear.

"Do you want one?" I asked Beverly, silently hoping she didn't turn me down.

"That's fi—"

"Mom," Milo said.

"Yes, please. Thank you."

She totally still hated me. I got her a blue one as well and handed it over. She wore it, but only for Milo; that much was blatantly clear.

"Milo!" Cammy yelled, running at him. Her arrival caught the attention of my family.

"Oh hey. Snacks is here!" Orlando called. I hated my brother.

Cammy slid to a stop in front of Milo.

"Energy level?" he asked.

"Mom said six."

"We can work with that."

"Look, we brought you these just in case." Cammy held out a package of earplugs with a sticky note that read: *Child Noise Blockers*.

Milo grinned. "Perfect. I'll keep them on me always." I loved that he didn't tell her he already had a pair in his pocket.

"Are you Milo's mom?" Cammy asked Beverly, who had already met Rachel at the store.

"Yes, I am. What's your name?"

"Camilla, but everyone calls me Cammy. Milo is super fun. I wanted to marry him, but Mom said he likes boys and is too old for me."

"Hey, stop trying to steal my man," I joked, wrapping an arm around his shoulders.

Her eyes widened. "I knew it when you held hands on the beach!"

"She sings Milo and Gideon sitting in a tree every time I see her." Milo handed me his backpack, then knelt so Cammy could jump on. She wrapped her arms around his neck and her legs around his waist before the group of us walked over to join my family.

Beverly's eyes didn't fall away from her son as she watched him carry Cammy to go talk with Rachel, something close to awe in her gaze.

We introduced everyone to Beverly, and when we finished with all the hellos, Milo again said, "Hi, baby Jacob," to Heather's belly.

Milo let Cammy down just as Mom asked Beverly, "Are you a vegetarian too?"

"Oh, no. I can eat anything. Thank you."

Mom turned her attention to Milo. "Gideon gave us some ideas to get for you. I researched recipes too. We have vegetable kabobs, and I found what looks like a yummy recipe for a corn salad, black-bean burgers, and grilled ranch potatoes." Mom was trying, and I loved her for it.

"You didn't have to go through all that trouble for me," Milo said.

"Of course we do. You're Gideon's friend, so we want you to feel at home."

"His boyfriend," Milo replied proudly.

"Yes, his boyfriend. You've made him very happy."

"Mom." I rolled my eyes.

"Ew, gross. What do you see in this guy?" Orlando pointed to me.

"Oh, lots of things. He's funny and kind and really talented. He tries all my meals, even if he doesn't think he's going to like them. Sometimes he stops by the store and brings me something he thinks I'll like…this pomegranate tea that made him think of me or a hat when I was working outside and my face got too pink from the sun. He doesn't care that I eat eggs, toast, and oatmeal every Monday and that I get upset if I can't. I bought him better sandals that didn't torture his toes, and he wears them even though the flip-flops don't bother him. Plus, he's hot."

"Damn, I think I might be in love with Gideon too after that," Heather teased.

"Yeah, same here," Meg added. "You don't bring me pomegranate tea." She playfully swatted Kris.

"You guys could learn a thing or two from me," I joked with Orlando and Kris, before wrapping my arms around Milo and kissing the top of his head. I liked this boyfriend business. A lot. "You're hotter," I whispered close to Milo's ear.

The group of us hung out at the picnic tables for a while after that. Meg wasn't feeling well again and had to go inside to lie down. Beverly was quiet. She replied when spoken to and joined in here or there, but I could tell she was trying to figure out what she thought about us, about this whole situation. Every time I looked at her, she was watching me, or Milo, or Milo with me, Cammy, or Rachel.

"Let's go swimming," Orlando said after a while.

I looked at Milo, who nodded. Beverly stayed on shore with Heather, Mom, and Dad, but the rest of us went out. I'd forgotten Beverly grew up here, but since she was older than my parents and having had Milo later, they didn't really know each other.

We played water games, splashed each other, Milo getting into it particularly heavily with Kris once. I was pretty sure he was taking his jealousy out on him.

Rachel kept ahold of Cammy the whole time, but every once in a while, the little girl would ride on Milo's back so he could swim around with her.

But then he came to me, tangled his arms around my neck, and floated. I held his waist, looking at him, taking in the blue of his eyes and the droplets of water clinging to his lashes, some of them matching up with freckles on his nose and cheek.

"This is one of the best days of my life," he said.

I felt like he'd just handed me all the happiness in the world. "Mine too."

And then I kissed him…and my brother and Kris sneak-attacked us, splashing us with water until we broke apart.

"I hate you," I told them.

They laughed. When Milo and Kris got into it again, Orlando said just for me, "I'm happy for you, little bro."

I was too.

CHAPTER TWENTY-FIVE

Milo

"I TRIED TO get Mom to come by with me, but she said no," I told Gene when he let me into the house. She'd decided to spend a month in Little Beach, which I couldn't believe. If you looked up the word *workaholic* in the dictionary, there should be a photo of Mom too; she never took time off. Her secretary had actually called me to make sure she was okay. I think they thought she might have been kidnapped and wasn't really with me, but then I'd never been away from her for so long. If I had, she would have more reasons to travel.

The good thing was she could still take care of some of her responsibilities remotely. It was what she often did when we weren't together.

I wondered how we would move forward. I wasn't leaving Little Beach; I loved it here. Even if Gideon and I broke up, I would want to stay. I'd be devastated and miserable if I didn't have him as a boyfriend, but Gideon had promised we would always be friends, and I believed him. We were totally bestie goals. And Little Beach was home. *My* home, and that wasn't something I ever thought I'd have.

"You can't push her, Milo." Gene closed the door, and the two of us went into the kitchen.

"She pushes me."

"And do you like it?"

"No, but she still does it."

He chuckled. "She has to want to hear about Wilma, and she has to do it in her own time."

"Well, her time sucks."

We went out the back door to the yard, where Gideon had delivered my supplies earlier. It was beautifully landscaped with tons of flowers, bushes, and cobblestone walkways weaving throughout.

It was my day off, and I'd told Gene I would start building him a porch swing with a canopy so he could enjoy Wilma's garden without the sun frying him alive.

There was a chair in the shade beneath a tree, where Gene sat. He liked being close to me when I visited, I'd noticed. That worked because I enjoyed his company and liked hearing stories about Wilma.

"So...you and Gideon," Gene started.

I grinned. "Oh, do you mean my boyfriend, Gideon?" I put my goggles and hard hat on and then handed my spares to Gene. He wore his without arguing. Rachel and Gid needed to be more like Gene.

"That's what I've heard around town."

"This is the kind of gossip I can get behind. Everyone is talking about me having a hot boyfriend." I sighed while pulling the plans I'd drawn out of my bag. "But it's more than just that, ya know? How did you know you loved Wilma? I asked Mom, and she gave me her advice, but I figure I should get as much information as possible before I tell Gideon how I might feel." I blurted things out a lot, but I was determined not to with this. I didn't want to do anything to screw it up. What if I pushed Gideon away? What if he liked me okay, but he didn't love me and I ruined everything? Or what if I thought I loved him and told him but then figured out I didn't? I wanted to be sure.

"I think it's something that happens slowly. One day I realized I was never quite as happy with anyone else as I was when I was with her."

"Oh, I definitely feel that."

"Things that might embarrass me or cause me to feel silly in front of other people didn't feel that way with her because I knew she liked me just the way I was."

"I think Gideon does too...like me that way. He says he does, and he never makes me feel incapable or like he's embarrassed of me." There was the one time with Orlando, but it had been a misunderstanding, and nothing like that had happened since. I always felt safe with Gid.

"I wanted nothing more than to see her smile, to make her happy, to be there for whatever she needed."

"Gideon's smiles are one of my favorite things in the world. It's even better when they make an appearance because of me. It's like, even if I screw up a lot of things, I at least got that right."

Gene nodded. "Sounds to me like if you're not there yet, you're on your way. He's sure smitten with you, couldn't stop talking about you when he came by earlier."

I reached out and anchored myself with a hand on the porch railing, like hearing that would make me float away. Even if this wasn't love, it was fucking awesome. "It's all because of Wilma, because she loved me even though she didn't know me. And she left me the store, so I moved here, and I'm happier than I've ever been. I wish I could thank her."

"You can," Gene said. "I don't know what I believe about afterlife or where we go when we pass, but I talk to her, and I believe she hears me. But even if you don't, I think she knows. If there's any way for her to watch over you, I know she is."

"Just tell her I don't wear pants at home. I wouldn't want her seeing anything she shouldn't," I teased, making Gene laugh. "You must miss her a lot."

"Every second of every day." He looked out just as the wind blew through the flowers. "But it's better now that you're here."

I didn't know what to say to that. It was a lot, but in a good way, so when he glanced at me again, I offered a grin and got to work. We talked about Mom and Wilma, and apparently they were both stubborn. He told me more stories and said he'd made a photo album for me. I kept thinking about what he said, though, about how it was better now that I was there. I liked Gene a lot; he was family to me. I'd never had that besides Mom—and Dad before he left. Now I had Gid, Mom, Gene, Rach, Cammy, and Gideon's family.

But Gene, he was something special.

It was hours later, and I was almost finished with his swing, when I asked, "Gene?"

"Yes?"

"Do you think I could call you grandpa? I've never had one before, but now I have Wilma, my grandma, even if it's just in spirit, and you."

His hands shook while he wiped the tears off his face. "Milo, I would be honored if you called me your grandpa."

"Thanks...Grandpa." And it didn't even feel weird to say. I couldn't wait to go home and tell Gideon.

GIDEON HAD LATE appointments and said he wouldn't finish up at the tattoo parlor until nine or ten. I hated when he had long nights, but I tried my best not to complain about them. I liked being home with him, eating dinner with him, and curling up together on the couch before we shared our nighttime routine and then went to bed together.

Rach was at the bookstore, so when I finished at Gene's, I just walked there.

It wasn't incredibly busy when I arrived, but there were people sitting in the café, drinking coffee, reading, or working on their laptops.

"Guess who has a new grandpa?" I asked.

"I don't know. I give up," Rachel replied.

"Me, brat! It's Gene. Don't tell Gideon. I want to."

"I wouldn't dare." Rachel smiled. "That makes me happy for both you and Gene."

I hung out with her for a bit, trying to find a way to

tell her the other thing I had on my mind. It was cool to have friends to talk to about this kind of stuff before I mentioned it to Gideon. When there were only two people left in the store, I said quietly, "I think I'm ready to have sex with Gideon."

She frowned. "Sweets, you and Gid have been doing that for a while now."

I rolled my eyes. "I know. I meant the other way. Him fucking me. He seems to like it a lot when I fuck him, but I'm still unsure about having a dick up there. Have you ever done it?"

Her cheeks sucked in slightly, and it was clear she was biting back a laugh.

"Not in your vagina; in your butt."

"God, I love you." She leaned over the counter so we were closer. "No, I've never had anal. Have you ever stuck anything else up there? Gid play around with his fingers or anything?"

"No. And he says he doesn't care, that he doesn't need to fuck me, but I want him to. I want to know what it's like to have him inside me."

"Then you should. And talk to Gideon about it ahead of time. You guys can work your way up to it. He can finger you some and—"

"Please don't ever say finger me again. It's weird coming from you."

She flicked my hand. "Hey, you're the one who started this conversation. Plus, you just asked me if I'd ever had a dick in my ass."

"That's what friends do!"

"But they can't say finger you?"

She had a point.

Rachel turned serious. "If you're ready, you should do it. If you're not sure, then you should wait. Either way, you should talk to Gideon. He'll accept whatever you decide and support you either way."

I knew he would, but sometimes I just wanted things to be easier for him so he didn't *have* to. "I might just play around back there myself first to see if I like it…"

"I have much more fun with myself than I do with a man; maybe you won't need Gideon anymore."

Her words were said playfully, but I still couldn't help replying with, "But I love him. I'd want him regardless." Oh. Well, now I knew the answer regarding my feelings for him.

"I know you would." She kissed my cheek. Having good friends was the best.

CHAPTER TWENTY-SIX

Gideon

"How are things going with you and Milo?" Orlando asked. We were at his place, putting together a crib, changing table, and all sorts of other things they would need in the nursery when Jacob was born. Heather was getting more and more anxious, and I could tell my brother was too, though he wasn't as free with talking about it as she was.

"Really good," I replied. "I care about him a lot."

"I can tell you do."

"Beverly still hates me."

"Good thing you're not dating her."

Which was true, I got where he was coming from, but... "That's real easy to say when Heather's family loves you. Milo and his mom are close. She's important to him." Though Milo was independent as fuck too. He was the kind of man who wouldn't let someone else's opinion change how he felt about someone. That wasn't always easy to do, but he managed it. That didn't mean I wasn't firmly on team *Do anything to get Beverly to like me.*

"Why wouldn't she like you? You're almost as cool as me, and most people don't even come close."

If there were a biggest-idiot-in-the-world award, my brother would win it. "Please don't say I'm like you." I worked on screwing the back of the crib into one of the sides. "She doesn't trust me," I admitted. "She thinks I'm using him because of the shop and—"

"Fuck her, then. You would never do that."

No, I wouldn't. "I don't even know if she really believes that or if it's just because she's worried about Milo and it's an excuse she can grab on to. Seeing him with someone is new for her, and she's his mom; she wants to protect him. I get that, but…" I rubbed a hand over my face, wondered if I was really going to admit this or not. "I think I'm in love with him."

"You should probably just reword that and say what you really mean—you're in love with him; there's no think about it." No, no there wasn't. "The two of you are good together. I didn't totally get it until the night of the bookstore opening, and then it was slammed home at Mom and Dad's. You fit well, and like I said, I really am happy for you."

I didn't look at Orlando, just kept working on the crib for my nephew. "I feel like I fit with him…and I've never had that, even with Kris. I love him. He's my best friend, and I know he loves me, but I don't *fit* with him, if that makes sense. I've always sort of felt like an outsider."

The room was quiet for a moment, so long that the silence sat heavy on my chest. When I forced myself to look up, Orlando was watching me. "With me?"

"With everyone." I shrugged. "It's not your fault. I think people spend too much time looking for the *why* in everything, and sometimes we're just built differently; this is how I'm built." I couldn't believe I was saying this to him, didn't think I would have if it wasn't for Milo. He didn't realize how much he'd changed me. He was so open, so honest and real. I loved that about Milo and strived to be more like him.

"Jesus, Gid. Why didn't you ever say anything? You're my favorite fucking person in this world. You might be younger than me, but I've always looked up to you. You're completely who you are and don't let anyone influence that. You never felt the need to be just like Dad, to follow those footsteps that have been mapped out for you."

"And you did?"

"Yes and no. I love my life. I love practicing law. Most days, I feel like this is exactly what I'm supposed to do and who I'm supposed to be, but there were times I've wondered if there could have been something else out there for me. If I'd ever allowed myself to consider other options—not when it comes to Heather, of course. But just…staying on the island, law school, following the exact same path Mom and Dad did."

"Dad loves you more because of it."

"No, he doesn't. Dad loves us differently…and Dad and I have more in common and talk more because of it. He loves you for who you are, Gid. He respects the hell out of you. I don't think you see yourself as clearly as the rest of us do."

Maybe I didn't, but did anyone?

"He talks about how proud of you he is all the time. When he brings up the shop or money, it's not because he's disappointed, but because he wants the best for you."

"Maybe he should tell me all that."

"Probably, but you could talk to him too."

He was right. I didn't try any more than Dad did. I'd just decided how he felt and accepted it. "Maybe I will."

"*Maybe I will*," Orlando teasingly mocked before tugging me into a hug. "I love you, little bro. I hope you know that."

"I love you too. Now get off me; you stink." Playfully, I tried to pull back, but he tightened his hold until I managed to get him off. We laughed and got some more work done on the nursery.

I thought about how excited Milo had been to come home last night and tell me about his conversation with Gene—how he'd asked Gene if he could call him grandpa—and I knew it was his strength that had made me talk to Orlando today.

We were finishing up on the changing table when Orlando said, "Next Friday, for my birthday, we're having a guys' night at the Lighthouse. This'll probably be one of the last times I do something like that since Jacob will be here soon. Kris is coming, Dad too, some of my other friends, and a few guys I work with. I'm going to get falling-down drunk, just so you know. I'm going to party like it's college one last time before I'm a mature, responsible dad. Do you think Milo will be able to come with you? I want him to feel welcome, but I don't want to pressure him either."

Fuck. I'd forgotten my own brother's birthday was coming up. A party sounded really fun. We hadn't done anything like that in a while, and Orlando was right; it would be even harder after the baby was born.

I thought about Milo, about how he didn't like parties, a lot of people, or loud noises, about how hard the opening night of Little Beach Books had been for him, and discomfort settled at the base of my spine. He'd been wrecked afterward and had felt like shit about it. What if he tried for me and it ended up even worse? I didn't ever want to put him in that kind of situation. He wanted my family to like him so much that I could see him going, even though he didn't want to. Especially if there was going to be a lot of drinking. I loved my brother and Kris, but they could get a little wild. Hell, I could too. It was fun to let loose like that every once in a while. "I don't know if that's such a good idea."

"Ask him and see what he says. I don't want him to think he's not welcome." I nodded, and he continued. "You should come about eight. We're going to have dinner first and all that. I can't remember the last time I partied with just the guys. It'll be fun to do something different. I want Heather to have a girls' night like that after Jacob gets here. That way she can have all the fun she wants to."

Orlando chuckled, and I joined in, but I couldn't stop remembering the night of the bookstore opening, how helpless I'd felt seeing Milo so upset. As much as I wanted to hang out with my brother and friends, I would do anything not to have Milo go through that again. Ever.

CHAPTER TWENTY-SEVEN

Milo

TONIGHT WAS THE night. I was ready to let Gideon fuck me. Or, I was ready to try and let him. I'd made a couple of clumsy attempts at using my fingers on myself, but it was just too awkward and weird. It was one thing to have something in Gideon's butt, but I didn't like putting things in my own. I figured that was something better experienced with someone else trying to give you pleasure. Maybe once I was used to it, things would be different, but as of now, I wasn't a fan.

I did want to try and share that connection with Gideon. I wanted to know what it would be like to feel him the way he got to feel me.

It was Friday night, and I'd told him he had to come home at eight o'clock and no earlier. The cool thing? He didn't even argue or ask questions. He'd just looked at me and nodded, accepting me exactly the way I was. My boyfriend was perfect.

I'd told him to eat dinner before he came home, and I did the same. Then I'd spent the last little while cleaning myself out and showering, so I guess there were some ways I'd always have to put something inside myself—there was no way I could risk not being totally clean back there, I would die if I made a mess of things in that way.

So now it was seven fifty-nine, and I was lying in my bed, *naked*, waiting for my boyfriend to come home so I could ask him to fuck me.

What was this life?

All I knew was that it was *awesome*.

At exactly eight, I heard the front door open and couldn't help smiling. I bet he'd stood outside and waited.

"Lo?" Gideon called out.

"I'm in the bedroom!" Whoa. My voice was shaky. That was new.

Gideon's footsteps moved toward me until he stepped inside the room, his brows pulled together in confusion until he saw me. His face immediately relaxed, a smile pulling at his lips and his eyes sparking with a desire I still couldn't believe was for me.

"Well, isn't this a nice surprise?"

"I hope so," I replied.

He tugged his sneakers off, then went for his pants. While he worked them open, Gideon asked, "Do you want me to jump in the shower real quick?"

I shook my head, trying to find a way to make the words come out before I just…let go to be myself. "You don't have to. And I was thinking we could do it the other way around. I mean, you fucking me. I can't promise, but I want to try. I showered and cleaned out, and I was going to light candles and put flower petals all around like you see in movies and stuff, but that just felt dumb and…why are you looking at me like that?" It was like I'd just offered him the world instead of my ass.

"Because I like you and I can't help looking at you like this," he replied softly, the words making me tremble. Tremble! How did he even do that just by speaking to me?

"I like you too." *I love you. I love you, I love you, I love you.*

Gideon walked over and pressed a gentle kiss to my lips. "I'll be right back. Don't move."

He slipped out of the room, but I did move. I sat up and listened. I heard the bathroom door close, my heart hammering in my chest as I waited and counted for three and a half minutes for Gideon to return.

He was naked and hard when he slid into bed beside

me, and I smelled mint and soap. He'd brushed his teeth and maybe had the quickest wash-up in the world, which just made me love him even more.

He moved over and straddled my thighs, sitting on my lap and looking at me with so much unrestrained want, it stole my breath.

"I can't make any promises, Gid. If I don't like it, I'll tell you, and we'll have to stop. That doesn't mean we won't ever be able to do it, just that we might have to take it more slowly."

Gideon cupped my cheek, his hand shaking. He was nervous too, which was strange since he'd done this so many times before. "I'll always stop. Even if we do it a hundred times and then you don't want to anymore, I'd stop. And if it doesn't work out, that's okay too. I don't need to top you, Lo. I just need you."

Thud. Thud. Thud. "Oh my." I pressed a hand over my chest. "I feel like I'm having a heart attack, like it's trying to beat its way out of my chest and into yours." People had confused me my whole life. In some ways, Gideon made perfect sense, and in others, he mixed me up even more. How could he need me? How could he want me and all my quirks that much?

"Don't do that." He leaned down and kissed the corner of my mouth. "Please just let me make this good for you."

I nodded, and he kissed the other side, then lashed at my lips with his tongue. I opened them up for him, and Gideon took advantage, dipping inside, kissing me with all the hunger in the world, like maybe he would die if he didn't taste me.

We made out like that, kissing and nipping, tongues chasing one another's and playing inside our mouths. Both his hands cupped my face the whole time before one drifted back to my nape and rested there.

When we pulled apart, I bent close to his chest, licked his nipple piercings, and savored the sound of Gideon's sharp inhalation. Our cocks were standing hard and tall between us, precum at the tips. I moved from one nipple to the other, tasting the cool metal, before leaning back and looking up at him. "Hi."

Gideon kissed the tip of my nose. "Hi." When he climbed off me, I missed the weight of him immediately. "Lie on your stomach. I want to try something. If you don't like it, just tell me."

I didn't hesitate before doing exactly what he said. There was no one I trusted more than him.

"Spread your legs," he added.

I did that too, and he moved between them.

"Oh God," I said when he spread my ass, leaned in,

and swiped my hole with his tongue. Delicious pleasure shot through me.

"Good?"

"Amazing. Do it again."

I looked over my shoulder to see him grin before lowering his face so it was *between my cheeks*. He did it again and again, licking me, tracing circles on my rim, and fuck, why did this feel so good? Why was it the best thing that had ever happened to me?

"Gideon…Gid," I said breathlessly, pushing my butt close to him, and he nuzzled in deeper, basically *feasting* on me. "I can't believe you're doing this…like…where you're putting your tongue… I don't know if I can do this to you, but then I feel like I'm robbing you of one of the most incredible forms of sex."

He laughed with his tongue on my asshole, which was another whole new sensation.

I bit the pillow. Fisted my hands in the blankets. Kept pushing my ass against him. Even if I couldn't let him fuck me, would he keep doing this to me? Like all day, every day, for the rest of our lives?

It was like his tongue somehow melted my muscles and made my body relax. My nerves stepped out of the way for the pleasure while he licked me and pushed his tongue in me, and I tried not to come as I fucked the mattress.

Getting eaten out was the *best*.

"This is great…like really good…so fucking incredible…Gideon…I might come…"

He pulled back, and I silently cursed myself for telling him. He kissed one cheek, then the other, rubbed my rim with a finger or a thumb—who the hell knew? I just thought it was amazing.

"We can't have that. Not yet. Can you reach up and grab the lube for me? And a condom."

"Yes. Are you going to fuck me now?"

"Not yet. We'll get some fingers in you to test the waters."

"If it's anything like having your tongue in me, I might become addicted." I reached over, pulled the nightstand drawer open, and grabbed the supplies.

Gideon took them both. He licked, then kissed my hole again before pumping some lube onto his fingers. I immediately tightened up.

"Lo?"

"Sorry. I tried it myself and didn't like it."

"Do you want me to stop?"

"No." I shook my head.

"Roll over." I did, and he grabbed a pillow and stuffed it under my hips before kneeling between my legs.

Gideon sucked the crown of my erection into his mouth while his finger teased my ass.

"This helps. This is nice." I looked down to see him smile around my dick.

Gideon kept sucking me. I'd gone a little soft, but was already hardening again. He licked my balls the way I liked before blowing me again, his finger circling, then pushing inside, and… "*Oh.*"

"Good *oh* or bad?"

"Good. Put my cock back in your mouth, please."

"So bossy."

"I said please!"

He did, bobbing his head on me while he fingered my ass. It felt so much better with Gideon doing it.

I watched him because it was totally hot. I liked looking at my dick in his mouth and seeing his hand move between my legs, matching the sensation I felt inside me. Gideon was *inside me*; not his cock yet, but still.

"You can try another one now."

He nodded and did. This one went in easier than the first, my body already learning to open and accept him. He used those two on me for a while before I felt more pressure and knew he was trying to work a third finger in. I thrust into his mouth, threaded my fingers through his hair, trying to hold on, but it was too short to grab much.

"You okay?" he asked, nuzzling my sac. "I have three in you."

"Yeah...it's different. I feel really full, but I'm getting used to it."

"Good." He kissed my balls—one, then the other—before going back to my cock. He sucked me, savored me, treated me like I was the most precious thing in the world to him, like I was to be cherished, and Gideon was making it his mission in life to do just that.

Each push of his fingers became easier. There was still pressure and fullness, but it wasn't bad, just something I was getting used to.

"Jesus, Lo. I can't believe I get to do this. You're so fucking sexy, so fucking *mine*."

"Yes. That. Will you fuck me now?" I mean, the man had just said I was his, and I wanted to be that because Gideon felt like he was mine.

He chuckled. "Yeah, let's do this."

It was weird when he pulled his fingers out. I felt empty, which should feel normal, but it didn't. Gideon ripped open the wrapper, then rolled the condom down his erection. He pumped some lube into his hand and slicked himself up.

"Is this how you want to do it?"

"Yes. I'm pretty bendy when I want to be. I don't

think I'll be able to relax if I'm not looking at you." And I wasn't ready to try and ride him yet.

"Okay. We got this." He positioned the pillow better. I opened my legs more, lifted them back some, while he knelt there, holding the base of his erection, then nudging at my ass.

"Go slow."

"I will. I'll take care of you." Most ways I hated that; I didn't want to be taken care of, but I remembered how it felt to do that with Gideon, and in this, with sex, I needed that from him.

Gideon didn't let his gaze stray from mine as he started to push in. The stretching sensation was a little uncomfortable, but I wanted this. I wanted him. I stroked myself as he slowly worked his way in…pressure, fullness, stretching. "Can I talk to you? I know you don't always like it."

"Yes, please do," I replied.

"You feel so perfect. Hot and tight. I've never been more turned on in my life, Lo. Never felt so goddamned fortunate. I still can't believe you chose me. You're the sexiest thing I've ever seen."

I didn't know about that, but hearing it did help. Gideon kept talking to me, telling me what it felt like, touching me, easing in, watching me, until he smiled.

"You took it. I'm all the way in. How do you feel?"

I felt... It was... I looked down, saw our bodies, knew he was inside me, that we were a part of each other in this totally new way—and my cock jerked. Oh yes, I was going to like this. "I feel full, but good. Connected to you, but not just in the obvious way. Like I feel it in my chest too." His lips stretched wider. "Should you move now?"

"It's killing me not to."

"Please don't die."

"I won't."

Gideon pulled back, then thrust in again, and... "Oh! Again." He did, over and over and over. "God, Gideon. Fuck me. Please fuck me." This was why people asked for it. This was why people told their partners to do what they were already doing; because it was perfect, and wonderful, and each time his dick moved inside me, pleasure zinged down my spine.

I stroked myself faster, closed my eyes.

"Look at me. I want you to look at me while I fuck you."

And that should be so annoying, but it wasn't. I opened my eyes and watched him, our gazes locked as Gideon pumped his hips, fucking me and loving me and making me feel even more like I was his. Topping was fantastic, but having someone in your body, being full of them and stretched by them was indescribable. I had a feeling it was only like that because it was Gideon.

He bent forward as if he was going to kiss me, and I wanted it, wanted it so bad, but then I remembered what he'd done to me, where his mouth and tongue had been. As if he could read my thoughts, Gideon stopped, then just rubbed his cheek against mine.

This was perfect. It was everything. I wondered how long we had to wait to do it again.

"Fuck, I'm not going to last," Gideon admitted.

"Me neither."

The sound of our bodies slapping together filled the room, dancing with sporadic words and sharp breaths.

It felt like it came out of nowhere, like one second I was fine and the next my body was shattering in the best possible way. Like I was feeling everything I had ever enjoyed in that one moment when my sac tightened and my load spurted from my cock. Cum splattered on my stomach and chest, another pulse each time Gideon thrust his hips forward, until he'd drained my balls.

"Fuck!" he growled, his dick spasming, his jaw tight, and his muscles flexing as he came inside me. That was exactly what it felt like, as if there was no condom between us and my body had milked an orgasm out of him to keep it deep inside.

My vision was fuzzy, my body loose and so relaxed I felt like I could melt into a puddle on the bed. Gideon kissed my forehead, my lips, my neck as laughter bubbled from deep in my chest, spilling from my lips. I was so happy and sated and in love. "I like that…a lot. I like you. I want to do it again. Not tonight, because I'm going to be sore, but soon. Gideon…you were *inside me*."

He smiled. "I know. I liked it too."

I pulled him down so he was against me, not caring about the cum between us. I just needed to touch him everywhere. I squeezed him tight, never wanting to come down from this high.

I was half-asleep when I heard his phone go off. "Who is it?" I asked.

"Just my brother. It's no biggie." Gideon turned it off, and I slipped into darkness.

CHAPTER TWENTY-EIGHT

Gideon

I COULDN'T GET over last night.

I'd lost my virginity at eighteen, and I'd hooked up with a lot of guys since then, but none of it had ever felt like that. It wasn't the sex so much as it was the fact that Milo trusted me, that he gave me that piece of himself even though he was nervous and wasn't sure if it would be for him; that he knew if we started and he didn't like it or wasn't comfortable, that I would stop, no questions asked, and would never make him feel bad about it.

But entangled together with all that was guilt because I hadn't gone to Orlando's party, and I hadn't told Milo about it. So, I'd not only ditched my brother, but I'd kept his birthday get-together from my boyfriend. I had to admit, that wasn't a good look.

I'd wanted to tell Milo last night, but it hadn't seemed right after the sex. I knew Milo well enough to know he'd put thought into our night before it happened, and I hadn't wanted to be like…*Well, my bro is getting drunk at the Lighthouse. Wanna go hang out there when we both know you'll probably hate it?* But what excuse did I have for not telling him earlier? And hell, if I was being honest, I still could've said something after we'd been together. We could have gone late. Orlando had texted to ask where I was. That would have been the perfect opportunity.

I tried to tell myself Orlando would understand. People didn't make it to parties all the time, but I still felt uncomfortable about it, and I hated that. When we'd woken, I'd planned to tell him, but then Beverly showed up with doughnuts for us and coffee for her since neither Milo nor I drank it.

Every time Milo looked at me, he would blush. I figured Beverly had to know something was up, but she didn't say anything, and thankfully Milo didn't either. She didn't need more reasons not to like me.

After breakfast, Beverly went to the bookstore with Milo. She did that often. She would work on her laptop there, just to be close to him. It was clear how much Milo meant to her, which was why I couldn't be too angry with her for hating me. She wanted what was best for her son, and even though I loved him and would do anything for him, she had no reason to believe that.

My first appointment wasn't until two, so I cleaned up the apartment and texted my brother, who was probably hung over and still asleep. **Sorry about last night. I'll make it up to you.**

I didn't tell him I hadn't gone because I didn't think Milo would want to. My choice had been my own. I could have gone without him. I'd chosen not to.

A few minutes after twelve, my phone buzzed with a text. I expected it to be Orlando, but it was Milo. **Mom wants us to go out to lunch with her!**

I was fairly certain she wanted to go out to lunch with Milo and not me.

You too! She said. She's trying, he added as if I'd spoken my concerns to him.

I'll be right down.

I locked up and went to the bookstore. Beverly and Milo were waiting outside. He grabbed my hand, knotted our fingers together, and kissed my cheek.

"Hey, you," I told him.

"I missed you."

"I missed you too."

When my eyes darted toward Beverly, she was watching us.

"We should get going. I figured we could go to the

Lighthouse," she said, and we agreed easily.

She didn't talk much on the walk there, but she never did around me. She was so different from Milo, so much more closed off, keeping the walls high to protect herself. "Is it pretty easy to get work done remotely?" I asked, trying to make conversation.

"There are some things I can't do, but a lot I can."

"Yeah, I bet. It's nice that you have the freedom to come here and stay so long, though. Maybe Milo and I can come out to San Diego sometime too."

He stopped, pulling me with him. Milo's gaze bore into mine, all soft and mushy like I'd just saved a kitten from sudden death, while I tried to figure out what the fuck I'd said to cause that look.

"I don't have to go," I told him. "You can always go by yourself too." I hadn't meant to make it sound like I was hijacking his hypothetical trip to see his mom.

"I want you to go. I just didn't know you would want to. That's serious."

Fuck, he was so adorable. "Lo…we're boyfriends, and we live together. It's pretty serious."

"I guess we are."

"I'm glad you agree."

"The two of you are ridiculous," Beverly added, but I could have sworn there was amusement in her voice. "Are we going to lunch or standing on the sidewalk all day?"

"We're going to lunch." Milo began walking again.

The Lighthouse had its typical lunch rush, so it was fairly loud and busy inside. I risked a glance at Milo, but he seemed okay, so I didn't mention it. When my gaze locked on Beverly next, I was pretty sure she had just done the same thing.

We plucked menus from the lobster claws and looked them over just before Drea, our waitress, came over.

"How's everyone doing today, and what can I get you to drink?"

Milo and Beverly just got water, and I asked for Sprite.

"What do you like here?" Beverly asked.

I kept reading my menu until Milo nudged me and I realized she was talking to me. Anytime we spoke, it was typically me who started the conversation.

"Oh, um, just about everything is good. I often get a burger or a steak, but they have great lobster and crab too. Their shrimp scampi is the best around."

My leg bounced against Milo's, and he rested his hand on my thigh. *Holy shit, your mom just asked me a question*, I wanted to tell him, but I bit it back.

"I'll try the shrimp scampi, then," Beverly said. "That was always my favorite when I was growing up too."

She ordered first when Drea came back. I got fish and chips, and Milo a tomato, mozzarella salad, and a baked potato.

"How is the tattoo business on the island?" she asked me next.

"I can't lie and say it's the best, but it could be worse. Some times are busier than others. I'll never be a rich man, but I don't really care about that. I just want to be happy." Though a little more money wouldn't hurt.

"Me too," Milo replied. "As long as I can keep the store in the black, I'm okay."

That reminded me I wanted to talk to Milo about paying more in rent. He was lucky the building was paid off, but there were still taxes and other expenses to consider. It was important to me that it didn't ever feel like I was taking advantage of him. Now wasn't the time, though.

"You boys need to consider your future. Even with the money I have put aside for Milo, you never know what will happen," Beverly said.

"Then I'll do taxes on the side," he replied, but I was stuck on the whole *you boys need to consider your future*. She'd said it as if she was sure I would be a part of Milo's and that she was okay with it.

"Yes, ma'am," I replied. "I've been thinking about

trying to find something else part-time anyway."

"What? Why?" Milo asked.

"Because we both know I pay less than the going rate for rent."

"I don't care about that." Milo waved his hand.

"But I do."

"Oh," he said, and I knew he got what I was saying. Milo had said before he didn't want to need me, and I didn't want to need him either. We were a unit, yes, but I wanted to carry my fair share. "Okay."

We talked for a few more minutes before Drea showed up with our food. I waited while Beverly took a bite, and she said, "Just as good as I remembered."

"I'm glad you like it," I told her.

"Beverly! Look at you. I can't believe you're really back," Gillian Withrow said, approaching our table. She was a few years younger than Beverly and had lived on the island her whole life. I was surprised this didn't happen more often, that more people didn't approach Beverly when she was out. Some did, of course, but it could be worse. Maybe everyone knew Beverly wasn't to be fucked with—well, everyone except Gillian.

"How have you been?" Beverly asked.

"Not bad. I was real sorry when Wilma passed away. It came as a shock to everyone when we learned about you…being her daughter and all."

There were some things one shouldn't say to people, and Gillian's statement was firmly on that list.

"Gillian," I started, just as Beverly said, "Well, I wasn't, and really, it's no one's business other than mine and Wilma's. But then you've always had a habit of sticking your nose where it doesn't belong."

"Oh…I'm sorry. I didn't mean any offense." Gillian feigned innocence, though she clearly just wanted to gossip and see Beverly's reaction.

"Of course you didn't, dear," Beverly replied, and I actually fell a little bit in love with her when she did. A small chuckle escaped my lips.

"My Alfred was at the bar with friends last night," Gillian said, looking at me. "Everyone was surprised you weren't at your brother's birthday party. Orlando was pretty disappointed from what I heard."

I felt Milo tense beside me. Goddamn it. He turned to me, and the second he did, I knew I'd fucked up—and I'd fucked up big-time. The devastation in his eyes felt like he'd punched through my chest and ripped my heart out; no, like I'd torn my own out.

"Orlando had a birthday party, and you didn't go?"

"It's not a big deal. I wasn't in the mood."

Milo shook his head, then rocked, similarly to what

I'd seen the night of the grand opening. "Don't do that. Don't lie to me. He had a party, and you not only didn't go, you didn't tell me about it… You didn't tell me because…" He cocked his head. "You didn't want me to go?"

Worry, shame, and guilt created a storm inside me, one with enough power to tear my world apart. "What? No. That's not it at all." He was shaking slightly, pulling away from me. "Let's go home. We'll talk about it there."

"No." He shook his head again, repeating, "No, no, no."

"If you'll excuse us, Gillian, we'd greatly appreciate it," Beverly said, but I didn't pull my gaze away from Milo to see if she'd listened.

My heart didn't feel like it had been pulled out anymore; it was there, banging against my chest. My stomach twisted up, knots of discomfort and anger at myself tying tighter and tighter. "I'm sorry. I fucked up. I just didn't want…"

"Didn't want me to freak out like I did last time. You didn't think I could handle it, but we'll never know if I could, or even if I would have wanted to try, because you didn't give me a choice, Gideon. That's not fair. You don't do that to boyfriends, and you don't do that to *friends*. You should have given me a *choice*."

Without another word, he shoved to his feet and walked out of the Lighthouse. Gillian was gone, but I didn't care. I just wanted to fix this, wanted never to have done something so stupid in the first place. Why hadn't I just told him? "Fuck." I rested my elbows on the table and buried my face in my hands. My legs were bouncing, unable to keep still. "I have to go talk to him."

"Give him some time," Beverly said. "He's angry, and he's hurt. When he's like that, he needs some space to process what he's feeling. Then, you fix it."

I dropped my hands and looked at her.

"You love him," she said. It wasn't a question because she knew the answer.

"Yes."

She nodded before looking down. "Good. That's good. He deserves that. I didn't give you a fair chance at first, but I see it now. You're good for him."

"He's good for me."

"You're good for each other," Beverly replied.

"Yeah, we are." I didn't know why he'd chosen me, but I would spend every day of my life making sure it was the right decision. "It wasn't that I thought he couldn't handle it, and I wouldn't be embarrassed if he struggled. I just…"

"Didn't want him to get hurt."

"Yes." But instead, I'd done that myself. I'd been the one to hurt him.

"We can't protect him from the world. Milo can do that for himself. I forget that sometimes—maybe more than sometimes—but he won't have it, nor should he have to deal with it." Beverly stood. "The two of you will work it out." She reached into her purse.

"No, I got it," I said. There were three basically untouched meals on the table.

"My treat next time." Beverly smiled, reached over, squeezed my hand, and walked out.

I hoped like hell she was right.

I WENT BACK to the shop but didn't let myself look inside the bookstore on the way there. Beverly said I needed to give him time. He'd walked away for space, and he deserved for me to respect him enough to give it to him. Approaching him at work would be a dick move. I couldn't stop myself from sending him a text, though, just to touch base. **I'm sorry. I fucked up. Can we talk later?**

I'm really upset. I'll let you know when I calm down. I might stay at the hotel tonight. I have to sort through my feelings.

You can stay at the apartment. I'll stay with Orlando. You won't be able to sleep if you don't have your bed. It was silly that the thought made me smile. I remembered picking him up that first morning and how grumpy he was… Jesus, even back then I was crazy about him. From the first moment I met him, I had been.

I can handle it, Gideon. I'm going back to work now.

Okay, I replied and put my phone away. I wasn't going to push. I'd respect what Milo asked of me.

I had a few pieces that day and ended up working until about six. When I finished, I didn't have a message from Orlando *or* Milo. I'd managed to piss them both off.

I didn't go straight home. I got into my truck and drove around until I ended up at my parents' place. I didn't know what I was doing there. Part of me wanted to back right out of the driveway and leave, but I didn't. Instead, I got out, knocked, and went inside. Mom was cooking dinner. "Gideon, what a surprise," she said, then frowned. "What's wrong?"

I sat on a stool at the island, across from her. "I screwed up with Milo. We had a fight because I didn't tell him about Orlando's party. And Orlando's mad at me because I didn't go. I managed to fuck it up with both of them." I couldn't believe I was sharing this with her. It wasn't my typical MO, but I was so fucking tired. And sad and angry with myself.

"Well, I'd imagine neither of them is really mad at you, but they're hurt."

"I know." And I really did. I could also understand why they were. "Do you wish I were different?" I found myself asking.

She turned off the stove. "What? No, absolutely not. Why would I wish that?"

"I don't know. Sometimes I think Dad does, that he wishes I were straight, or that I went to law school like him and Orlando, or hell, that I went to college at all. He doesn't talk to me like he does with Orlando. He—"

"Do I really make you feel that way?" Dad asked from behind me. I hadn't realized he was there.

I turned to see him standing in the doorway. He was in slacks, a button-up shirt, and a tie, likely having gone to his office on the mainland even though it was Saturday.

"I never meant for you to think that. I guess sometimes…sometimes maybe I don't feel like I know how to talk to you the way I do with Orlando. We don't have as much in common, and maybe I thought in some ways *you* wished *I* were different. You're so independent and fearless. You are who you are, and you've never shied away from that. While I've always followed the rules, you've made your own. And sometimes, maybe I envy your ability to march to the beat of your own drum in a way I never had the courage to do. But no, I don't wish you were anyone other than who you are. Clearly, I don't always do a good job of showing you that."

I opened my mouth but wasn't sure what to say. How did one respond to that? I'd spent my whole life not feeling up to his standards, and then he says this? "You think I'm fearless?"

"Yes, though maybe that's not the right word. We all fear something, don't we? But you never let it hold you back. I went to school to be a lawyer like my father because it was safe and all I knew. I ask you how the shop is doing because I can't just let go and trust that everything will be okay the way you can. It's a gift, Gideon, and I'm so proud of you."

"I worry about things too. If the shop will last, what will happen with me and Milo. If I'm making the right choices."

"I know, but you keep going regardless. You follow your dreams, and you take chances. That's something to be proud of, Gideon," Dad said, and I could see it, his pride in me, his insecurity when it came to how to talk to me. Orlando was right; it was a two-way street.

"I love you, son," Dad added, making my eyes sting.

"I love you too."

Mom was crying, and I shoved to my feet, hugged her, then went to my dad and hugged him too. We saw each other often, yet I couldn't remember the last time I'd hugged him. We stayed that way for a long time, then sat down to talk.

I had dinner with my parents, just the three of us. It was another thing I couldn't remember the last time we'd done it. Orlando and Heather were always there, and often Meg and Kris too.

After we ate, Dad and I made a promise to spend more time together and share more of ourselves with each other.

When I got back into my truck, I called my brother. "I'm a dick," I said instead of hello.

"Obviously."

"I'm sorry."

"As you should be."

"I shouldn't have no-showed, and it was an asshole move to ignore your text."

"No," Orlando replied. "You shouldn't have ditched me. You could have told me you were staying with Milo. I would have understood."

"Yeah, I see that now. I fucked up this whole situation. I didn't even tell Milo about the party, and now he's mad at me."

"As he should be," Orlando repeated. "You gonna fix it?"

"I am." Because now that I had Milo, I couldn't imagine my life without him.

CHAPTER TWENTY-NINE

Milo

"MILO...YOU DO KNOW that stomping across the hotel room all night isn't going to solve anything, right?" Mom said, and I stopped and crossed my arms.

"I had no idea. Thank you for telling me."

Mom sighed. "Sit down." She patted the bed beside her. She was perched on the end of it, watching me.

"I don't want to sit down."

"Please, Milo."

I groaned but walked over and joined her. "He didn't think I could handle it, and I hate that he may have been right," I admitted. "I don't want to be held back, and I don't want to hold him back. I want to go out with my boyfriend and his brother and their friends."

"Did you ever stop and think that maybe that's why Gideon didn't tell you?" I opened my mouth to argue, but she continued. "I'm not saying he was right—at all. I'm saying he knows how bad you want them to like you and how bad you want to be a part of his life, so he knew you might not be thinking clearly when you answered. Would you have pushed through and said yes, even if you had your doubts?"

I looked down, not liking that the answer would be yes. "He still should've given me the choice. Or he should've gone himself. That's the worst part—not that I didn't know, but that I held Gideon back. He missed an important day with his brother because certain situations are hard for me. I love him, and I don't ever want him to miss out on parts of life because of me."

It wasn't fair. I finally had a boyfriend, but he'd chosen to stay home and not go out and enjoy himself because of my issues. How long would it be before Gideon got tired of that? Before it made him break up with me?

"That's understandable because you love him and don't want to be the reason he doesn't do certain things. But first, Gideon made that choice himself; you had nothing to do with it. Second, all couples make sacrifices for each other sometimes. That's not reserved only for you and Gideon, just like wanting to protect those you love isn't either. I know how independent and capable you are. I'd bet Gideon does too. If he didn't, you wouldn't love him. It's everyone's first instinct to try and protect those important to them. If you knew something might hurt me, wouldn't you try to keep that from happening?"

Oh, I saw where she was going with this. I nodded.

"And if you worried about Gideon or Rachel or Cammy, wouldn't you try to protect them too? That's part of what love is…and Gideon loves you. No, he shouldn't have kept the party from you, and yes, you absolutely deserve the right to make your own decisions. There are boundaries the two of you need to discuss, but every relationship has those, not just yours. You've always wanted to live a normal life, whatever your definition of normal is. I don't like that word at all, but that's what you wanted, and that's what you have. Couples fight, people screw up, and sometimes people we love hurt us, but that doesn't mean they don't love us or…*oh*."

With that one last word, I knew Mom was seeing her own situation with Wilma and Gene. Wilma had hurt her, but that didn't mean she hadn't loved her. Wilma was gone, yes, but Mom could still make her peace with her and hear her story.

"Adulting sucks," I said, and she chuckled.

"Yes, it does."

"But it's kind of amazing too, isn't it?"

Mom smiled. "Yes, it is. And so are you." She reached over and held my hand.

"Do you really think Gideon loves me? He's never said it."

"I do, but maybe you should talk to him about that. Have you told him you love him?" I shook my head. "And that doesn't mean you don't, so buck up. Go talk to your man and tell him how you feel."

She was…God, she was the absolute best. "I love you." I scooted closer and pulled Mom into a hug.

"I love you too, Milo. More than anything in this world. And I'm so damn happy for you. You've built a beautiful life here. The place I always felt stifled me is the one that has helped set you free."

It had. Life was funny that way sometimes. I'd never thought I totally knew who I was or what I wanted, and through her love for my mom, Wilma had helped me find myself…in a bookstore, on an island, with my tattoo guy and my best friend Rachel, her daughter, Cammy, with Gene and Gideon's family too. I had those people because of Wilma.

"We're so alike, you and I. We don't want to need anyone, but make sure that stubbornness doesn't cause you to miss out on life the way I let it."

"It's never too late to change, Mom."

"I suppose it's not." She swiped at a couple of stray tears. "If I expect you to be brave and put your faith in people, I guess I should too. Maybe tomorrow you and I can go see Gene. The two of you can tell me about Wilma."

I smiled. "I'd like that. He would too."

Mom nodded, straightened her spine, and I knew the emotional stuff was over for her. "Now maybe you should go home and talk to that boyfriend of yours."

"I will." I practically bounced to my feet. "Thank you. You're the best mom ever, and I love you, even though you annoy me sometimes."

Mom laughed. "I love you, even though you annoy me sometimes too."

"I need to order a car. I'm going home…to tell Gideon I love him."

I'd still give him a piece of my mind, though, too.

CHAPTER THIRTY

Gideon

WAS IT RIDICULOUS that I sat on the couch with my cell in my hand, trying to will a text message from Milo? Because that's exactly what I was doing.

Can I come see you, please? I'd sent it an hour ago, and still no response. Not hearing from him was eating me alive.

I wanted to tell him I was sorry and that I loved him.

I wanted to tell him about talking to Dad and Orlando.

Basically, I just wanted him.

My eyes shot to the door when I heard a key in the lock. It opened just as I pushed to my feet, and there he was, his hair actually messy like he'd run his fingers through it in nerves or frustration.

"Hi," I said.

"I need to take off my pants for this."

I grinned, struggled to breathe slightly because my chest swelled so big. "Listen, I—"

"Gideon! Don't talk yet! Let me finish."

God, he was ridiculous and adorable, and I loved him so fucking much.

I waited while he took his shoes off, then his socks, and finally his pants. He stood straight before sighing, his shoulders rising and lowering in a dramatic shrug. "I've never had a fight with a boyfriend before."

"I've never done such a dumbass thing as a boyfriend before."

"Gid," he said softly, walking over to me. "I understand why you did what you did. I'm your best friend and your boyfriend, and you didn't want to see me get hurt. I want to protect you when I can too, but there are some things we can't shield each other from. You can't handpick every social interaction we have. You can't shelter me from every possible uncomfortable situation. I'm autistic. This is my life. This is who I am. And if we're going to be together—and I really, really want us to be together—then you have to respect that. You have to give me a *choice*."

"I know. Fuck, I know, and I did it for completely selfish reasons too. It's hard to see you like that." When you loved someone, you wanted to fix things that hurt them, and I couldn't do that for Milo.

"Too hard?" he asked.

My pulse jumped. "No, fuck no."

"Because this isn't a temporary thing. I will always have my idiosyncrasies, and sometimes they might change. And sometimes we won't know what one is until it happens. There might be days you'll invite me out and it'll be fine, and times I might hate it, and there will be times I'll tell you I don't even want to go. I know it doesn't always make things easy, but I'm not sorry about who I am. I like me."

"Jesus, Lo." I stepped close to him, risked reaching over to cup his cheek, and he let me. "I'm not sorry about who you are either. I'm so fucking crazy about you. Don't you know that?" He looked up at me with big, blue, trusting eyes that had the key to unlock everything inside me. "I'm in love with you."

His pupils blew wide, but then he jerked backward. "Noooo. You weren't supposed to say that."

My insides froze up. My heart stopped beating. Holy shit. He didn't feel the same. It wasn't every day you spilled your heart to a guy, and he answered with, *Nah, I'm good.* "It's okay if you're not there yet. I just, um...wanted you to know?" Fuck my life.

"What? Oh! No. That's not what I meant. I just

wanted to tell you first. I had it all planned out! Mom said you loved me, but I didn't believe her. I was going to tell you anyway because it's true, and I wanted to be brave and tell you, regardless of whether you felt the same."

His words shocked me back to life, a defibrillator pulsing electrical currents through my heart. "Say what?"

"I love you."

"I just wanted to hear the words. You didn't actually use them."

"But I'm still frustrated you said it first."

"Milo, your boyfriend just admitted he's crazy in love with you, and you're annoyed he said it before you?"

"Yes, yes I am."

I laughed. "God, I love you."

His face split open in a smile. "I love you too. You make me happy in ways I didn't know I needed. You're smart, kind, funny, and talented. You accept people as they are. You accept me, and you love me for it, for all those pieces of me that other people think are strange. You are…" He stepped in closer again, wrapping his arms around my waist. "My favorite person in the whole world…even when you make mistakes."

"Thankfully, it's regardless of my screw-ups. If you'd come home earlier, you would have realized I forgot to add tomatoes to the shopping list. Don't worry, I fixed it."

"Gideon! You should just do it when you use something so you don't forget."

"I'm learning." I wrapped my arms around him. "You're my favorite person too. You make me feel wanted, and that's even better than feeling needed. I never had that before you. I didn't feel wanted or like I belonged. Even if it doesn't make sense to others, and even if we're different, we fit together, Lo." I brushed the back of my hand against his cheek. "I'm sorry I hurt you. I don't ever want you to feel like I don't trust your judgment or that I'm embarrassed of what might happen. But you have to understand that I'm not perfect, that I'll make mistakes and so will you."

"I know." He looked down. "I think I put you on a pedestal. You've always been different with me than other people. That's why it hit me so hard."

"We're both going to have to get used to this. There might be some stumbling along the way, but we can do it. I want to be with you."

He nodded. "And I also wanted to say that it's okay if sometimes you don't…like, if someone has a party and you just don't want to risk it or to worry about me, all you have to do is tell me. The worst part was that you stayed home instead of going. Orlando messaged you that night, and you still didn't go. You can't do that, Gideon. Ever. You can ask me if I want to go, or you can tell me you'd rather go alone, but don't keep it to yourself and stay home. I won't be the guy who makes you miss out."

"You also need to be honest with me if you're unsure about a situation," I said. When he agreed, I added, "Everything is better when you're there."

"Are you trying to get into my pants? Because yes, you totally can. I'd really like to kiss you now."

"I'd like to kiss you all the time."

"Me too. I like that. I change my answer to that."

I dropped my mouth to his, and he immediately let my tongue inside. I would never get used to the way he melted against me, to the want that thrummed through him and seemed to say my name.

We kissed our way to the couch before I lay down and pulled him on top of me. We made out for a while, and then Milo took off our clothes, got on his knees, sucked me until I was close to coming, then finished me off with his hand, my load painting his chest.

He cleaned us up. Sometimes he did that; sometimes he didn't. When he was done, I tugged him down to lie with me again. "I talked to Dad," I said, and relayed the whole conversation to him.

He pressed his lips to mine. "I'm so proud of

you…and you're worthy and wanted and awesome at sex."

I chuckled. "Well, thank God for that."

"Mom wants to talk to Gene," he added. "I'm going to take her there tomorrow. I don't think she hates you anymore."

"I don't think so either."

We lay there quietly for a few minutes, my fingers dancing up and down his spine, Milo's cheek on my chest. "Gid?"

"Yeah?"

"Know how I talk about us being bestie goals? Like all other best friends should want to be like us?"

"I do, and you have a point."

I didn't have to see his smile—I could feel it. "Now we're boyfriend goals. We're basically the best boyfriends ever."

"Oh, for sure."

"Everyone should want to be like us."

"I agree." Our bodies vibrated together in laughter. There was nothing like being with him, having fun with him.

"I love you, Gid."

"I love you too."

"I said it first this time. I win."

"You're ridiculous."

"Hey, do you think you can get it up again? I kinda want to have sex."

I let loose another chuckle. "What am I going to do with you?"

"Love me, laugh with me, have sex with me."

"Totally boyfriend goals."

That sounded perfect to me.

EPILOGUE

Milo

Three years later

"EXCUSE ME? MR. Sign Guy? It's not straight," I said to the man who was currently on a ladder in front of our building. "We should have done it ourselves. I told you, Gid; we should have done it ourselves."

"He's not done," Gideon replied just as one of the sign guys said, "We're not done yet."

We'd just finished another remodel, this time knocking down part of the wall between Conflicting Ink and Little Beach Books. We put in glass doors. We wouldn't always want them open, and maybe to some people it was strange, this combination of bookstore and tattoo parlor, but we liked the idea and we were us, so who cared what anyone else thought.

"Oh my God. What are they doing? They're not doing it right."

"Lo…it's fine. Relax."

"How many times do I have to tell you that saying *relax* doesn't work?"

"I love you? Wanna have sex?"

"Cheater!" I teased. "It really is a cute sign." In large letters it read: INK & INK. On the left side, in small print, it said *Conflicting Ink*, with an image of a hand holding a tattoo machine; on the right were books and my store's name.

It was basically perfect.

Kind of like us.

It had been an interesting three years. Gideon had taken a part-time job for a while, determined to pull in more money. He'd wanted to pay me more, but that was just silly. We were in love, and I owned the building. I didn't want his rent for the apartment or the tattoo parlor. So he'd put it away and had paid for this remodel, and we would now split the taxes every year. It worked.

"Let's get out of here," Gideon said.

"Absolutely not."

"Lo…"

"Ugh. Fine. I hate you sometimes."

"We have to go to Mom and Dad's for lunch anyway."

He was right, we did, and I loved going over there, so

I didn't pout too much.

Rachel had graduated from college, so she didn't work with me anymore, but we still hung out all the time. Besides Gideon, she was still my best friend. She had a new boyfriend, and I'd been a little worried how that would go. I wasn't for everyone, and what if Rach fell in love with someone who didn't like me? She'd said she would kick him to the curb if that was the case, but I would never expect that.

Luckily, Dontrell was really great. He treated Rachel the way she deserved, loved Cammy, and got along with me and Gid. Cammy was still one of my favorite people too. Sometimes, she'd just hang out with me and Gideon for the day.

A woman named Serena worked with me now, and I liked her a lot too. She was older than us, in her forties, loved reading, and wasn't just looking for something to fill her time while she finished school, so she was perfect.

We headed for Gideon's truck. The whole time to his parents' house, I stressed out about the sign. "Why is micromanaging such a bad thing?"

"Do you like it when people do it to you?" Gideon asked.

"We're not talking about me."

He laughed. "Point proven. They'll do a great job. If

we have an issue, they'll do it again."

Everyone was already in the backyard when we arrived. Jacob was three now. He and I weren't sure about each other, but we were making it work. That's what family did.

Heather was pregnant again. We wanted them to keep having all the babies so no one asked us about them.

Kris and Orlando were building a sandcastle with Jacob and Aria, Kris and Megan's little girl.

"Snacks!" Orlando waved.

"Be nice to my boyfriend," I told him.

"Yeah, be nice to Milo's boyfriend," Gideon added.

"Unca Gid! Unca Lo!" Jacob climbed to his feet and ran over to us. Apparently today was a good day between us. He was even more finicky than I was.

"What's up, little man?" Gideon scooped him into his arms. It was totally adorable but not enough to make me want to adopt kids of our own. I liked being able to spend time with them and then give them back if they were too loud or hyper. It was a good gig.

"Hello, Jacob." I shook his hand. It was our thing. I possibly liked him more than I wanted to admit. I was the first person to have said hello to him, after all.

"Milo, I made a new vegetarian recipe. Come taste it," Annemarie said. She was always trying to make new things for me, which was really sweet.

I kissed Gideon's cheek just as his dad came over. They'd gotten closer over the past few years, making it a point to spend time together, just the two of them.

I said hello to him, then went over to taste Annemarie's new creation. It was a cauliflower cake with a kick of spice. "I approve."

She laughed. "I'm glad. How's your mama doing?"

"Good. She'll be here next month." She'd bought a small, one-bedroom house on the island. While she still lived in California, she spent about three weeks here, three times a year. Gideon and I went to California to see her too.

Grandpa Gene had told her she could stay with him, but Mom was funny about things like that. They spent a lot of time together every visit, though, and even when she was in San Diego, they talked on the phone at least once a week.

I didn't know how much longer he would be able to live on his own, so Gid or I stopped by to check on him every day. I didn't want him to go to a home, and we'd actually talked about moving into his house to help take care of him, though no decisions had been made.

Also, Mom had forgiven Grandma. I still loved calling her that. Wilma had become Grandma to me the day

Gene became Grandpa. Anytime someone annoyed me and I wanted to stay mad at them, I thought about Grandma and how she had died before I got the chance to get to know her. Life was too short to hold grudges.

Lunch was good, with lots of laughter and nitpicking, but it wasn't long before I needed some space. Before I had the chance to mention it, Gideon said, "We better head out. We need to go see Gene for a while and then check on the store." We'd invited him, but he hadn't been feeling great.

I loved that no one argued or asked why we were leaving so early. I hugged Megan and Heather, then told the kids goodbye, including, of course, baby Penelope in Heather's belly.

It was a quick drive to Gene's. We knocked, then opened the door. "Grandpa?" I called out. I still couldn't believe sometimes how much my life had changed. I had a grandpa and a boyfriend and so much more family.

"Out back," Gene replied.

He was sitting on the swing I'd built him in Grandma's garden. "How are you today?"

Grandpa smiled at me. "Feeling a bit better. Life is good. Just wish she were here to enjoy it with us."

"Me too," I replied, and Gideon squeezed my hand in support.

We spent about an hour there with him before heading home. Everything was good at the store, and the sign was right, which helped me relax.

Later that night, we were home, naked in bed, after Gideon had fucked me. We didn't use condoms now, and I still couldn't swallow, but I was okay with him coming inside my ass, which we both liked a lot. It was really hot.

"We should get married," I said. I'd thought about it, but hadn't planned on actually saying it to him. I didn't regret it, though. Using the words out loud just told me how much I wanted it.

"What?" Gideon fumbled to turn the lamp on.

"We should get married," I repeated.

"Are you serious?"

"If you want to. If you don't, that's okay too, but I just thought—"

"Yes," Gideon cut me off. "Yes, I would love to marry you."

"Really? Oh my God. I totally just proposed to you. I can't wait to tell Rachel."

"I can't wait to be your husband."

I smiled. "I can't wait for that either."

He kissed me, and we maybe got each other off again.

I loved that none of this was too weird for him. That it didn't matter if we didn't have rings yet and no one had gotten down on one knee. It had just happened and was just right, like everything about Gid and me.

Who knew that a phone call from a strange man named Chester would change my life? I had my grandma to thank for it—Wilma, who always loved me, though she'd never met me.

"Gid?"

"Yeah?"

"Can we still say we're boyfriend goals even when we're husbands? I mean, we can say husband goals, but it'll take me some time to get used to it."

"We're us, Lo. We can say and do anything we want. That's how we roll."

Yes, it was, and even though neither of us was perfect, we kind of were together.

Find Riley:

Newsletter

Reader's Group
facebook.com/groups/RileysRebels2.0

Facebook
facebook.com/rileyhartwrites

Twitter
twitter.com/RileyHart5

Goodreads
goodreads.com/author/show/7013384.Riley_Hart

Instagram
instagram.com/rileyhartwrites

BookBub
bookbub.com/profile/riley-hart

Thank You

Each and every day, I wake up thankful that I get to do what I love, thankful that I get to tell stories, give happily ever afters, and that there are people who enjoy reading them. As always, to each and every person who has picked up my books, thank you. I couldn't do this without you.

This book... There are no words for how much I enjoyed telling Milo and Gideon's story. I wrote the whole thing with the biggest smile on my face. Thank you for taking this journey with us. I hope you enjoyed hanging on Little Beach Island with the crew. I'll tell you a secret... We're probably not supposed to have favorites, but Milo is one of my favorite characters I've ever written. I wanted to do him justice so badly, and I hope I did.

If you have time, I'd love a review for Boyfriend Goals on your favorite review site like Goodreads or BookBub. They help authors immensely. Also, if you'd like to keep in touch and get updates on future releases, giveaways, and any upcoming news, you can always join my newsletter and my reader group.

Thanks for reading!
Riley

Series by Riley Hart

Secrets Kept
Briar County
Atlanta Lightning
Blackcreek
Boys In Makeup with Christina Lee
Broken Pieces
Crossroads
Fever Falls with Devon McCormack
Finding
Forbidden Love with Christina Lee
Havenwood
Jared and Kieran
Last Chance
Metropolis with Devon McCormack
Rock Solid Construction
Saint and Lucky
Stumbling Into Love
Wild side

Standalone books:
Strings Attached
Beautiful & Terrible Things

Love Always
Endless Stretch Of Blue
Looking For Trouble
His Truth

Standalone books with Devon McCormack:
No Good Mitchell
Beautiful Chaos
Weight Of The World
Up For The Challenge

Standalone books with Christina Lee:
Science & Jockstraps
Of Sunlight and Stardust

About the Author

Riley Hart is the girl who wears her heart on her sleeve. Although she primarily focuses on male/male romance, under her various pen names, she's written a little bit of everything. Regardless of the sub-genre, there's always one common theme and that's…romance! No surprise seeing as she's a hopeless romantic herself. Riley's a lover of character-driven plots, flawed characters, and always tries to write stories and characters people can relate to. She believes everyone deserves to see themselves in the books they read. When she's not writing, you'll find her reading, traveling or dreaming about traveling. She has two perfectly sarcastic kids and a husband who still makes her swoon.

Riley Hart is represented by Jane Dystel at Dystel, Goderich & Bourret Literary Management. She's a 2019 Lambda Literary Award Finalist for *Of Sunlight and Stardust*. Under her pen name, her young adult novel, *The History of Us* is an ALA Rainbow Booklist Recommended Read and *Turn the World Upside Down* is a Florida Authors and Publishers President's Book Award Winner.

www.ingramcontent.com/pod-product-compliance
Ingram Content Group UK Ltd.
Pitfield, Milton Keynes, MK11 3LW, UK
UKHW011311280725
7110UKWH00030B/429